THE
TRUTH
AND
LIES
OF
~~ELLA~~
~~BLACK~~

Emily Barr worked as a journalist in London but always hankered after a quiet room and a book to write. She went travelling for a year, which gave her an idea for a novel set in the world of backpackers in Asia. This became *Backpack*, an adult thriller which won the WHSmith New Talent Award, and she has since written eleven more adult novels published in the UK and around the world. She lives in Cornwall with her partner and their children.

Follow Emily Barr
on Twitter @emily_barr
and Instagram @emilybarr01
#EllaBlack

THE TRUTH AND LIES OF ~~ELLA~~ ~~BLACK~~

EMILY BARR

PENGUIN BOOKS

PENGUIN BOOKS

UK | USA | Canada | Ireland | Australia
India | New Zealand | South Africa

Penguin Books is part of the Penguin Random House group of companies
whose addresses can be found at global.penguinrandomhouse.com.

www.penguin.co.uk
www.puffin.co.uk
www.ladybird.co.uk

Penguin
Random House
UK

Digital edition first published 2017
Paperback edition first published 2018

001

Set in 10.5/15.5 Sabon LT Std
Typeset by Jouve (UK), Milton Keynes
Printed in Great Britain by Clays Ltd, St Ives plc

A CIP catalogue record for this book is available from the British Library

ISBN: 978-0-141-36700-2

MIX
Paper from
responsible sources
FSC® C018179
www.fsc.org

Penguin Random House is committed to a
sustainable future for our business, our readers
and our planet. This book is made from Forest
Stewardship Council® certified paper.

For Craig

1

40 days until she dies

I am huddled on a bench, shivering, but I don't care about being a bit cold because I'm busy. I have a pencil and a sketchpad balanced on my knees, and I'm sitting in a park in front of a view that has the Houses of Parliament in it, leaning on Jack, who is reading a book. I'm totally focused on my drawing. I'm not actually drawing the view in front of me; I do have a few pages of Big Bens in my sketchbook, but it's just not the thing that seems to be appearing on the page.

'Are you nearly done?' says Jack. 'I mean, you have to take as long as it takes, but it's going to rain and . . .'

He shifts around and looks at my drawing.

'Oh,' he says. 'Oh right – a metaphorical interpretation of the view?'

'Yep.'

'Ella Black has made me shiver on a bench for an hour so she could draw a picture of . . . Ella Black.'

'It's not Ella Black.'

'Sorry to break this to you, sweetie, but I think it really is.'

I look at it. She looks like me but she isn't me. I wish

Jack could see that, though I don't know how I could possibly expect him to. If I told him, he'd probably understand in the end, but I have never told him and I never will. I laugh a bit, from nerves, and he does too.

'How's your book?' I say.

'Brilliant, actually. The apocalypse is well underway. Hey. You know, you're right. This doesn't look quite like you. It's like you with psychotic eyes, isn't it? It's you thinking about something you really, really hate.'

I look at him. I steady my breathing. 'Yes,' I say. 'Yes, actually. It really is.'

'You're not thinking about me, are you?'

I look at Jack: blond, unexceptional-looking and one of my two best friends in the world. One of my two only friends in the world. I love his face. I love the way we know each other's secrets. Though really I know his big secret, but he doesn't know all of mine. I might not know all of his. I probably don't.

'Of course I'm not thinking about you, you dick,' I say, and a raindrop falls right on to my drawing and blurs its face. I close the sketchpad, and Jack puts away his apocalyptic thriller, and we run to a big tree and stand underneath it, looking at the rain and the people putting up umbrellas and hoods and walking fast to unimaginable places, and we wait for it to ease up enough for us to walk to Trafalgar Square and catch a train home to Kent.

We ran away to London because it was half term. We spent the morning going to free galleries and looking at art, and then we bought some books, and then we went to sit in the park and I tried to draw the lovely view but I drew myself with psychotic eyes instead, and I know why I did and I'm glad I did.

By the time we get to Charing Cross the rush hour has started. It's later than we realized, even though I was literally looking at one of the most famous clocks in the world for quite a lot of the afternoon.

'Massive miscalculation,' says Jack.

'I know, right?'

We stand and look at the people on the concourse. It is extremely busy, not just with commuters (though mainly with them) but also with half-term people like Jack and me, people who have come to London to look at the sights and then forgotten that you need to get a train home either earlier or later than this. If we get the right train it will only take forty minutes, but it might be an uncomfortable ride. We live in a commuter town, and people are going home in their thousands.

We're about halfway back when my head starts ringing. I'm standing up, separated from Jack by two business types who got on at London Bridge and who are pretending they're still at work. One is pressing right up against me, reading some boring financial thing on his iPad. The other is hanging on to a pole as desperately as if he were a stripper and making a very important phone call about a shareholders' meeting. My head is ringing, I tell myself, because I'm standing up, and tired, and fed up. I haven't got my phone for distraction because I lost it yesterday. I can't talk to Jack because he's too far away. I have to live in the moment, and everything is blurred around the edges because I am standing up and tired and fed up. I mutter to myself to try to keep it together. No one cares. No one notices.

By the time we're walking back to my house, though, I know things are going wrong. I should not have drawn that picture. My ears are ringing with a high-pitched sound even though we're out in the open air, hand in hand, looking normal. I grabbed Jack's hand because sometimes he can ground me, and he never minds me doing that. I try to make the ringing stop. I try to use his energy to balance myself.

It gets louder.

It

gets

louder and louder.

And although I am walking towards my house, and although I look normal, I know that I'm not a normal girl and that I have to get to the safe place; I have to get to my bedroom, with the door closed. I have to be on my own now.

I squeeze Jack's hand, and he squeezes back because he has no idea. The pavement is dark with recent rain, and the clouds are gathering again, but right now the sunset is turning the sky into a purple bruise, and everything looks like a painting.

Please go, I say internally. *Go now. You can come back later.*

She makes my vision go a bit blotchy around the edges, and that's her way of saying, *NOT. LATER. NOW.*

'Actually,' I say to Jack, 'I need to do some art homework.' I'm trying to breathe evenly, to appear normal. He doesn't seem to have noticed anything different. I do wonder whether he sees it, particularly after today, but doesn't ask because he knows I don't want him to.

'I will not impose upon the artiste any longer,' he says. He flings a hand dramatically across his brow. '*I need to paint! I live for my art!* Is that you saying you want me to bugger off?'

'Would you mind? I mean it in a nice way.' It is pressing on the inside of my head. I have to get him to go. I wish I could tell him but I can't.

I can't because I'm not brave enough. In the part of me the world sees I'm a bit of a walkover, easily bullied, easily ignored. That's the better version of me: I don't dare to try to be stroppy, particularly at a time like this, because anything could happen. The girl in my drawing might come pouring out and poison all of it. That would be the end of everything.

'Come in for a minute anyway,' I say, feeling Bella listening carefully to every word I say, 'and then – well, then yes, you can bugger off. I've got, like, a whole painting to finish and you know I'm not very sociable when that happens. Only Humphrey can come anywhere near.'

Jack laughs. 'You spoil that cat,' he says.

Then it's raining again so we run the last bit, hand in hand, up the hill to my house. We run past a woman with

5

long tangled hair who's struggling to put up an umbrella, and a man pushing a bike with a toddler on the back. The toddler waves at us and shouts: 'I gettin' wet!'

I wave back with my free hand and feel Bella in the other, gripping Jack, trying to use her powers to electrocute him, wishing he would die because he is normal and happy and she doesn't think that's fair.

Jack is not really normal and happy, but he is, compared to Bella. I love him. Along with Lily he is my best friend. Everyone thinks he's my boyfriend, but he's not: he's better than that. We have a thing that works for both of us.

I don't want a real boyfriend. I don't think I'll ever want a relationship. My school is a posh girls' school, but a lot of the sixth-formers live in a world in which they defer absolutely to boys. It's pathetic and it makes me mad, but I haven't been brave enough to say anything. Actually, if I tried to argue with them, Bella would jump out and smash the nearest simpering handmaiden with a fire extinguisher, so it's probably best that I bite it back.

Jack likes the best side of me, which is the only thing he sees. Hanging out with me has helped him in all sorts of ways, and for a while he raised my status so I was not a top-level target. But it didn't last long and soon after that the girls at school started on me again.

I've never told Jack about the things that happen to me at school. He would only get upset and mad, and nothing would change, apart from him being a little less happy. And I want Jack to be happy. Only Lily knows what happens, and Lily protects me from it as much as she can.

When we burst in Mum is standing in the hallway, pretending she just happens to be there, holding something in her hands and smiling in smug anticipation.

I look at it. 'My phone!' I say, and she grins and holds it out to me.

'Someone handed it in,' she says. 'The police called and I picked it up. I thought I'd lost mine too but then I found it again. It restores your faith, doesn't it?'

Mum is just saying that because it's a cliché: she doesn't need her faith restored. She's not disillusioned or cynical about anything, though she does make sure to keep us as safe as she possibly can at all times, from dangers that don't actually exist. I take my phone from her and quickly check it; everything is exactly as it was when I last saw it, yesterday morning, just before I lost it in town.

I don't think Mum has looked through it. I hope she hasn't.

Bella is inside my head, clearing her throat, demanding attention. I push her aside.

Mum doesn't look as if she's had a shock insight into my school life. She is happy to see us, Jack and me. She lives for us. She stands around in the hall waiting for me to come home because I am her life. It's weird. Obviously it's nice for me, but I do feel bad for her because her life must be boring. Sometimes I try to imagine my way into her head, and I just can't. I don't think she has a dark side at all.

She would be so upset if she knew what happened to me. That's why I can never tell her. Right now Bella is knocking on the inside of my skull and I need to get away.

As soon as we are through the door, Mum clicks all the locks shut behind us. No house is quite as secure as ours. For as long as I can remember, keeping me safe has been pretty much Mum's career. She is compelled to make sure I am always safe; always, always safe, all the time. It's almost funny that she relaxes when I'm tucked away in my bedroom, considering that this is actually the danger zone.

Jack is grinning back at her.

'How are you, Mrs Black?' he says in his polite way. 'You're looking lovely.'

She loves that. Mum adores Jack. She wants us to get married and give her lots of grandchildren. Again, she has no idea that that can never happen, which is sweet. I mutter something because Bella is in my head and I can't talk very well at the moment.

'Biscuit?' she says. 'I've just made some. Still warm from the oven.'

I'm not going to stop to have a biscuit, but I'll save some for Bella because she might like them later. Unless they're the spelt-and-sweet-potato ones Mum made last week too, in which case no one will ever, ever want one.

'Yes please,' says Jack. He's hoping for the chocolate-chip cookies, I know it.

While he follows her into the kitchen I walk straight ahead and go into the loo and close the door and lock it and lean against it and try to breathe. I have to get rid of them both. I have to make Jack go home in the next few minutes. My head tightens. Black spots dance across my vision.

He is sitting at the table flirting with Mum. They both do that. I think Jack finds it funny. God only knows what Mum is up to. She grins at him and looks coquettish and reminisces about her youth, and he laughs in all the right places and says the right things back to her. Neither of them particularly cares whether I'm bothered or not; and although it's gross I just roll my eyes and look away.

The biscuits are ginger and sultana. That's just about acceptable, so I take three and wrap them in a piece of kitchen roll.

'Sorry, Jack,' I say, and under Mum's approving eye I walk over and kiss the top of his head. 'Got to do some painting. See you tomorrow.'

He laughs. 'Sure. See you tomorrow, Ells. I won't hang around.'

'You're welcome to –' Mum starts to say, but I silence her with a glare and leave the room, gasping for breath, taking the stairs two at a time.

I close my bedroom door and try to breathe. My head is ringing so loudly I wouldn't be able to hear anything else, not even a fire alarm or a nuclear siren if it went off. Maybe one of those things is happening right now. I don't care if it is. I roll up my sleeves and look at the tiny lines on the insides of my arms. I'm ashamed of them. I'm never going to let that happen again.

Be nice, I say to Bella.

BE NICE, she replies, imitating me. *BE NICE.*
ALWAYS BE NICE.

Oh, please stop.

PLEASE STOP. PLEASE STOP. PLEASE STOP.

Leave me alone.

LEAVE ME ALONE.

Leave

me

alone.

LEAVE.

I don't know what is me and what is her.

I put my hands to the sides of my face and scream silently like the painting. All I want is to be normal.

I draw in a shuddery breath and press the palms of my hands on the carpet, feeling the floor, being here in this moment, myself in my room. One thing I have learned over the years is how to pretend; and when this door is closed I don't have to pretend any more. It can all come out.

I pull the pictures out from under the bed. They are meticulous explosions of horror. They are filled with death and maiming and nightmares. Bella drew them and she likes to look at them. Perhaps I can assuage her with them.

I call her Bella because she is the dark side of me. It's Ella but not. It's Bad Ella. Bella. I thought of that a few years ago and it made it a bit better, because before that I called it the Monster. Anything is a tiny bit better when it has a name. Bella is better than the Monster. I didn't know then that Bella means beautiful: my Bella isn't beautiful at all. She is the opposite. But she's still Bella.

Bella is desperate to own the whole of me: I am alert and battling all the time. Sometimes I have to let her out before everything explodes. It's scary, but after that happens I feel calm and peaceful and, I think, kind of happy. Everything is balanced for a while. That's when we draw these pictures. I look at them now. They are done in black ink – huge sheets of tiny detail like Hieronymus Bosch, but with modern bits in them. Children are decapitated here. Body parts are everywhere. There is blood and murder. These pictures take us ages and I hope no one ever finds them, but they're definitely the best art I've ever done.

She doesn't want to look at them now. *LATER*, she says.

It's hard to breathe. The ringing grows louder. I push my hands down on the carpet and try harder. Humphrey is waiting, I see. Humphrey always turns up when Bella's here.

'Have a biscuit,' I say desperately, and I unfold the kitchen roll and let them all fall across the carpet. I grab one and shove it into my mouth, but Bella spits it out because she's seen something much better than a biscuit.

Humphrey has carried a terrified bird into my bedroom, somehow getting it past Mum, who would have screamed and shooed him away if she'd seen. The bird is tiny. It looks like a baby. I wonder if Humphrey pulled it out of its nest, whether its mother is missing it.

The bird is flapping its little wings and trying to fly away, even though its body has been punctured by Humphrey's teeth.

He does this often, my cat. He's very much on Team Bella rather than Team Ella. He knows.

I crawl over to it. I can't even hear the ringing any more: it's just a white noise that blocks out the mundane world. I feel Ella leaving and then I am Bella, and Ella has gone and that's good because she is pathetic. I can hardly breathe as I reach for the hammer that Ella keeps under the bed. It's a little hammer that looks ladylike and inoffensive: when Mum found it Ella said it was part of her sculpting kit for art, and she totally believed her.

I pick the tiny thing up by a feather and place it on top of a history essay, which is on top of a textbook on the floor. I straighten it, stroking it with a finger.

'Hello,' I whisper, and I am Bella through and through.

Humphrey gives me a look. He is excited. He is a bad cat and he never pretends to be anything different.

My breathing quickens as I stare at the little bird.

I can't hear anything. I can't see anything but the bird.

And I know what I'm going to do. I wouldn't have arranged the creature and got out the hammer if I didn't. I know what I'm going to do because it is what I live for.

The world is dark around the edges like a spooky photo. Everything else has faded away. Bird, book, cat, hammer.

Bella.

I feel sick, but not in a normal way. Nothing about this is normal for anyone but me.

I can see the bird trying to fly away, and I know it will never fly again. I am Bella, and I can do anything. I have the power of life and death.

I pick up the hammer, wait for a moment with it raised just high enough, savouring every second, and smash it down on top of the creature.

I

feel

it

crunch.

I

watch

it

shatter.

I stare at the remains. I love doing this.

'Thanks,' I breathe to the cat, and he inclines his head towards me in a *you're-welcome* sort of way. A *we're-in-this-together* way.

This is what it's all about. I love it when I get to take over. I want to be her forever; I want her to stop being Ella Black and let me stay here, in her body. I could do anything.

The white noise starts to fade. I try to hang on to it.

I hate doing this, says Ella's pathetic voice.

GO AWAY.

I am scared.

NO YOU'RE NOT.

'Ella?'

The voice slices through everything and I am shrinking away to nothingness.

The ringing is back, but it's quieter. I am Ella, cross-legged beside my bed, on the other side of the room from the door. It takes me seconds to come back to myself, to know that I am Ella again and not Bella, and when I do I push the hammer under the bed and jump to my feet. My legs wobble. My heart pounds so hard they must be able to hear it downstairs.

Lily is standing in the doorway.

I look around, gasping for breath, drawing in great lungfuls of air and trying to use them to force the last bits of Bella away. I am in my bedroom. The walls are pink and blue, with anime posters and my sketches of Rio de Janeiro. My clothes are on the floor. There is a photo collage of me and Lily and Jack, laughing, doing ironic duck-faced pouts, posing with our arms round one another. Everything looks normal.

Everything

looks

normal.

But I know nothing is normal.

I don't know what she's seen. I don't know if she saw Bella lift the hammer and kill the bird. Bella is not here. She is not. Lily cannot see her. She cannot see this. She cannot. I push the darkness away, away, away.

In my head I say the words that bring me back to myself. They only work after Bella has done her thing and nearly gone.

The universe the universe the universe, I say.

The universe.

The universe.

The

whole

universe.

The only thing that chases Bella away is that cosmic perspective. If I think of the entire universe and how tiny I am, everything feels manageable because nothing matters. Nothing at all matters. Ella doesn't matter and neither does Bella. Unfortunately, this really does only work when she's on her way out. It doesn't stop her arriving.

I discovered the universe thing by mistake. I was in the downstairs loo, aged about eleven, battling a demon I understood even less than I do now. I had my back against the locked door and I was pulling the wallpaper off the wall because I couldn't control myself and I had to destroy something. As I did it, Bella started to fade, and I read a line in a poem that is still hanging up on our downstairs loo wall.

> *Whether or not it is clear to you, no doubt the universe*
> *   is unfolding as it should.*
> *No doubt the universe is unfolding as it should.*
> *The universe is unfolding.*

It made Bella leave me alone. Now I've refined it to just the words *the universe*. I say them over and over again.

Bella has gone.

My lips move but I don't think any sound comes out.

I must be nice.

Be nice.

Be normal.

I

have

to
be
normal.
Smile.
You
must
smile.

'Oh, hey, Lily,' I say. My voice trembles but the words are kind of right. 'Um. Don't come in!'

I snap the last bit as she steps into the room. She stops. I take a wobbly step towards her then sit on the bed because my legs give out.

'Oh, Ella.' Lily is lovely. She is confused by my snapping at her because I never do that. 'Are you OK? Your mum said I could come up. I just came by because you haven't got your phone and I wanted to –' I see her look at my bed. I see her notice my phone. 'Oh, you got it back?'

'Yes. Back. Um.'

Be normal.

'Sorry,' I say. I form the word carefully, trying to say the thing that Ella would say. 'The cat brought in a bird. It's *really* grim. It's made me sick. Sorry. Really don't come in. I had to put it out of its misery. I . . . had . . . to . . .'

It's too difficult to come back to myself. It's harder every time. One day I won't make it. One day I will be stuck as Bella. I know she wants that. I would hate it. It can never happen.

The ringing is fainter still, and then it just about stops. The edges of the world are sharp again.

'Oh, shitting hell,' says Lily. Lily could never understand, and I would never tell her because if I did she might not be my friend any more and I need her. *I need her.* She pulls me back, often, and always without knowing. 'Oh, Ella. You poor thing. I've got a tissue. Hang on.'

She is walking towards me. Humphrey crouches, then runs, streaking past her legs and out of the room and down the stairs.

I pull her down to sit next to me on the bed and take her face in my hands. I cannot let her look at what I did. Her springy hair on my fingers grounds me. I am with Lily now.

'Seriously,' I say, my face right in front of hers. 'Don't look. I'll clean it up. Could you maybe run down and get a plastic bag from my mum?'

I am hiccupping. It is all too much. I've always managed Bella better than this. I've always kept Lily away from her. Lately it has been getting worse.

'Sure. Shit, Ella. You poor, poor thing.' She puts an arm round me, and just for a moment I lean in and bury my face in her shoulder. Her hair is loose. It tickles my face. I cling on, and then I force myself to let go.

When she has left I put my head in my hands. This is awful; I can't keep it up. Jack must have wondered why I needed him to leave. Lily actually walked into my room and found Bella in it. Next time it will be worse and then everyone will know. I can't get my thoughts straight or stop shaking, but I have to clean this up. I can't let Lily know, and I can't let Jack know either.

They cannot know.

They
cannot
know.

I leave the poor smashed bird where it is, and fold the history essay around it. I am shaking, and a feather falls out of the package. I kick the textbook out of the way and try to pick up the stray feathers, though I really need to vacuum to get the carpet clean.

Mum will be pleased to see me spontaneously using the vacuum cleaner. So that will make everyone happy for a bit.

When Lily comes back with the bag I drop in the bird in its essay coffin, and drop most of the feathers in too.

'I'll just wash my hands.'

Lily ties the handles of the bag and takes it downstairs while I lock myself in the bathroom and try to breathe without it catching, without gasping or taking such shallow breaths that I feel dizzy. I wash my hands with lots of soap. I splash my face with cold water and soap, and I put on some moisturizer to make it soft and smooth. I take off my old eye make-up. I breathe in and out. In. Out. In, deeply. Out, deeply. I close my eyes. I remember smashing the bird. It made Bella happy, and Bella is part of me.

I do not want that to make me happy.

I do not want to be part Bella.

I do not want it to build up inside me like this.

I do not want to be someone who smashes birds with a hammer.

I do not want to be this girl.

2

37 days

'Ella!' she shouts up the stairs. I notice that Lily is keeping away from my room after what happened on Wednesday. I grab my bag and run down the stairs, smiling, ready to be relentlessly nice all day long.

'Hello!' I say, super-enthusiastically.

She grins. 'You look gorgeous.'

I don't, but it's lovely of her to say so.

'*You* do,' I tell her. She's wearing skinny jeans and a big white shirt. 'You really do. Classic and beautiful.' I immediately feel messy beside her, in my leggings and long-sleeved T-shirt. I feel like a child, but that doesn't matter.

Lily and I have been best friends for nearly ten years: that's more than half our lives. We became proper friends at the age of eight, when we were put together for a school nature walk and let loose in the forest with a sheet of paper and a list of random things to collect. We went further and further from the base. I wanted to get lost to see what would happen (Bella was young then too, and she took a more random approach), and Lily was happy with that plan because she likes an adventure.

It didn't go brilliantly, but we ended up friends.

As we walk into the kitchen to say goodbye to Mum and Dad, they stop talking and plaster on fake smiles. I wish they'd just argue properly – they are always breaking off a whispered fight as I come into a room. Dad is off work today because of his recent trip, and that means they get an extra day to hiss at each other, which is nice.

'Hello, girls!' says Mum.

Dad looks up from his paper as if he were absorbed in it. He might as well be holding it upside down because he definitely wasn't reading.

'All right?' he says.

Mum is clattering about, cooking. I wish that sometimes she would read the paper while he cooked, but no. They just don't do it like that. I'd like her to have a break sometimes. Dad does occasionally offer, but she insists on doing it all herself; she'll only let us lay the table or take the compost out to the wormery.

Yes. My mother seriously has a wormery. It's like three hundred pets that eat all our kitchen waste and poo out compost. I love them. Sometimes I take off the lid and stare at them. Once Bella tried to make me pour boiling water on to them and I had to run all the way to my room and slash one of my own paintings to pieces with a craft knife just to save them.

So Mum is cooking. She's tall and blonde, just like I used to be (I am still tall unfortunately, but no longer blonde), and she beams as we walk through the kitchen, and says: 'Would you like some soup, girls?'

Lily says: 'That's really kind of you, but we're just off to Mollie's.'

'It smells great though,' I say, even though it really doesn't. Mum's lentil soup is so thick you can literally use it as wallpaper paste. Once I stuck a sketch I'd done to the wall with it, just to see if it worked, and it's still there today. It's a picture of Humphrey stalking a mouse, and it's on the wall to the left of the window.

Mum was out and I was messing around with Jack. I bet him that it would stay up, and it has, for months now. We laughed so much we cried. I do love Jack.

Dad and Mum both pretend we haven't walked in on another silent argument, so it feels insanely awkward. Dad smiles at me and Lily and turns a page of his paper. Generally he is much easier to live with than Mum, because he does his thing and gives me all the space I need, which is a lot. I can talk to Dad about things and he'll engage with me. The other day he said abstract art was rubbish, and I told him why he was wrong and he totally got it and changed his mind.

'Watching movies?' he says now.

'Yep,' I say.

'It's *Psycho* today,' says Lily.

'The Bates Motel,' says Dad.

I don't answer. Lily humours him for us both by singing a version of the shower music and Dad makes a stabbing motion, which I notice he aims at Mum.

We get on our bikes and cycle off. I love cycling. Even when you're wearing a helmet the wind is in your hair.

I like the way your legs hurt and you feel as if you've done something good. Sometimes I have even managed to cycle Bella away from me.

As I follow Lily, her hair springing out from under her helmet, I think about the fact that Mum and Dad are unusually happy to see me leave the house today, and I know it's so they can carry on their secret arguing. I was always glad that my parents weren't divorced like most people's because I'd rather live with Dad (judging by what happens to other people I'd probably have to live with Mum), but now I wish they'd just do it already. I'm seventeen so I could live where I liked. I have no idea what is going on and why, and I certainly don't want to think about one of them having an affair, so I guess I'll just leave them to it.

Lily hasn't seen her dad since she was eight, though she still gets money from him. That must be horrible, but she says it's all she knows and so it's perfectly fine, and she is indeed one of life's happy people.

A couple of hours later we are in Mollie's massive living room, almost at the exciting part of *Psycho*. I can't relax here because I don't belong: I know I'm only here because I'm with Lily. Mollie and the twins and Lily are all A-list and I'm a hanger-on, so I sit quietly on the squashy sofa with Lily, our legs pressed together, and that grounds me though I couldn't say so. Mollie's dad put a bowl of Maltesers in front of us a minute ago and they're already half gone and I've taken most of them out of nerves.

Everyone's staring at the screen so they don't even notice. I will do extra exercise later to make up for it. Mollie will be angry if she sees that I've taken all the Maltesers.

I know they don't like me because I'm boring and scared and awkward. I look like one of them (or I did), but I'm not one of them. I say the wrong thing, or I say nothing at all, and generally they just act as if I wasn't there. They don't hate me though, so that's something.

Mollie is applying for film studies at college and she's trying to watch every important film ever made so she'll be able to talk about them at interviews and get offers from everywhere. We are all watching them with her (or rather, she invited Lily and the twins to watch them with her, and Lily brought me along) because we will be off to uni next year too, and they all like the idea of being seen as cool and stylish film buffs. I do too, obviously, but mainly I just enjoy switching off and watching the movies. When I'm absorbed in someone else's traumas, my own can fade into the background. It's the same with books. It's why I love reading and why I love painting too.

The idea of going away from here is weird. Unlike Mollie, I don't know what I want to do or who I want to be. I only want to apply to art school, but you can't exactly have a career as an artist (not according to the careers advisers at school anyway). Whatever it turns out to be, I can't wait to leave this town because I only have Lily and Jack here and no one else cares about me, and if I was far away from Kent I might be OK. I might become a full-time Bella or, just maybe, I might finally manage to fight her and kill her off. I could be Ella all the time. I could be someone good.

I take a deep breath. Perhaps I should apply for film studies too. I'm enjoying this film. I wish the rest of them would stop talking so I could concentrate, though of course I can't ask them to.

Unfortunately Lily is telling them about the bird. She didn't tell them after it happened, but she's telling them now.

'God, Ella,' says Mollie, looking as if she's actually a bit scared of me, and perhaps she *should* be. 'That is so fucked. I mean – here's a bird in distress.' She laughs. 'Let's get, like, *Ella Black* to put it out of its misery.'

She and the twins all burst out laughing. I look at Lily. She mouths, 'Sorry.'

'But,' says Nisha, 'that is seriously so gross. I literally couldn't have done it.' She looks at me as if I might be a monster, as if this is a story that might travel like a bush fire around the common room, as if it is something that could make my life just that little bit worse, and I know it is.

I try to give her a bright smile, though I bet it comes out all wrong. 'I just did what I had to do,' I say. 'That poor thing.'

I think those were the right words. I have to measure my words all the time when I'm with the Alpha girls. The slightest misstep and they become vicious. These aren't the worst, not at all; but they are still bad, and everything is reported to everyone.

I imagine for a second what might happen if I told them that it wasn't actually me who killed the bird, that it was my other self, Bella. My inner monster, who takes me over from time to time, who is scaring me by being brazen every time it happens. It would be the beginning of the end of everything. Within a couple of minutes I would be notorious throughout the school and beyond it.

The woman in the film has just got into the shower and I know this means the famous scene is about to happen. Everyone seems to have lost interest in me and we all stare at the screen as the *Psycho* music starts and Janet Leigh is murdered.

'Ella, I'm so sorry,' Lily whispers, right into my ear. 'I didn't mean them to –'

'It's OK.' I cut her off. 'Truly it is.' And it is. I could be annoyed with her for telling them about the bird, but I'm not. She said it to make them sympathize with me, and it's not her fault it didn't work.

She takes my hand. 'Love you.'

I spend the rest of the day as the hanger-on, being as nice as I possibly can. I always try to do that. Because I'm scared of the bad thing that lives inside me, and because Lily walked in when I was under Bella's control, I work on being normal more than ever before. I concentrate all my efforts on being kind and helpful, not that anyone but Lily cares what I do. I sit with Mollie and talk her through the essay on *Sons and Lovers*, which I've done and she hasn't, and she accepts my help and says, 'Thank you.' That feels like a breakthrough.

'Why *did* you do that to your hair?' she asks, picking up a strand of it in her fingers as we work side by side, and looking at it in distaste.

I shrug. 'I just fancied a change,' I say. That is the biggest lie ever. My hair used to be long and blonde like Mollie's, but now it's lopsided (much longer on one side than the other) and purple. The lopsidedness came after a horrible incident at school with Tessa, whose hobby is making my life, and the lives of everyone else who doesn't quite fit in, as difficult as she can. The purple was part of a complicated accommodation I made with Bella to stop her attacking Tessa back with her own knife. Anyway, my public position is that I fancied a change, and actually I like the purple. I'm different from everyone else, so I might as well *look* different.

'Right.' Mollie is smirking. Actually I can't wait to get away from here.

'So it's about Mrs Morel controlling Paul even after she's died,' I say. 'That's what I put. I looked it up online and that's what it said. She ruins all his relationships because she wants to make sure he loves his mummy the best.'

'Hey, Anusha,' says Mollie. 'That sounds a bit like Dean.'

Everyone looks at Anusha and laughs about her boyfriend, and the heat is off me and I am pleased.

3

35 days

'Lily?' says Mrs Browning. 'Perhaps you'd like to answer.'

I look at Lily. She is fiddling with her fingernails, staring down at the desk. She hasn't got a clue what to say. I know she didn't hear the question because she was drawing a picture of herself as a manga character in her notebook under the table. She has coloured her skin light brown and her hair pink, and has given herself huge eyes. Underneath it she has written: *Lilichan*.

We are supposed to be sensible now that we're in our last year of school. We're meant to be adults. We should be doing these subjects because we are committed to them. We are not meant to yawn and mess around and draw cartoons under the desk; and yet of course we do, because this is school and we have been here for years and years and it's boring.

'Sorry,' says Lily.

There is a muffled snicker from the rest of the group.

'Lily – answer my question about the text. This is A-level year. If you don't want to answer a very basic question, you should not have picked this subject.'

Mrs Browning is a good teacher and I like her. No one else does. However, I don't like it when she picks on Lily, who daydreams her way through English because she didn't know what to do for her third subject and picked it because I was doing it. Lily's heart is not in English and, although she is the most focused person I know, when she's in an English lesson that focus is never on the book. She's generally thinking about music and drama instead.

Now she shifts in her chair, pulls her skirt straight and stares at the book in front of her. I take the drawing from her under the table, just in case. The rain has turned to hail and the stones are battering at the window. A year from now we'll be out of here, and Mrs Browning will still be behind her desk, trying to get people whose minds are elsewhere to talk about books they haven't read. I wish I could communicate that thought to Lily right now.

I know *Sons and Lovers*. I like it. I heard the question. I clear my throat and speak quickly before I can decide not to.

'Mrs Morel's jealous of Paul's relationship with Miriam,' I say quickly. 'And that's –'

'No, Ella. I asked Lily, thank you. I know *you* know.'

The silence is tangible. It is a thick thing, a fog, heavy in the air. There are only ten of us in the class, and when I look around I see that I am the only one who is not staring down at a piece of paper, desperate not to be picked on.

My head rings and I start a frantic internal bargaining with Bella. She cannot take over at school. She cannot. She never has, not in class, and she never will.

CAKE.

No.

ANOTHER HAIR COLOUR.

No. Later. We'll do something later.

HURT THE TEACHER. SHE'S BEING MEAN TO LILY.

I can't hurt the teacher.

Mrs Browning, unaware of the danger she's in, is staring at Lily, who is hunched in on herself, looking down at her lap. No one gets to make my best friend feel like this. Lily is an angel. My vision narrows.

This cannot happen at school. It can't. It did once before, and I only just got through it by locking myself in a loo and taking it out on myself until Bella went away. Not now; not in class. No. The edges of my vision black out, and I look frantically at the edges of things to make them come back into focus.

'Your hair looks nice today, miss,' Bella says to Browning, using my mouth. I am horrified. I only ever speak in class to give an answer. I never do anything like this.

She touches her hair, which is as flat and scraggly as it always is. 'Well, I wish I could say the same for *you*, Ella,' she says, her lips tight.

'Yeah, but it does. Where do you get it done?'

Everyone is staring at me, wide-eyed.

'Lily. Answer the question.'

'The question?' Lily says, very quietly.

I close my eyes and take some deep, deliberate breaths because I can't let Bella do anything more than this. Being rude to Mrs Browning was not enough. I can feel it happening. It's rising inside me. I can't look at everything quickly enough to stop it blurring. I am becoming Bella. I want to fly at her. I want to shout. I need to hurt her.

PULL HER HAIR.

I can't.

THROW HER BAG OUT OF THE WINDOW.

I can't.

PUNCH HER.

I have to stay in control.

WELL, HELP LILY. LILY IS THE PERSON YOU LOVE MOST. YOU CAN DO THAT.

Bella and I are in tentative agreement.

I pull my notebook down under the table and start scribbling, breathing deeply, pushing away the ringing and the blurring. I focus only on the words, and when it's done I push it towards Lily, who reads it quickly, then says:

'Mrs Morel is jealous of Paul's relationships with Miriam and Clara. This has a damaging effect on Paul. So, though she dies, I would argue that she has still won.'

Browning rolls her eyes. I can see that she is on the brink of walking out, even though there are still twenty minutes until break. I hope she does. I will her to. That would end this.

'*You* would argue that, would you, Lily?' she says.

'Yes, miss.'

'Ella, you are doing Lily no favours whatsoever,' she says. 'Yes, I know *you* can do it. I know you've read the book and can produce a considered argument. You won't be able to pass Lily the answer in her exams, will you? She needs to do the work herself, or otherwise drop the subject. If she can't be bothered to read a novel that is not at all difficult – or even to read the bloody York Notes – then this class is not the place for her. And as for your rudeness, we'll be discussing that later.'

'Lily's going to get an A,' I say. I reach for her hand under the table and squeeze it. She squeezes back, clinging on. *The universe the universe the universe.* I chase Bella away with the words. I hang on to Lily's hand.

My breathing comes more easily. I can hear properly; I can see properly. It is the biggest relief, the best thing. I close my eyes and appreciate having my head to myself. Bella left, and I didn't hurt anyone. I didn't even hurt myself.

The lesson staggers on for fifteen minutes that manage to be both dull and tense, and then I take Lily's hand in mine and we walk out of the room together. Mollie walks on Lily's other side (though I don't know where she was when Lily needed backup), and none of us look back. We go straight to the common room.

Lily blinks back tears and tries to laugh. I notice that she is tiny these days. I want to look after her like she looks after me.

'Oh fuck,' she says. 'She's kind of right. I know. I was going to read the book. I just . . . didn't.'

'Read it,' I say quietly, 'and you'll be fine. You *will* get an A, and then we'll be out of here. All the teachers will have to stay until they die.'

Lily smiles at that.

'Coffee?' says Mollie, to both of us.

'Sure.'

I am still shaky but I don't think anyone is looking at me. I reached a compromise with Bella and it was just about OK. It was a horribly close call. If I'd done what she wanted and punched a teacher I'd have been expelled by now. It doesn't bear thinking about.

Nothing like this can happen again.

I don't know how to stop it. It's getting worse and I don't know how to make it stop. Bella wants to come out every day. I use almost all my energy pushing her back down. It's beginning to feel impossible.

I watch Mollie as she tips the old coffee out of the jug and refills the filter. The common room is big, with sofas and bean bags, and a kitchen corner with kettle, coffee machine and a fridge that stinks of gone-off milk. The room as a whole smells of coffee and perfumed deodorant. It is always filled with teenage girls making a big point of relaxing, or desperately trying to do overdue homework before it slips out of control, or going through crises and breakdowns, alone, together, collectively. I know I'm not the only one with demons. I imagine I am the only one with *a* demon though.

I don't want to be here. On my bedside table I have a list of places I would rather be. Only Jack has seen it. He made his own at the same time. We didn't compile the tragic 'bucket lists' terminally ill kids make; we just wrote down some places we would rather be. I added the last two items when I was alone. Mine says:

ELLA'S WISH LIST

1. *Go to Rio – particularly Copacabana beach. Draw it from life, not from a photo.*
2. *Visit a tropical island anywhere in the world, with sand and palm trees. Find a beach that is the opposite of where we went last year, in Cornwall.*
3. *Live in a huge exciting city, e.g. New York.*
4. *Find a job and earn money doing something fulfilling and interesting, independent of my parents.*
5. *Be away from my life in Kent. JUST BE ANYWHERE AWAY FROM STUPID ENGLAND AND MY FRUSTRATING LIFE.*
6. *Be someone different from Ella Black because I am SO DULL.*
7. *Learn to live with my dark side.*

We had a laugh writing them. Jack's is full of shocking ideas, and I bet he added some extras when I wasn't there too.

I have written my list out several times, and this is its current incarnation. Each time I try to make it measured, but Bella takes the pen and adds her thoughts and it degenerates into frustration and anger. I'm going to apply to universities and art colleges in cool places (though not as cool as Rio or New York obviously) and I'll probably get into more than one of them. I do well at school, and this summer I'll have qualifications in English, art and history.

I don't want to get my head down and go to university and then find some dull job like my dad and work all the time. No one here thinks I'm adventurous, but I am in secret. I long to be free of everything I currently know. I don't belong in this common room. I have two friends in the whole world, Lily and Jack. I want to run from everything: from being seen as pathetic by everyone, from Bella, from my mother's constant locking of the door once I am safely inside. I want to be free.

'Thanks, Mollie,' I say, taking the stained mug of black coffee she's holding out to me. It's a big thing, Mollie making me a coffee. It's because I was so rude to Mrs Browning. I smile broadly at her and take a sip: it's hot, and pretty much nasty, but it's what we drink.

'Well, Ella,' says Mollie. 'You were epic.' She is staring at me with something like awe. 'Seriously.' She turns to the twins, who don't do English. 'Browning was giving Lily a hard time. And then Ella just goes: "Your hair looks nice, miss."'

'Ella?' Anusha gasps.

'I know, right?'

Everyone within earshot bursts out laughing. I try to smile along with it. The moment is reported again and again to people who didn't hear the first time. I shrink into my seat and look at Lily.

'You OK?' I say quietly.

'Yeah,' she says. 'I'm fine. But where the hell did that come from? *Your hair looks nice, miss?*' She giggles, and I giggle too, and then we are both laughing. We don't notice that there's a teacher in the room, heading right towards us, until she's almost beside us.

No one really takes any notice when teachers come into the common room. When they do they try to be cool. They make a show of 'treating you like adults'. They do this by saying: 'Hi, girls!' and 'Ooh, you look relaxed.' They try to slouch a bit to show us that, impossible as it seems, they were young once.

Today, though, it's our form tutor, Mrs Phipps, and she isn't trying to be *down wiv da kidz* at all. She is walking purposefully, looking only at me.

Mrs Browning said we would talk about my rudeness so I was expecting something like this. I'm trembling. I never get into trouble.

'Ella,' says Phipps. 'Ella, I need you to come with me, please. Bring your bag and your coat.'

I widen my eyes at Lily and Mollie to hide the fact that I am cold all over. They are sending me home for being rude to a teacher. I pick up my bag and toss the long side of my hair and try to smile.

'Coat?' says Phipps. She is looking at me strangely. It's unnerving. She normally loves me. She usually says things like: 'Thank goodness for you, at least, Ella,' which makes the others hate me even more.

'Actually – I don't have one?' I say. I talk in the slow, slightly Australian way I've heard other girls do when they want to annoy the teachers. They hate a sentence to sound like a question. I don't know what else to do. My heart is pounding.

'Really?'

'Really.'

She starts to say something but then stops. She's wearing a horrible dress, and Lily points at it behind her back and makes a face to the others, who snigger. I appreciate her support.

Everyone in the room is looking at me and I want to bolt. I keep my head down and follow Phipps out of the room. Tessa the bully looks up and rolls her eyes at me as I walk past.

I find myself going slightly out of my way to kick her bag.

Bella is stirring.

I am out of the common room and heading straight into trouble.

My mother is in the head's office. She is sitting on a chair, and Mrs Austen, the head teacher, is, as ever, swigging from the bottle that says 'water' on it, which everyone knows really contains vodka. Neither of them looks happy.

This does seem over the top, considering.

I imagine myself saying: *It wasn't me. It was Bella. She's a kind of demon who lives inside me. She's been there as long as I can remember but you thought I was just having tantrums, and when I was about seven I realized I had to hide it. And actually I can't remember much anyway from before I was six or so, which probably means I was such a vile child that you had my mind wiped. That would make it all kinds of worse. My parents would send me away to some upmarket asylum and I'd be forced* to sit quietly in group therapy until I could convince someone I was 'better'. Everyone in the school would talk of nothing else for weeks, like they do when someone goes away to have their anorexia treated, and I would never go back.

'Here she is,' says Phipps, standing in the doorway, a hand on my shoulder. I know it must be a *stop-her-running-away* grip, though it feels more like a *don't-worry* one. I want to push it off violently, but of course I can't. In fact Bella has already scoped out the House Cup sitting on a shelf behind Mrs Austen and wants to use it to smash everyone in the room, but she's just about under control at the moment. 'Apparently the pounding hail outside is no reason for a sixth-former to bring a coat to school, but she's got her bag.'

'Thanks, Sarah,' says Mrs Austen, and the door clicks shut and there are just the three of us there.

My mum is in the room. I was a bit rude to a teacher, which admittedly has never happened before, but it wasn't that bad. I was defending my friend, and all I actually said was 'Your hair looks nice.' They called my *mother*. They have no idea how much worse it could have been.

No

idea

at

all.

Mum is looking at me with the strangest expression. Her hair is plastered down with rain. She hasn't brought a coat with her either.

I wait for someone to say something, but they don't. I'm certainly not going to be the first to speak. I feel the moment stretch out. We are all suspended, waiting. Something is about to happen, but if no one says anything, then it won't. I'm good at not speaking. This is easy for me. Bella's happy just watching, for now.

'Ella,' says Mum, cracking first. 'Ella. Darling. We have to go. It's a bit sudden. Sorry, darling.'

'I don't know what I even did,' I say, straight at Mrs Austen. My words tumble over each other. 'It's not fair. I was a bit rude to Mrs Browning but –'

I stop talking because I can see from both their faces that they don't know what I am talking about. I have just confessed to something they have no idea that I did.

'Were you?' Mrs Austen says, inclining her head. She has helmet hair and looks like Angela Merkel. 'That's not like you, Ella. But this has nothing to do with Mrs Browning.' There is a big question on her face, but she doesn't ask it. 'Your mother needs to take you away, my dear.' She tilts her head towards Mum.

'Yes. Darling. Ella. We need to go right now. It's not in the least bit your fault. Of course it's not. Though you shouldn't be rude to teachers . . .'

Her voice drifts away somewhere. I see that she is hugely stressed. I feel bad for her but I have no idea what's going on.

'Where are we going?'

'I'll explain on the way. Somewhere that will make you very happy. But we have to get going quickly or we won't make the . . .'

I stare at Mum. She doesn't meet my eye. I need her to finish the sentence, to tell me what we won't make. All my muscles tense. I don't know what's happening but I'm terrified that she might have found my drawings under the bed, the dark, dark drawings of the inside of my head.

If she found them she would take me straight to some kind of psychiatrist. I know she would. This must be something big. *We have to get going quickly or we won't make the . . . appointment?*

Everything is going to unravel. I work so hard to keep myself separate from Bella, and now they're going to pull my life to pieces. This is why, since I was seven, when I realized how bad I was, I have tried so hard to keep it secret. I'm trembling all over, waiting for the ringing in my head to get louder, because I know Bella won't take this lying down either.

'Absolutely right now, I'm afraid,' she says, her lips tight. She is always dressed like a hippy, my mum, but today, I notice, she is trying to look upmarket. She's wearing a floaty dress with flowers all over it and the seashell necklace she puts on to go to weddings and parents' evenings.

I try to gauge from her face whether she is scared of me. My parents have no idea what goes on in my head and I need to keep it that way. I have worked hard to make them think that I'm awkward and shy (both of which are true) and absolutely nothing else.

Mum is worried about me. She is treading carefully. She is going to take me to some clinic.

I have always known that she would do anything for me, within a carefully defined range of things. If I said I wanted to learn the oboe, for example, she would have sorted it out for me instantly. Ballet would be a yes (and it was, for years) but cheerleading would be a no. If I wanted to see a counsellor to talk about the monster in my head, I imagine she would work hard to convince me there was no need for that sort of thing at all.

Mum could have done things with her life because she's clever and lovely, but all she did was have one baby and then chain herself to a healthy cookbook and a drawer of craft materials for evermore. She opted out of everything. I kind of respect her for that. I love her for devoting her entire life to me. How can you not love that? She waits for Dad to come home from work and puts healthy food in front of him. She buys me the things I need for my art. She looks after us. She considers it to be her job. If I thank her for a lift, or anything at all, she says: 'Oh, that's OK. It's my job.'

She could have done anything, and she chose to look after me instead. It's not a choice I'd be making if I ever had a child. We have talked about this, though we never argue. She says, 'Part of feminism is having a choice, and my choice was to stay at home.' I tell her that is a bit of a cop-out as it's a choice you can only make if you have a spouse who can support you while you do it, and instead of arguing her point she says: 'Yes, you're probably right, darling.'

She is already on her feet. 'Now, Ella,' she says. 'We have to leave now. *Right now*.'

I don't know where to start.

'But, Mum,' I say. 'I'm at school. It's education. I should really stay here. I'll see you at four. OK?'

I wait for backup, but it doesn't come. I realize that the head teacher of my expensive school had me collected from the common room for whatever this reason is.

She would only do that if it was an emergency. She wouldn't do it for no reason.

She would do it if someone was dead.

Mum is here.

It could be Dad. I'd rather it was her.

I push that thought away and pretend it never happened.

'Is Dad OK?' I say, talking to my shoes.

'Yes,' Mum says, though she doesn't sound surprised to be asked. 'He's perfectly fine. He's meeting us here. Now.'

'What, then?'

Mum is alive. Dad is alive. They wouldn't collect me from school if it was the cat. Still, I hope it's not Humphrey.

'I'll tell you on the way,' says Mum. 'Like I said. Come on.'

I look at Merkel.

She nods. 'Off you go, Ella,' she says. 'We'll see you when we see you.'

That fills me with horror. She should have said *tomorrow*. She doesn't know when I'll be back. But I have studying to do. I need to be at *school*. I don't want to go to therapy. She will see me when she sees me. That opens up a chasm. I hold on to the edge of her desk, trying to tether myself.

41

Merkel looks calm, but she is holding a little piece of card and tearing it into tiny pieces, dropping the shreds into a pile. There was handwriting on it. I wonder what it said. When I look into her face she looks away. I look at Mum, who is standing by the door now. I don't know what to do. I don't want to go. I hate it at school but I want to stay.

'*Why?*' I manage to say. 'What's going on?' My voice is tiny.

'We'll talk in the car.' Mum's not looking at me.

'Do I really have to go?' I say this to Mrs Austen. My voice is trembling.

'Yes, Ella,' she says. 'You really have to go. Don't worry about school for now. We'll still be here. You'll be all right. Off you go.'

On the way to the car I text Lily and Jack. Mum seems to be kidnapping me, I write to our group.

'Put your phone away,' says Mum.

Dad is parking in the teachers' car park as we get there. He is all right, and I am surprised to find that I'm so swamped with relief that my legs nearly give way. A part of me didn't believe Mum at all and thought she would tell me in the car that, actually, he was in a coma or something. Dad is so much more straightforward than she is. He is just Dad.

It's still raining, but just drizzling now. Dad gets into Mum's car, apparently ready to leave his Audi behind without a backward glance. Parents aren't allowed to park in the teachers' car park. They're certainly not allowed to abandon their cars there.

Abandoning his car is very much not a thing my dad would do. He is very organized.

I am so glad he's still alive that I actually hug him and whisper: 'What the hell is going on with her?'

'So sorry, darling,' he whispers back. 'It's not Mum. I promise. We'll tell you in a minute. Let's just get away for now.'

I swallow. 'OK.'

I turn round in the back seat and watch the school disappearing through the rain-splattered window. I don't know when We'll be back. I am utterly terrified. I can feel Bella inside me, biding her time, waiting to see what this is before she starts to deal with it. I hope Dad really will tell me in a minute.

The car radio beeps the hour. Everyone in the common room is talking about me and I am not there.

'*The news headlines at eleven o'clock,*' says the radio. '*Nuclear tensions increase as the stand-off continues. Amanda Hinchcliffe is released from jail after a third appeal. Two more cases of simian flu have been confirmed in the United Kingdom –*'

Mum jabs at the car radio and it goes off, flicks on again, then goes back off. She and Dad both inhale sharply. Her hand is shaking. Dad wobbles the steering wheel and almost runs over a long-haired woman who is standing at the end of the school drive, texting.

'What?' I say. 'Tell me. What is it?'

'Let's just have some peace and quiet so we can talk,' says Mum. 'Sorry, darling. I know this is weird but it's nothing to worry about. It's to do with Dad's work. We're going to be away for a little while, but it will be fine. In fact it'll be fun. You're going to enjoy it.'

It turns out that this is all they are planning to say. This is the promised 'explanation' in all its pathetic glory.

'Dad?' I say, my voice so quiet it barely comes out.

'Later,' he says.

Mum passes me a Twix, and I put it in my pocket for later. Bella loves bad food, and I might need it to pacify her.

'Where are we going?' I ask. 'You have to tell me that, at least.'

'Heathrow,' says Dad.

I text Jack and Lily the word Heathrow without looking at my phone. I don't know what word it actually sends.

'And after that we're going to Rio.'

Dad and I sit in a coffee shop while Mum goes and sorts some things out. I am drinking 'coffee' that is actually mildly flavoured milk. I hate milk. I'm drinking it anyway. It gives me something to do with my hands now that they've taken my phone away. Mum just picked it up from the table and walked off with it, and she pretended not to hear me calling after her.

'Did you look at my list?' I say. 'My list of the places I'd like to be? Why are we going to Rio?'

He smiles. 'Ellie, you've talked about Rio a lot. You did

that huge painting which your mother and I thought was wonderful. What list?'

Only my dad calls me Ellie. I like it.

They know that everything about Rio enthrals me. It seems wonderful and alive and full of samba and life and excitement. Before I stumbled on Rio while looking for a tropical setting to paint (from photographs), I had no idea that there could be a place like that. I want to be someone who is at home in Rio de Janeiro, rather than a nervous schoolgirl in Kent who can't do anything more daring than dye her hair an outlandish colour after a tense internal struggle.

I don't want to go there like this though. I would prefer to get myself there when I'm older and braver, rather than being escorted by weird shifty parents who apparently no longer trust me with my own phone.

But right now? I can't even express how weird this is.

'I know, Ellie,' Dad says, and he looks exhausted. There are big things he's not telling me; I wish he would just spill it all out, whatever it is. 'This thing came up for me, workwise, and we know how much you'd love to visit. So we thought we could make a family trip of it.'

'Right.' As if I would believe that. As if.

His eyes are begging me to pretend. 'Aren't you a little bit pleased?'

I sigh. I take a sip of coffee and wipe the milk froth off my top lip with a napkin. I contemplate pretending to be delighted at being taken along on this 'work trip'. I imagine myself saying: *It's amazing! Thank you so much!* It wouldn't work really, would it?

'It's just a little bit too weird,' I say. 'You like me going to school. If we were all going because of your work, then you would have arranged that and sorted the time off. In no universe do you just decide on the spur of the moment and grab me from school and drive to the airport. Then take my phone. Fuck's sake. I'm not *that* stupid.'

I said 'fuck' to my dad. That's never happened before. I look at him. He looks at me. His eyes crinkle. We both know I would never have said that if Mum was here. I push Bella away again.

I'M WATCHING, she says.

I know, I tell her.

'We thought you'd love the idea,' he says.

'What about Humphrey? Who's looking after him?'

I can see from Dad's face that he has no idea. My poor Humphrey will be baffled. He will hate me when he realizes I've gone away, and if no one is going to feed him then he might die.

He won't die. There are feral cats. Humphrey's vicious enough to survive. I know that better than anyone. But still. When I get home he'll be thin and tough and he won't bring me presents any more.

'I'm sure your mother's got that covered,' Dad says after a while.

'And Jack,' I say. 'Jack's coming over tonight. I won't be there.'

I know that Jack won't actually turn up because I told him I was going to Heathrow. The rest will have been filled in for him by my schoolmates: he will know that I've been swept off halfway through the morning, immediately after being rude to Mrs Browning.

'Oh.' Dad is way out of his depth. This is actually scary. It feels as if we are running away, but we can't possibly have anything to run from because we are normal and boring and law-abiding; or at least *they* are. We're running away from something they're not telling me about. This is spiralling into something very, very weird; but at least they're not dropping me off at an asylum, I suppose.

'Can I call him?' I say. 'Can I at least tell Jack that I'm off on the "trip of a lifetime" and will be back . . . next week? Shall I say that? How long are we going for?'

'Oh. I'm not sure. Look, you know you can't call him. We don't really want anyone to know that we're going to Rio.'

'Yeah. You've got some work stuff to do in Brazil and it's Top Secret?' I think of something. 'Have we even packed? Oh my God, Dad. Where's my stuff?'

I look around the concourse purely as a dramatic move, but I'm glad I do because someone is walking in our direction, and even from this distance I can see that it's Jack. I know his blond hair and his tall skinny body. I know the way he walks.

'It's complicated,' says Dad. 'Mum's packed some things. We'll buy stuff.'

'Jesus.' But I'm not looking at him. I'm looking at Jack and I'm grinning. I hoped he would do this. Jack has a car and we both use Find my iPhone.

Dad turns to follow my gaze and then closes his eyes and breathes deeply. 'Ellie,' he says. 'Oh, for God's sake.'

But I am on my feet and running towards Jack. He sweeps me up in his arms.

'Thank you so much,' I say. 'Thank you for coming.'

'What's going on?'

'No idea.'

My dad is right next to us, of course. He says, 'Good to see you, Jack,' in a tone that makes it clear that he means the opposite.

'Ella sent me a couple of texts,' Jack says, seeing that he needs to explain, 'and I had a free period and I had my car at school and I just thought I'd come and say goodbye.'

'Well, that's very romantic.' Dad doesn't see what's right in front of him. They were both so pleased when I started hanging out with Jack that neither of them noticed that we're not boyfriend and girlfriend at all. That's fine by me and fine by Jack, though I found it hard to keep a straight face when Mum insisted on ceremonially handing me a bag of condoms a few months ago.

'Dad,' I say. 'Can Jack and I just have a minute? I promise I won't say anything about the thing you just said not to say about.'

He rolls his eyes. 'I'll get you a drink, Jack,' he says. 'What'll it be?'

'Flat white?' he replies. 'Thanks so much.'

Those minutes with Jack are exactly what I need. We lean forward, chins on hands, and talk with our heads close.

'What's the thing you're not meant to tell me?' he says as the airport bustles around us.

'That we're going to Rio. Don't tell anyone.'

'Fucking Rio! Can I come?'

'I wish! I don't know what's happening.'

'Enjoy it, babe. Whatever it is.'

'Will you be OK?'

Jack sighs. 'Yes. I will. I'll miss you. I had a close call on Saturday. I went to the Admiral Duncan with Tony, and there was a teacher from my school there. Mr Jones. He's quite new. Young. Fit. Anyway he saw me and I saw him and I was scared that he'd tell the other teachers, because why wouldn't he, and also he could see I was technically breaking the law by drinking. So I had to grab him at school this morning and beg him not to tell anyone. He said he wouldn't. I hope he means it.'

'He will. He'll know what's at stake. He'll have been there himself. And you'll be out of there soon.'

'I will.'

'You'll be OK without your girlfriend for a while?'

'Yeah. Will you be OK without your boyfriend?'

'I have no idea.'

There are tears in my eyes. I don't want to leave Jack. We met in Wetherspoon's one night when I was tagging along with Lily's friends and he was pretending not to be on a date with a boy. Poor Jack. He was having a drink with someone, and then half the girls' school walked in. I watched him leap in the air and walk away from his date. That was intriguing: I'm always on the lookout for other misfits. We started talking, and then I found I had a new best friend. When everyone assumed

49

that we were going out it worked for us both, so we kept up the pretence.

Obviously it's fine to be gay. Obviously it's not the nineteen-fifties any more. Try telling that to Jack's parents and their church though. He just needs to avoid them taking him to conversion therapy until his exams finish and he can leave home forever. I've never seen anyone fit into their environment quite as badly as Jack does.

I reach out and ruffle his blond hair. He grabs my hand and squeezes it.

'I'll miss you,' I say. 'Email me. Keep in touch. I'm sure I'll be back soon.'

He laughs. 'Yeah. You'll probably be home in a couple of days and my dash to the airport will look ridiculous.'

'It's the best thing anyone's ever done for me.'

Bella has gone silent. She doesn't want to leave Jack either.

When he's gone Dad and I sit quietly. There are echoing announcements that I cannot quite hear, and there are people all over the place, none of them looking as if they are travelling for fun.

This morning Mum drove me to school and told me to have a lovely day. A few hours later she abducted me to take me to Brazil and now she has my phone.

That doesn't happen.

'Going to the loo.' I say it in an offhand way, hoping that this will make Dad casual too.

He shifts in his chair, runs his fingers through his hair. 'Can you wait for your mother to get back?'

'No. No, I can't. Am I not allowed to go to the *toilet* any more?'

I walk away before he can reply, aiming for a distant yellow and black sign with a lady in a sticking-out skirt on it. Dad actually gets up and follows. I cannot begin to address how weird and embarrassing this is, so I pretend he's not there. I'm not going to bolt for Jack and his car (someone has to behave properly around here, and it's clearly not going to be them), so I walk across the concourse with my father gaining on me all the way. When we get there I stand aside and gesture for him to go into the ladies' ahead of me.

'I'll just wait here,' he mutters, and he stations himself there, a toilet guard.

I sit on the loo and try to think. My parents are boring. They can't have done anything they have to run away from.

I THINK THEY'VE DONE SOMETHING TERRIBLE, Bella says helpfully.

Like what?

STEALING. ARSON. DRINK DRIVING. WHATEVER PEOPLE DO.

They must have done something, she's right, but it feels impossible.

Dad works as a financial adviser. He does go away for work from time to time, so I could half believe it, but he never actually has to drop everything and flee the country.

I flush the loo and wash my hands, staring at myself in the mirror as I do so. An Asian woman is washing her hands next to me. She looks at me in the mirror and grins, nodding at my hair. I smile back.

I still look like me. My hair still looks great. It looks very un-Ella. It is more Bella than Ella.

I am, however, wearing school uniform. I will be flying to Brazil in a black school skirt and white blouse and green V-necked jumper. I hope Mum has done some halfway reasonable packing. I hope she has brought me some books, my pencils, my little sketchbook. I quash the thrilling idea that, having produced a massive painting of Rio as part of my GCSE art, I now have the opportunity to draw it from life. I have headphones, but until they give me my phone back I can't use them. I need all that. I need it. If I don't have my world around me – my books, my music, my art – there will be too much blank space, and I know who will leap in to fill it. I must have my stuff to keep my head full of normal things, to ward off the badness.

I can't tell them that.

Dad escorts me back to our table in the café, where we discover that no one has stolen or blown up our bags, or taken away the dregs of our coffee. I stare at him over the top of my cup while he looks anywhere but at me. I wish I'd got Jack to stay right up to the last minute. I wish he was here now.

When Mum comes back she looks different again. She is grinning, though she has also been crying, and she is brandishing boarding passes. She's been gone for ages.

'Right. I've checked us all in. I've dropped off the bag.

We can go through security now.' She smiles with her mouth but not with her eyes. Her eyes look at me with huge, unnameable emotion. 'Let's get you to Rio, darling.'

It's quite nice to be locked in a metal structure that has been flung, by the power of the burning fossil, into the air. We are trapped, but no one cares. Everyone has chosen imprisonment. We are in a massive bomb, and it's slowly exploding in a controlled way that means it lands in one piece when we get to Rio. And it's messing up the environment as it does so.

I'm not completely sure about it being a bomb (I might be thinking of a space rocket), but I like the idea.

I am on my way to Rio. Although it's freaky and weird, this is also interesting. It is the very thing I wished for when I sat bored and ignored at school.

However, I have a bad, bad feeling.

I alternate between staring out of the window at the clouds and staring at a film about a woman who has a surrogate baby and then doesn't want to give it up. I'm not interested – I am barely even following – but it gives me moving shapes to look at. I have a book on my lap, and it's one I really want to read, which I bought at the airport, but I can't focus on that either. The people in front of me are talking loudly about their trip to Latin America.

'She'll meet us in Lima,' says a woman, 'if we get there before the twenty-fifth. If not, she says we can try to hook up in Cusco.' It goes on and on, the discussion of complicated arrangements. The people behind are also talking non-stop, but I can't understand them at all. I put my headphones back on.

I won't understand anything anyone says in Brazil – I don't speak even a little bit of Spanish, and I gave up French last year, although I was actually good at it. French won't get me far in Rio anyway.

Flying to Brazil, for the three of us, can't be cheap. Is it from my parents' savings? Is it embezzled? Stolen? Laundered? I can't imagine any of those things. It can only be money they had in the bank.

My parents are too normal for this. That is a fact. Yet here we are. It smells slightly of sweat in here. It smells of recirculated air. I have drunk a little bottle of white wine, and now Mum says I have to have soft drinks. Even though I am seventeen they are acting as if I was five. I could have sat here and got drunk on my own, and it wouldn't exactly have been *fun* but it would have distracted me. I'll be eighteen next month.

Both my parents are constantly looking at me, quickly and sneakily. Every time I look round one of them is doing a surreptitious check. It's extremely unnerving; this could still be about Bella. If they found out about my mental state they might take me off on a huge strange holiday as a way of avoiding a difficult conversation.

I can't think why else they would take me on a bucket-list sort of holiday. I'm obviously not ill.

Obviously.

There is nothing ill about me.

Nothing

ill
about
me
at
all.

If I concentrate I can almost make a fantasy life in Brazil come into focus. I pretend to myself that I could finish my education at a school beside the beach, with those mountains I painted as a perfect backdrop. I could make new friends, and they would be cool and international and they would like me and not despise me. In a few weeks from now I might be wearing a bikini top and little shorts to school, and I could have friends from Latin America and all over the world. My new friends will be glamorous and beautiful, with glossy black hair, and they will make everyone at home look dull and drab. I will fit in just fine with my purple sideways hair: I will be the cool quirky English girl.

If Dad had been embezzling, then he would be caught and arrested and taken home. There would be camera flashes, and everyone in the whole world would know that he stole money and we ran away to Rio. Everyone would be terrified of us as we were taken off the plane in handcuffs.

Dad couldn't have done a thing like that. He just couldn't.

I take off my headphones.

'What is it really?' I say to Mum, who is pretending to read an in-flight magazine.

'What is what?'

'The thing we're running away from.'

I look into her eyes for a while, and I can't read what's in them, but the look still feels like the most honest conversation we've had since she turned up at school, which was only this morning. Mum's eyes are a greyish blue. Mine are light brown like Dad's. Hers would go better with my hair: they're almost purple.

'Just enjoy the holiday,' she says after a while. 'I promise no one's in trouble. It's not like that.'

'What is it like?'

We stare at each other some more. She wants to tell me. I hold my breath and will her to do it. There is a tidal wave of emotion in her eyes, but she doesn't say another word. Still, she's worried about me; I can see it.

This is about me.

This is not about Dad's work or Mum having a breakdown.

It

is

about

me.

They would only whisk me away to the place at the top of my list if they thought this was my only chance to go there.

If they knew something terrible was about to happen.

If they wanted me to have fun while I still could.

I need to stop thinking.

I put on the headphones and turn back to the film. After a while a woman appears beside Mum with a trolley of food, but although I ask for the chicken I don't want it. I stare at it and smell its horrible smell and wonder why this chicken and I are meeting right here, right now, in a sealed tin thirty thousand feet up in the sky.

Someone farmed and killed this chicken. It probably grew up on a battery farm, too fat to be able to stand up on its legs. It never flew. It never even stretched out its wings. It was a crop, farmed like a cabbage, kept alive only because its life force was the thing that kept the meat fresh.

Then it was executed, sent off to a different sort of factory and made into an airline dinner, nestled in with potatoes and slimy broccoli, covered in a gloopy grey sauce, sent up into the sky, warmed through and presented to me.

I eat it quickly. It is, oddly, delicious and I smile at the way the world is set up for humans to do what the hell we like.

Later I wake with my face creased from the little pillow. I make the parents move so I can queue for the loo. I have no concept of what time it might be, but I suppose it's night back at home.

I wonder who is thinking about me. Jack, and Lily. Girls at school will talk about me for a bit and then move on to something else. Only Lily will actually miss me. Only Jack actually knows where I am.

I yawn and remember the first time I met Lily. She was the only mixed-race girl in the class and I was in love with her bouncy hair from afar. When we were put together for the nature walk I remember that my head was ringing and I knew I had to do something naughty to make it stop, and I was glad I was going to do it with Lily.

'I think there's a whole pile of fir cones just over there,' I said, and took her hand.

'Maybe some blackberries,' she suggested, and we headed away from the path together. We climbed over branches and pushed our way through brambles and past nettles, and ended up in a clearing deep among the trees, where we sat down and talked. We hadn't really talked before. Lily told me that her dad had just left and her mum was taking her back to Ghana for the summer. I told her that I was getting a kitten next week and I was going to call him Humphrey.

We stayed away for ages. I loved being away from the rest of the class, who ignored me or laughed at me even then because sometimes I was quiet and shy and at other times I lost control and had huge tantrums and they all thought I was mad. I didn't really know Lily at all, but suddenly she felt like my only friend.

It took ages before they started shouting for us. We passed the time by talking about any old thing. I told her some stories I'd half stolen from books. I adapted tales about orphans and castles and forest adventures, realizing that I could be myself with Lily. She has a beautiful voice, and she sang some songs to me very quietly. She taught me some words of Ghanaian.

We heard the others shouting, but I wasn't scared about being in trouble because there were two of us, and the ringing had stopped and I was back in my own skin. We stayed tight, giggling. Our dresses had been ripped by brambles and our hair was all over the place.

They shouted our names, and after a while we went back.

'It's OK,' Lily whispered, squeezing my hand. She and I were friends now.

The teachers were frantic. All the other girls were standing in pairs at the base at the edge of the forest, holding hands and looking scared. We ran towards them, and then I let go of Lily's hand and flung myself at Mrs Barrett, throwing my arms around her waist and sobbing.

'We got lost,' I said. 'We went off the path because we saw a rabbit and then we couldn't find it again. We were so scared.'

I could hear her heart pounding. She put a hand on my head.

'Well,' she said. 'You're safe now. No going off the path again, girls.'

I looked round Mrs Barrett and saw Lily standing a little way off, crying and being fussed over by other girls who all wanted to look after her. Our eyes met and we both smiled tiny little smiles.

'Here you go.' My mother hands me my passport and a white form. 'Your immigration form. I filled it in for you.'

'That's lucky, since I can't read or write.'

She sighs. 'Ella. You were asleep.'

I look away. We are in a queue of tetchy travellers. They all want to get out into Rio, and I want it more than any of them. Lots of them are talking fast in languages I don't understand; or at least in *a* language I don't understand. I let it drift past me. None of these travellers look as if they're being kidnapped by the people who are supposed to look after them.

None of them looks as if there might be something wrong inside their bodies.

Actually some of them do.

'Hello,' says the immigration man, and he gives me a quick, bored smile. I pass over my passport and white form, and he stamps the passport and hands it back, part of the form still in it. I say, 'Thanks,' and join Mum and Dad, who are, of course, both right there, waiting for me. Mum extends a hand and I give her back my passport and its form. She puts it in her handbag. I am five years old.

We have one single suitcase between us, and not much hand luggage either. 'We'll buy the right sort of clothes when we get there,' Mum said (God knows what she's packed). I'm trying to make my school uniform look the least uniformish I can, but if you're wearing a short black skirt, black tights and a white shirt, and you're not at school, you look like a waitress. I twiddle the long side of my hair around my finger, self-conscious about my stupid clothes rather than my purple hair. I don't want to be wearing tights in Latin America. The air, even indoors, is humid and heavy. Everything feels strange.

Then we are getting into a taxi. A man is throwing our suitcase into the boot. I ignore both parents' attempts at conversation and climb into the front. I slam the door before either of them can tell me to sit in the back with Mum.

It's dark, but I can still see trees with huge green leaves in strange shapes. There are lights twinkling all around. People live in this city: it is their world and I know nothing at all about it. This is wild and exciting.

The driver goes fast, using his horn often. It's totally brilliant. He swerves round corners and through tunnels. I'm happy to be his passenger. I can sense both parents tensing behind me, nervous, scared of crashing, but I don't care.

There are buses everywhere: they hurtle along, taking their unimaginable passengers to unimaginable destinations. They are awesome buses, the opposite of the stupid ones that hardly manage to speed up at all between stops at home. One veers towards us from the next lane, but our driver stops it with liberal use of his horn. Dad clears his throat, and I know that he wants to ask him to slow down and drive like he does, all sensible, checking his mirror and indicating and following the highway code. I also know that he won't say anything because he hasn't got the words, and even if he did he would feel that it was too rude.

I am giddy with excitement. I knew this would be my place and it is. Everything is different. Everything is wonderful and exciting and dreamlike, and none of it feels real. My head is not ringing. My vision has never been clearer. I am entirely myself.

There are mountains silhouetted against the dark sky. I have been longing for the mountains. A light is shining on top of one of them, and the driver points to it and says something to me. I say: '*Que?*' and hope he understands.

'*Cristo Redentor,*' he says, turning towards me and taking his eyes off the road in a way that makes both parents gasp behind us.

'*Cristo Redentor,*' I repeat, and he nods, pleased.

Then there are buildings all around, and I stare at them. When people say city centres are all the same, they are not talking about this city. There are no chain stores here; no Boots, no Smith's, no Sainsbury's. Shops flash by, all closed, and sometimes there are restaurants and bars with people sitting outside, and I can't look properly at anything because we're driving too fast for anything to come into focus.

I am a bit scared but I stamp that out. This is amazing. It's the place in my head, but it's real and better. I am absolutely longing to draw it all.

Soon we are outside a hotel with a shiny front, and a man in uniform opens my door. I am the first out of the car, the first to set foot on the Rio pavement, which is made not of normal paving stones, but of black and white mosaic tiles in swirling patterns. The air is hot. It smells exciting – like the sea, and tropical plants, and adventure.

I smile at the doorman. I watch my parents fumbling, thanking the driver, thanking the hotel doorman, wondering whether they ought to be tipping either one of them, and if so how much, and what Brazilian currency is all about anyway. I see them looking agonized, and I know that they are trying to remember what they paid for the cab when they bought the voucher at the airport, and working out the right percentage for a tip. While they're doing that the cabbie drives off without a tip, and the doorman carries our suitcase into the hotel. I follow him in, from the warm damp outdoors to a sharply air-conditioned lobby that is all shiny with marble.

I stand in the cool. Mum and Dad scurry after me and walk up to the desk, where a friendly man welcomes us all in English, and they start to fill in forms and hand over bank cards.

The three of us are sharing a room. I know it would be twice as expensive if we had two rooms, but I'm sure the reason they're making me sleep in the same room is so they can watch me all the time, awake and asleep. I had my own room when we went to Cornwall a couple of months ago, but now I am demoted to theirs. I might as well still be a baby. I feel like an object they have to remember not to lose.

It's a big and beautiful room though, and I would be monstrous to complain about it. My single bed is quite far away from their double, but they will still be able to sit up in bed and check on me whenever they want.

I sit on my bed, then lie on my back. The room has a high ceiling, a marble-tiled floor and a minibar and a safe, and it's clean and shiny.

'What time is it?'

Mum is fiddling with the suitcase. She has opened the wardrobe. The way she's fussing around while trying to look casual catches my attention, and I start to watch her closely, pretending to be undoing my shoe. I see her take a bundle of papers out of her handbag and put them into the little safe: from the haunted expression on her face I can tell they are important. I lean over and try to see them, but I can make out only a handful of official-looking envelopes.

She looks round to see whether I'm watching, and then presses buttons carefully until they beep and the safe is locked. Then she looks at me again. I pretend I didn't notice a thing.

'Nearly midnight, local time,' says Dad. He is pacing about, trying to force himself to relax. 'But that's nearly two back home.'

'Is this the southern hemisphere?'

'Of course it is.'

'We crossed the equator.'

'We did,' he says. 'I believe it goes through the north of Brazil. It's nice to see you excited, Ellie, if I'm allowed to say that.'

I smile at him. I am seized with an urge to jump up and down and sing. If you had told me this morning that my day would end in Rio, I would of course have thought it was unimaginably amazing, as well as impossible. And it is. And I am here. I am in this magical place; the place of my dreams.

I don't jump and sing. I just tell him that he *is* allowed to say it. I don't say that Mum wouldn't be – that's not fair but it's true.

I walk over to the window to check out Rio. In fact it looks out over a courtyard with other people's windows. There are lights on in two balconies that are crammed with flowerpots and bikes and clothes lines. Those are not hotel balconies; they are actual Brazilian people's lives.

'Fancy a shower before bed?' Mum says. Her eyes are wild. She is hanging up clothes. She seems to have brought a couple of random outfits for each of us.

'We're not going to bed now,' I say. I look at them and see that they both think we are. 'Mum! Dad? Hello? You turn up at school and pull me out in front of everyone and I have no idea why, but I bet Dad's not going to work tomorrow. You make me sit on a plane for hours without explaining anything that makes any sense at all – and now you're telling me to have a shower and go to bed? We're in *Rio de Janeiro* and I'm *not* going to bed. You saw it out there. It's amazing. I don't know what the hell is going on, but we're here and I think *you* think something bad is about to happen but I have no idea what. So take me out for a drink. Please.'

My head is ringing a bit but I'm not having that, not here, not now. My eyes dart around the edges of things, making them clear. I feel Bella stumbling out of her cave and I tell her to go back. I might need her later. I don't need her now.

She backs off. That's unusual. It makes me happy.

I make my way back to my bed and sit on it. I take deep breaths. I wait, but Bella really isn't there. Neither parent notices that I'm wobbly.

Mum sighs and puts both hands to her temples, which is just completely annoying.

Dad shakes his head. 'We can go out tomorrow, darling. Not now. It's two in the morning and we're in a foreign city. You have to be careful in Rio. You can't just wander around in the middle of the night. You're young and you have no idea how sheltered you've been.' Mum does a little huff when he says this, which is interesting. 'We might as well write big signs saying *Mug Me* and hold them above our heads.'

'People wouldn't understand them because they'd be written in a foreign language,' I say. My vision is perfectly clear, despite the fact that I'm annoyed. I shift backwards and lean against the wall. I am all Ella. 'It's midnight, not two, and I'm old enough for you to stop sheltering me – if that's what you've been doing.' I'm cross, but it's a mild, ordinary sort of cross. I just want to go out in Rio, to the nearest bar. It's nothing more than that. It feels

66

normal and amazing. 'Let's ask at reception if it's safe for us to go out,' I say, using the most reasonable tone of voice I can produce. 'Please. If there isn't somewhere right on this block, then we can come back and go to bed. I don't want alcohol or anything like that. I just want to sit out on one of those chairs on the pavement. Now that we're here.'

They look at each other. They look at me, their daughter, smiling at them, happy to be here. They both start putting their shoes back on. I close my eyes, my head against the wall, and feel the gratitude flooding through me and try to get myself together.

The man on reception laughs and says that of course it's absolutely fine to go out, and that there's a bar almost next door, and even though I'm still wearing school uniform I can't wait to go there.

It is right where he said it would be, and there's live music blasting out, and all I want to do is go inside and let the music go right through me, and dance and dance and dance. A band is playing. People are standing up, listening to the music. Some of them are, in an unshowy way, dancing in the street. I want to stay and dance in the street too, but obviously Mum and Dad don't, and anyway I don't want to dance with *them*. I look closely at the people as we pass by. These people are Brazilians. I am in their country. I am a foreigner now.

I am foreign.

I am a stranger.

I am an outsider.

It is thrilling and scary. I roll up the sleeves of my school jumper. The white threads of the old scars don't show at all under the streetlights.

When we get to the corner I see the name of our street on a sign.

'*Nossa Senhora de Copacabana*?' I read. 'Copacabana? Is that where we are?'

'Yes.' Mum looks far less happy with this fact than she should. 'Yes, darling. This is the area where lots of the hotels are.'

'Copacabana?'

'Yes.'

'We are standing in *Copacabana*? Actual Copacabana in Rio? Where's the beach? I want to paddle in the water right now! With the little mountains out to sea! I spent ages painting them.'

Dad sounds exhausted and I know that I'm pushing it.

'In the morning, Ellie. Absolutely not now. That beach is seriously dangerous after dark. It's a block or so away from here – I don't know in which direction. We'll find it in daylight.'

'Is it really dangerous? Or is that just something people think?'

'Really dangerous. I'm not comfortable as it is, leaving the hotel at night. We're doing it for you, Ellie, when both your mother and I want to go to bed. And if we don't see a decent-looking café in the next few minutes we're going back.'

'Come on.' I tug Dad's arm. 'Look. There's a place over here with tables out. One drink and we'll go back to the hotel.'

I order a Coke. Dad has a beer, which he attempts to order by saying, '*Una thairvaytha por favor,*' but the barman looks confused for quite a long time, so Dad points and says 'Beer?' and is immediately handed a bottle. Mum has a pale-green cocktail with mashed-up limes in it. It's not a drink I've ever seen before at home. Sometimes Jack and I go to the pub and drink lager. Sometimes Lily and I drink sticky-sweet drinks like Southern Comfort. Occasionally I get to tag along with Lily, Mollie and the twins, and we have cocktails with silly names and I am always the first to leave. Of course, as far as my parents are concerned, I've never drunk anything stronger than the occasional glass of wine with dinner.

'When in Rome,' Mum says, and she starts to drink it through the straw. 'Oh my *God*, I need this.'

I've seen her drinking wine. I've never seen her drunk. I will watch her in Rio with interest.

There are some other English people in the bar. They look like they're straight off the plane too. They are drinking beer but eyeing Mum's cocktail.

'This doesn't feel scary,' I say. 'You must admit – this is a lot less scary than Wetherspoon's.'

Dad inclines his head in a way that means it might not feel scary but it doesn't mean we're safe. He tries to look at me as if he knows everything and I am a little girl who needs protecting; but it doesn't work. He knows why we're here, and yet he is terrified of the very air we're breathing. And I'm not.

Dad drinks half his bottle of beer in a couple of gulps. I close my eyes and draw in a deep breath. I woke up this morning and had a shower and played with Humphrey and went to school feeling bored. Now I'm sitting at an outside table in Rio de Janeiro, watching my mum drink a cocktail very quickly through a straw and order another.

I have no idea what has happened.

4

34 days

I need to wake up. It's school. The light is coming in through the curtains and that means I've overslept. Even before I open my eyes I can tell it's brighter than usual.

Something strange happened. I lie in my bed. I am in my own messy bedroom. Humphrey is curled up by my feet. There is homework on the desk, and I've had a weird and messed-up dream that ended with me crawling into bed in Rio in the same room as my parents, who were already comatose after chucking back three boozy drinks each like rugby lads on a stag.

I yawn and prepare to open my eyes.

I need to go to school.

But I can't.

Because I am in Rio.

I

am

in

Rio.

It happened. This is Brazil. The room is light because the curtains weren't closed properly, and my dad is sitting

71

up in bed reading a book, with the air of someone who wants a cup of tea and has had a look for the kettle and found it missing because we are Abroad in a Foreign Place. If he wanted tea in bed he shouldn't have left the country.

Mum is asleep. Her hair is all over the pillow and her mouth is open and she was too tipsy to take off her make-up, so there is mascara all the way down one of her cheeks, and it's probably on the pillowcase too – though she has always told me that if I *must* wear make-up (and I don't need to because I am so pretty, and so on), then I should always take it off before bed because of pores and bed linen and things. She doesn't often wear make-up herself, and she isn't looking like such a classy lady now. If I had my phone I would pretend to Dad that I was going to take her photo (though I wouldn't really be that mean; I would mime it to make him laugh), but of course I haven't got it because they took it away from me and now it's locked in that safe.

I *have* to get my phone. Yesterday was one thing, but actually living daily life with my parents and without a phone is something completely different. I don't know what to do with myself, now that I can't check what they're saying about me on social media, or look at what's happened in the world, or just put on my headphones and listen to music or an audiobook.

Everyone else listens to music. I do, but I listen to books more. I don't know why everyone doesn't want to be read a story all the time. I listen to the A-level texts over and over again and that's how I know them so well. If I could I'd read a book with my eyes while listening to another with my ears.

Dad sees me looking at Mum. He gazes down at her sleeping off her cocktails, and smiles. I smile back, and haul myself out of bed and into the bathroom.

This is Copacabana. There is a beach nearby. No one robbed us when we went out, and no one looked as if they might be going to either, even though it was dark and we had no idea what we were doing or where we were going. My parents and I are going to be here for some unspecified length of time, for a reason they won't tell me.

I'm going to make them tell me.

They *have* to tell me.

Even if it's something awful I have to know, because I am starting to imagine things.

I brush my teeth and comb my hair with my fingers. I am far too pale to be here. I need to get a tan.

An hour later I trail into the dining room after my parents, trying to look independent and cool.

No one cares.

The room has a huge bank of buffet tables to one side, televisions on at either end, and tables with white tablecloths. The waiting staff are wearing black and white uniforms, but they don't look stuffy. I watch Dad talking to the woman at the desk, and then follow him and Mum over to a table.

'We just help ourselves, darling,' says Mum.

The buffet is enormous, covering table after table. I stare at it.

'I know!' says Dad. 'Right? As much as you like. Go for it.'

I pile a plate with scrambled eggs (or MIXED EGGS as the label calls them) and some balls coated in breadcrumbs that turn out to have lovely melted cheese in the middle, and a roll. I put that on the table and go back for a glass of fresh orange juice. A woman comes round with a flask of coffee and pours it for us, though Mum shakes her head and goes to find herself some kind of pathetic homeopathic-type tea from an otherwise-unvisited table round the side of a pillar. Dad, usually another fan of horrible weak tea, joins me in a coffee.

'This is an awesome breakfast,' I say, and it is. The cheese-ball things are wonderful, and for some reason I don't want to eat meat at the moment. I love animals so I don't really know why I've always eaten them. I don't take any meat; I look at Dad's bacon and things but I don't steal any from his plate even though he'd let me.

Mum is just eating fruit (she claims only to like things that grow in the ground), and it looks so nice that when I've finished all my eggs and cheesy things I go back and get a second plate of breakfast from the grown-in-the-ground part of the table. I end up with a pile of mango, watermelon and pineapple slices, all juicy and all gorgeous. I could eat like this every day.

Perhaps we *will* eat like this every day now. Perhaps this is the rest of our lives.

'So,' I say to Mum and Dad as we finish our drinks. 'What's the plan? What time do you need to be at work, Dad? Did your suit get crumpled in the suitcase? It must have been in there if you're going to work.'

I stare from one to the other. This would be a good time for them to admit they made that bit up, but of course they don't.

'Oh, Ella.' Mum is using her put-upon voice, which I think is a bit rich, considering. 'Ella. Just give us a bit of space to think, please, darling. Dad's work isn't today.'

'Of course it's not. How surprising. So what do you need to think about?'

Mum looks hurt by my tone. Hiding Bella from Mum has, I realize, been the single greatest achievement of my life. I would be horrified if she found out what I'm really like.

'We just need to make a plan. I know we have to buy you some more clothes, and we will. Let me talk to the front desk about the best place to go for that.'

I sigh. 'OK. Can I have the room key? I want to go and read my book. If I had a book, which I don't. I'll watch some Brazilian telly. Or am I not allowed to be away from your side in case someone kidnaps me?'

Mum looks at Dad, who laughs.

'As adorable as you are, Ellie, I don't think you'll be kidnapped between here and the bedroom. Here you go.'

He extracts the room key from his wallet and hands it over, and I walk as quickly as I can out of the breakfast room to get away from them.

Something happened when I mentioned being kidnapped. It was only a fraction of a second, but Mum reacted in a weird way. Dad did too, though he covered it instantly – he's more grounded than she is. I have no idea what the fuck that could mean. I am normal, and no one in their right mind would want to kidnap me. Who would want Ella Black? I come with baggage, and although my parents have enough money for this trip, apparently, they're not exactly the global super-rich, so it can't really be a ransom situation.

I am *not* normal, and that is all the more reason why no one should want to snatch me.

All I can think of is that I might be ill, but I don't want to be ill. I want to leave school (which I appear to have done, for the moment) and have adventures. I want to make myself better in my head and do things in the world. I want to see things, experience them. I want to do good things. I want to do them for other people as well as for myself. That's a new thought.

There is something in the safe that will help me work out what's happening. I know there is.

I will try all possible codes until I open it. It's sure to be my birthday. They always use my birthday. If it isn't my birthday I'll know there is something they really, really, *really* don't want me to see, and I will find it.

And then I see him.

As I'm charging out, three people – two boys and a girl – are coming in through the door from the lobby. They are Latin-looking, chatting in what seems to be both Spanish and English. Then I see the boy at the back, and I stop.

It is like being electrocuted. I recognize something in his eyes. He's a stranger; yet I know him. This boy is one of the main characters in my life. I know in an instant that the feelings I know from books and poems and songs are real. I know him; I just haven't met him yet. He has dark brown hair and olivy skin, and he is tall and broad and muscular. I never knew it before, but this is what my ideal boy looks like. Jack flits through my head and I smile. Jack would like this boy too.

The boy stops and looks at me. He smiles. Our eyes meet. I couldn't look away if I wanted to.

He's older than I am, but not much, and he's wearing cut-off denim shorts and a plain green T-shirt. He smiles the most perfect smile. He has even teeth, and his smile takes over his whole face. I am smiling too.

'*Hola*,' he says. He is staring at me in the same way I am staring at him. Am I imagining that? I don't think I am. I hope I'm not. No one has ever looked at me like this.

'*Hola*,' I say. I don't know what to do, and so I grin a bit more. He is looking into my eyes, and although I want to freeze this moment and save it forever, I have to be the first to look away. I need to get into the lift before my parents come along and ruin everything.

I break the eye contact and try not to fall over as I walk across the small lobby. I press the 'up' button and turn back. The boy is still looking. Our eyes meet again. I say everything I can through my eyes, and he says it back.

Then he gives a little nod and turns away, catching up with his friends.

If anyone else was here they would see a girl standing in a lift, smiling into the mirror. In fact I am being serenaded by cherubs with harps. I am being struck by that angel with the arrow. I am gasping for breath.

I have to talk to that boy. I don't know what I'd say but I don't care.

The lift chimes and I am on the eleventh floor. I open our room and sit down on the bed, and relive the almost-wordless encounter over and over again without stopping.

He is staying at the hotel. I have to speak to him. He is with two friends, a boy and a girl. I, however, am with my mummy and daddy. That might spoil everything.

I cannot let that happen.

All I want is that boy. I have no idea whether we will be able to speak to each other, but I'm sure one of his friends was speaking English.

He said: '*Hola*.'

I said: '*Hola*.'

It isn't really very much to work with, but I replay it again and again.

He was going to breakfast at half past eight. Tomorrow I will go to breakfast at half past eight too, and I'll do whatever it takes to get there without my parents.

The dress I am wearing right now, packed by Mum, is all right, but it's the only thing I've got that is. It's purple like my hair, made from T-shirt material, and although it's very plain and cost almost nothing from some high-street shop, it's nice. I need to do some serious shopping today in order to have something better to wear for breakfast tomorrow. At home I always wear sleeves. Here I can't do that. I'll just have to assume that no one will notice. Wearing sleeves is a habit and I need to lose it.

Now, though, I'm in the room alone, and I need to see what's in the safe.

I stand in front of it: it wants a four-digit code, so obviously I'm going to try and give it the exact one it needs. As well as all the big things, my phone is in there and I would really, really like my phone back. I try my birthday: 1711. It doesn't work. I try my year of birth, and Mum's birthday, and Dad's, but literally nothing works.

Whatever is in here, my parents *really* don't want me to find it. I start to panic.

SMASH IT UP.

That came from nowhere. I shake my head. I can't actually smash it up. Can I?

IT'S NOT REALLY SECURE. IT'S JUST FOR REASSURANCE. WE CAN EASILY BREAK IT.

We can't. I mustn't. I look around for an implement, just in case, but someone is knocking on the door. Bella fades away as I stare at it, picturing the gorgeous boy on the other side, forgetting the safe. He has asked reception for my room number and come to find me.

I'll open the door, and he will be out there, and I will step right up and kiss him. I would kiss him without knowing his name, or anything about him.

I pull my hair over my shoulder, arrange my body to what might or might not be its best advantage, take a deep breath and open the door.

'Oh,' I say, slumping. 'It's you.'

Dad laughs. 'Who were you expecting?'

'No one. We've got two keys, haven't we?'

'Yes. And both of them are here. We didn't think we'd need two keys for breakfast.'

'Ella,' says Mum. 'Are you all right, darling? You look pale.'

I turn on her. I can't help it.

'You always say I look pale. I'm pale because we live in a cold rainy country, and even though we're in Brazil now, we haven't actually been out of doors in daylight. We're like the vampires of Rio.'

'Ella!'

I cave instantly. 'Sorry. I'm just desperate to get outside. Because we're actually here. You know?'

Mum caves too. She hugs me, pulling me tight so my face is in her hair.

'Oh, I'm sorry, darling. I know it's a lot to deal with. Let's sort ourselves out and get into the sunshine. I know you need to have a look at the beach, and it ought to be safe enough in daylight if we don't carry valuables. There are shopping malls and things like that, so after you've seen the beach we can ask the hotel to call us a taxi, and get you all kitted out.' She flicks her eyes towards me and away again. 'And if you wanted to get your hair dyed back to your lovely blonde, we could do that too. I'm sure it would be easy.'

I frown. I don't need to answer that part. 'Clothes would be good,' I say. 'Thank you.' I am going to keep being nice. No outbursts, despite the fact that my parents are annoying and boring and forming a constant human shield around me, and that is going to stop me talking to the boy.

I want to talk to the boy. And I want to open the safe. But I want to talk to him more. And I need some clothes.

I know Mum is trying her best but I am very nearly eighteen. They have trusted me to walk around town on my own since I was eleven, and now they've gone completely, freakishly weird on me. However, I am desperate to get out into the sunshine and see the beach and breathe the air and embrace the fact that I am actually here, so I pull myself together. I'll have another go at the safe later.

'Thanks,' I say. I make myself smile at Mum. 'Sorry. The beach would be wonderful. Thank you.'

The relief that swamps her face, just for a moment, makes me feel bad.

It is the middle of the afternoon. We have been to the shops and now I'm sitting on the real, sandy, gorgeous Copacabana Beach, a sketchbook on my lap, drawing the beach and the rocks and the mountains in real life. The sun is on my face and I'm doing my best to look entirely absorbed in my drawing, while secretly listening to my parents' whispered conversation. I am frowning and concentrating hard (but not really), and after a while they start talking a tiny bit louder. I strain to catch the words, and then I hear Mum saying:

'The cattery are asking for a fortune.'

Dad says: 'Well, they always do.'

I carry on listening but it turns out they really *are* talking about how much it will cost for Humphrey to go to his own (downmarket) hotel. Apparently our cleaner, Michelle, is coming in tomorrow and Mum says she's asked her to drop Humphrey off when she leaves. Poor Humphrey. I bet he'd rather stay out in the wild, catching his own dinner, than go to that smelly place and be shut in a cage, having to listen to the yowling of all the other cats asking loudly why the humans have sent them to prison.

My parents didn't plan this trip *at all*. I feel bad for Humphrey. I would never have chosen to go away without saying goodbye to him. I would have cuddled him and talked to him and explained why I was leaving and when I would be back. He will be missing me, and he will also be missing Bella. I have had an almost Bella-free day today. I love that.

I have to find out what's happening.

And I have to find that boy.

I watch a tiny child splashing in the shallow water. Copacabana is not how I expected it to be even though I knew exactly what it looked like; even though I did a huge painting of almost this exact view in art last year. Then I was painting from a still photo; now I am sketching from life, and it is wildly lively. Everyone is here. A group of extraordinary boys wearing tiny swimming trunks run up and down nearby, and I cannot stop staring at the chiselled contours of their bodies. They are all black and glistening. Their muscles are defined and none of them has an ounce of fat. They don't look like humans in the way my parents and I are human. I have never seen anyone who looks like this in real life.

I remember the boy in the hotel again. Every part of me longs to be close to him.

The toddler's mother takes its hand. Vendors come past selling peanuts and sunglasses. Up by the pavement a string of little cafés sell food and coffee and beer. Everything anyone could want is right here. My drawing is full of as much life as I can cram into it.

A woman runs past wearing a tiny swimming costume, her body jiggling all over the place, and no one is taking any notice. I know that on a British beach people would be sniggering at her, but here they really don't care at all.

I fill in some detail of the bumpy little mountains out in the water. Mist floats around in the distance, and the green hills are sometimes hidden, sometimes revealed.

'Nice to see you happy,' says Dad.

I try to put on a sulky face but it doesn't work, because they both laugh. Mum is more relaxed than she has been since we got here, and it's actually nice to see that, and I do want her to be happy, because if she's less haunted and stressed, the emergency might have gone away a bit.

'You always said you'd love it here,' she says, looking at my picture and smiling.

I nod. I want them to think that this is enough; that Rio and the sunshine and the little denim shorts and tops and sandals, and the sketchbook and the pencils they've bought me are enough to stop me trying to work out what is going on.

I put down my sketchbook and smile at them.

'So,' I say. 'We can fit in some sightseeing now. Let's do something.'

They laugh and look at each other. Mum shrugs.

'I suppose,' says Dad, 'that this could be a good time to visit the famous Jesus up on the hill. What's its name? You know – the Christ statue.'

'Yeah – the *Cristo Redentor*?'

'What?'

'The taxi driver told me last night. It was lit up on the hilltop. He said it was *Cristo Redentor*.'

'I missed that,' says Mum. 'Christ the Redeemer. Well. The morning might be better really. I'm not sure the hotel will be able to arrange a trip immediately.'

'They organize all sorts,' says Dad. 'I asked about it. They book the Cristo thing, and the Sugar Loaf Mountain, and any number of walking tours. There are even tours to the favelas. You know, the slums. I think we can give that one a miss, don't you?'

I remember the film *City of God*. We watched that a few months ago as part of Mollie's education.

'A tour of the slums?' I say. 'That sounds like a horrible idea. Stare at the poor people! Point at them and take photos and then go back to the lovely comfy hotel? I actually think that's disgusting.'

'And those favelas are absolute no-go areas,' says Mum. 'We need to keep you safe.'

Her words hang in the air.

The man at the hotel, whose name badge says he is Pedro, tells us that this is a good day to go up the mountain because it's so clear, but that we'll have to hurry.

'You don't need a tour,' he says, smiling the conspiratorial smile of one who knows that he's supposed to be pushing them at us. 'You just need a taxi. Then you buy tickets for the train. It's very easy. When you get out of the taxi, don't speak to anyone trying to sell you a trip, OK?'

'Will it be OK that we don't speak Spanish?' I say, and he laughs.

'Well, that won't matter at all. Here in Brazil we speak Portuguese. But, no, you'll be fine with English.'

'I meant Portuguese,' I say, my cheeks flaming. I didn't really: I had no idea. But now I do.

The doorman flags down a yellow cab and tells the driver where we're going, and we are off, weaving through the streets again. I sit in the front, like before. I just get in and no one stops me.

The driver grins at me.

'*Hola*,' I say experimentally. I have just repeated everything I have ever said to the boy at breakfast.

'*Hola*,' he replies with a nod.

We set off into the traffic and I stare out of the window, trying to see everything.

I could look at Rio forever. I think you'd see new things every single time. There are people in Lycra. There are gyms with huge windows looking out on to the streets, filled with people doing weights. There are old people and children, black people and white people. There are juice bars and coffee shops and restaurants. There are drag queens and old men in suits, fat people and thin people. There are old people sitting in parks playing chess. Everything is here.

At school I thought I was pretty much educated. I barely scraped through the social side of things, but when it came to the education I thought I was doing all right. I felt I knew the things you need to know. Now I'm not at all sure I know any single thing at all. The world is so much larger than I ever imagined, and there is so much more to life than my small existence. When I listen to Brazilian people speaking, I can't make out a word of it because I know nothing about these people and their language, and I wish I did. The sounds are different: there are lots of 'shh' and 'chhh' things going on. If we stay longer I'm going to have to puzzle it out. I can't believe I didn't even know what language it was. That is mortifying.

A minute ago everything in my life was mapped out. Now it's not. No one seems to hate me in Brazil; I am coming alive.

I want to go online and try to work out what I'm doing here, so I have to get my phone.

I try to remember anything I've read about parents running away with their children. It's what one parent does to keep the child away from the other, but that's not us. Some parents ran away with their child a few years ago, I think, because the child was ill and they didn't want him to have chemo because they wanted him treated with crystals or something.

I would know if I was desperately ill. There would have been doctors' appointments and hospitals.

There were.

With a lurch of my stomach I remember that there *were* doctors' appointments.

My vision goes a bit fuzzy. This is important. I can't have Bella stirring. I need to focus. I force her away.

I remember. I was small, and I hated them. I only remember them in a fuzzy way, but I know they happened. I remember being upset, crying and crying, and everyone trying to comfort me and tell me it was all right. I remember a woman talking to me in a nasty pretend-kind way, but I didn't like her eyes and I wouldn't speak to her. I remember my mother crying along with me.

I had forgotten all about it. I think little-me made a decision to forget it, and then did.

I remember my mum saying: 'We'll always look after you.' I remember that making me feel better. What if I have a genetic condition? It could be getting worse. Perhaps I won't be able to live much longer before I start to deteriorate. That would be a reason to bring me to Rio.

I try not to think about that.

There was a nuclear stand-off last time I heard the news on the radio as we drove away from school. Maybe we're here to hide out from that. There was something about the simian flu, which has been around for a while. Perhaps, without my knowing, I have tested positive for it and they've brought me here to stop me being dissected and used for medical research.

Rio is not a place you visit to get *away* from terrifying viruses.

It all seems unlikely. Everything seems impossible, but the doctors' appointments feel like the biggest clue. I am probably very ill. I whisper that under my breath.

I am probably very ill.

The driver looks over, but he doesn't say anything.

If I was ill it might explain why I have Bella. I could have something in my brain, something real. A tumour with a name. I wish I had my phone. I would use it to google things I might have. I would wade through medical papers. Or I could use it for distraction, if Rio wasn't distraction enough.

I stare out of the cab into a bus, where a woman is holding a tiny dog up to the window. I wave at the dog, and she lifts its paw to make it wave back.

I focus on my toes. They feel well. My legs feel OK. So do my knees. Of course they do: this thing is in my head. I concentrate as hard as I can on each part of my body, inside and out, to try to diagnose anything that might be out of the ordinary, but as far as I can tell it all feels fine. If I was ill, or some kind of medical time bomb, they wouldn't be letting me out and about in Rio. Or would they? Perhaps they would. I don't know anything.

The secret illness is, weirdly, the most plausible of the possibilities. I feel sick.

I want my phone. I want my book. Before we left I was reading a sci-fi trilogy about a place called Area X that changed people when they went into it. I am in my own Area X and I want to go back to the fictional one, please.

I want to listen to music.

I want to talk to Jack and Lily.

I want to see that boy.

When we get out of the cab, ticket touts descend, as Pedro said they would, trying to sell us trips up the mountain. I bat them away, striding over to the ticket office because I know Mum would be swayed by anyone telling her the trip would be too dangerous unless she bought a special expensive tour. I ask for the tickets myself, and Dad pays, and we go into the waiting area where a man painted silver stands very still, a hat for coins at his feet.

On the train I sit a little way away from the parents, staring out of the window. I want to hear them speaking because I am consumed by the need to know. I think I'm going to die soon; perhaps this is my last able-bodied trip out into the world. I imagine my brain melting away until I can't read or speak or think or feed myself. I would kill myself now rather than let that happen.

The train judders into action and I stare out at the rainforest. *Live every day as if it were your last, because one day it will be.* That was a meme that used to be passed around at school. It felt like an easy thing to say, trite but kind of true. It was superficial and easy.

Now it feels terrifying.

After a while I see that Mum and Dad are leaning towards each other, muttering in their fighty way, so I slide over on to the seat behind theirs and they don't notice.

'Yes, I know,' Dad is hissing. 'But Ellie's not demonstrative. She never has been. She's not the hugging type. It's not *you*. It's because she's –'

He breaks off quickly because Mum stiffens. She has sensed me there and looked round.

'What?' I say. 'It's because I'm *what*?'

'Nothing,' says Mum. 'Don't creep up.'

I'm not the hugging type. That is true. I want to cry but I can't because I'm not really the crying type either; not when they're around, anyway. I would like to be the hugging type. I think I would like that very much.

'We went to the doctor's a lot when I was little.' It is hard to get the words out, but I say them carefully, one by one. 'What was it about?'

Both of them look straight ahead. Neither of them so much as flickers. I feel the panic coming off their backs; at least I think I do. I think I feel them sitting there, utterly frozen because they don't know what to say. I think I feel them wondering how on earth to handle this.

I wish they'd looked round at me, puzzled, and said something like: *What are you talking about? No, you didn't.* But they don't, and the time ticks by and they still don't.

I can look back and see that Mum's been protecting me all my life – the CCTV outside the house, the quadruple locks on the doors, the burglar and fire alarms. I have no idea what I'm being protected from. Or maybe she's just scared of the outside world and I've had to stay inside with her to be safe.

I'm nearly an adult. If I'm ill they have to tell me because that's what people do. Little children get told when they've got leukaemia, and yet somehow I'm not allowed to know what this huge thing is that's wrong with my life.

I want to ask them to look after me now, but I can't. It's easier to be nasty. It is getting easier and easier as my head is filled with a high-pitched ringing. She's been away from me all day but now she's stronger than she's ever been. She is blocking out the rainforest and the train so that all I can see is my parents. Like me, she knows that they have the answer and that there is something about me and that they are choosing not to tell me because they don't trust me, or because it's too awful.

I long to be the hugging type. I want to let my parents look after me, to have them stroke me and tell me that everything is going to be all right, that I'm not terminally ill, that this holiday is a weird treat because they love me so much.

THAT'S NOT WHAT IT IS.

I know.

THEY'RE LYING.

I know.

DO SOMETHING ABOUT IT.

Mum hardly ever tries to hug me any more. She will never know that my good self has often kept away from her so Bella can't hurt her, because Bella absolutely hates my mother.

I don't even want to be nice. Blotches dance across my vision.

'I'm nearly eighteen,' I whisper. They both have to lean back to hear me.

SAY THE THINGS THAT WILL HURT THEM MOST.

'I'm not your baby. I'm an adult now – I could get up and walk away from here and never speak to either of you ever again.' *I am holding the hammer, hitting the bird.* 'And I will. You don't have the right to keep this secret from me. If you don't tell me what's going on, you don't get to be my parents any more. You don't trust me enough to tell me anything – I don't trust you enough to live with you. That's how it is.'

A part of me gasps. I have never let Bella speak to them before. Not since I was tiny and I had what everyone called 'tantrums', before I learned that I had to hide them.

'Ellie,' says Dad. He puts a hand on my arm. I shake it off. I cannot let him come close to Bella.

'You . . . should . . . tell . . . me,' I say. I bite my lip until it bleeds. I clench my hands into fists and push my nails into my palms. I inhale deeply. I cannot shout and rage on a train that is juddering up a Brazilian mountain, that is otherwise filled with content tourists idly staring out of windows. I can't attack them in public even though Bella is begging me to let her. I walk quickly away to stop myself exploding, and when I get to the back of the train I sit on an empty seat, slide over to the window and press my forehead against the glass.

There must be some medication that would stop this happening.

I think it's Bella that's made me ill. She might be a symptom or she might somehow be a cause.

Go *away*

go away

go away.

I close my eyes and recite the words. I need it to go away.

The universe the universe the universe.

I picture outer space. I am not even a fraction of a dot. I am tiny and insignificant.

As we judder on it recedes, just far enough for me to take control of myself. It would have been better to cry. Then they would have come close and hugged me. They are my parents and I know I love them. Of course I love them. Everything I do is about trying not to disappoint them, about being the daughter they deserve and hiding the bad things. And I have just said terrible things. I am crying now, staring out at the wild greenery. I wipe my eyes with the back of my hand and sniff. My eyeliner must be everywhere. I cannot fall to pieces. I try to breathe.

Stay
away
Bella.
S
t
a
y
a
w
a
y
B
e
l
l
a

Someone taps me on the shoulder. I look round without bothering to tidy my face up, and see that a man in a baseball cap with VENEZUELA on it is holding out a pack of tissues. I shake my head, but then reach out a trembling hand and take them anyway. I wipe my eyes and blow my nose. I can't look round at him again but I am grateful.

I wrestle myself under control. I know my parents are looking at me, and I want to open up to them but I can't, because I cannot tell them that I am possessed by my own demon, and also because they haven't told me what I'm doing here. Dad's right: I've never been one for hugs and kisses, though he and I have always shared an understanding. I built that barrier up myself by trying to protect them; but they've strengthened it by bringing me here with a huge secret.

I started it and they've made it worse. I hate myself, and it's probably easiest if I hate them too.

There are two men with tattoos in front of me; they are smiling at each other and pointing things out and laughing at their own private jokes and I want to ask if I can walk around with them when we get to the top of this mountain. They probably don't want a strange foreign girl tagging along; least of all a strange foreign girl with purple hair and white legs and a tear-stained face, who didn't even know until a few hours ago that Portuguese is the language of Brazil.

The Venezuela man taps me on the shoulder again, and I hand back the tissue packet, but he gestures for me to keep it. He says something that I don't understand, and then when he sees I don't understand he says: 'I'm sorry you sad.'

I manage a little smile and a nod. That feels like the kindest thing anyone has ever said.

The forest parts, and then I am looking at the most breathtaking view in the world. The sun is glinting off the sea. There are the little mountains out in the water, and I can see the beaches, the sprawl of buildings, the tiny cars. I gaze and gaze and gaze. I breathe. I stare and breathe and I don't want the train to stop, but it does.

Outside, my parents come and stand beside me and I want to say the right thing. I want to say sorry, but the word sticks in my throat and I can barely breathe around it. I move instead, along with the crowd, and they walk on either side of me.

'Ella,' says Dad. I'm glad it's him speaking rather than her. 'Look. I know this is frustrating. There are a few things we just can't tell you right now. It's nothing terrible. Please just trust us for a while. You're not ill.'

I don't answer because I don't believe him, and I don't know what to say. I give each parent an awkward little hug – the best I can manage – and walk away.

The huge statue of Jesus towers above us. A crowd of people gathers at a distance from him, standing with their arms outstretched like his, while each one has a friend lying on their back on the ground in front of them, taking a photograph. I suppose the angle makes it look funny. In a way I want to try it out, just to be normal. But I can't, of course, because I am the only person on this mountain without a phone. A little kid of about three is sitting on the ground playing with one. I am literally the only one who doesn't have the piece of technology that connects you to the world, and your friends, and the things you love, and your life. And I don't even know why I haven't got it. Because I don't know anything.

Bella said horrible things to Mum and Dad. That has happened now. It is there: they have met her even though they don't know it. I want to say sorry, to make it up to them, to thank them for bringing me to the best place in the world and for giving me an amazing holiday. But I can't: I don't know how.

There are souvenir shops and stalls selling everything Christ-the-Redeemer branded, and I want to get a fridge magnet for our kitchen to remind us of this holiday, which is going to be amazing because I'm never going to be horrible ever again, except that I don't know how many days are going to pass before we'll be back in our kitchen, or if anything will ever be normal again anyway. A stressed-looking man wearing a Jesus apron and baseball cap strides past me into the café, and Mum appears, taking my arm and guiding me out of his way. I shake her off when I actually want to sob in her arms.

I want a cap. I want an apron. I want things with this place on them, to anchor me. I look at Jesus. I wish he actually would redeem me. I stare up at him. His arms are open. His skirt has lovely pleats in it. I like the drapes of his clothes.

I need to be able to make myself be nice. I do it at school every day. I can compliment Jesus on his drapery but I can't say anything kind to my own mother.

I will try.

'Sorry,' I say. My voice comes out very quiet indeed. 'Mum. I'm sorry I was horrible on the train. Really sorry.'

She puts her arm round my shoulders and tries to pull me into a proper hug. I let her do it because she is my mum.

5

33 days

I walk into the breakfast room, carefully dressed in my new outfit with my hair blow-dried and what I hope is just the right amount of make-up to make me look 'natural'. I scan the room, my heart fluttering, every atom of me longing to see him and also scared that if I *do* see him the magic might be over. Imagine looking at him and just seeing someone ordinary. Imagine his eyes looking me over and then, bored, focusing on something else. It felt so magical yesterday that it might not have been real at all.

I look around the room and I know that none of these people is him.

'Are you sure, darling?' Mum said when she saw me ready to go downstairs. 'I mean, that outfit is a little more "beach" than "hotel breakfast".'

I took a deep breath and reminded myself to be nice.

'It'll be fine,' I said. 'It's Rio, and I'm dressing for the day.' I wanted to snap at her, but I didn't. I walked over to give her a hug, but I didn't quite dare because I knew there was someone inside me who was very annoyed that she had questioned my outfit. At the last minute I dodged sideways, and she looked confused.

As it's our second morning I feel like someone who totally knows the way things are done round here. I go straight to the buffet for a glass of orange juice. I stand by the table of food on my own, wondering whether I could really attract the attention of the most gorgeous boy in the world over breakfast at a hotel in Rio de Janeiro.

If he turns up.

What if he went home yesterday? What if he isn't here at all? What if I never see that boy again? Yesterday morning's glance might be the only experience of love I'm ever going to have in my entire life.

The idea gives me a pain in the chest. It makes my brain hurt, my heart hurt. It would be unbearable – to stare into a stranger's eye and feel everything and then never see him again.

I put the juice on the table. Both parents are sitting there waiting for the coffee lady to arrive, and I know I should have offered to get them some juice too. I don't know why I didn't.

'D'you want some juice?' I mutter. They both look delighted to be asked, but they say no. I go and get two glasses anyway, and put them on the table, just in case they change their minds.

I go back to pile up a plate of fruit, which I eat with a knife and fork while Mum goes to get the same thing for herself and Dad helps himself to bacon and, oddly for breakfast time, ham-and-cheese toasted sandwiches. I still don't want to eat meat. In fact right now I am eating a raw vegan diet, consisting only of fruit, which would make my skin glow and my eyes sparkle if I kept it up, so I keep it up for several minutes, until I drink some coffee and then remember the cheese balls and go and pile a plate with them.

I have a cheese ball in my mouth when he looks at me. Not only do I have a cheese ball in my mouth, but I'm talking to my parents about whether or not there is too much cloud for us to take the cable car up the Sugar Loaf Mountain. I am saying: 'We probably don't need to go up a mountain *every single day*.' When I say the word 'day', however, I put so much emphasis on it that a big piece of cheese ball flies on to the table and stays connected to my mouth by a string of melted cheese, and that is when I look up and see that the boy is standing nearby, looking at me.

It is the worst thing that has ever happened.

He is standing beside the very next table with his two friends, and he is smiling at me, though his smile is now frozen. This is the worst moment of my life.

He was watching as I spat food out on the table. He was waiting for me to look at him, and then I spat out my food and it stayed connected to my mouth by a string, a helpful marker of exactly what had happened. He saw that, and he can see it now, and there is absolutely no way around that.

I want to die right now. I want the hotel to catch fire so we can all run out into the street and down to the beach and into the sea and swim forever. I want a long-dormant volcano to rise up from beneath this dining room and push us all away on a tide of lava. I have turned so red that my lipstick must be camouflaged against my face. My hair is probably dark red too. I move my hand to break the cheese string, but I can't pick up the piece of cheese ball because that would mean admitting that I spat it out. Dad raises his eyebrows in an annoying way, and I only see him do it because I am looking anywhere but at the boy. Mum tuts, picks up the pieces of food with her napkin, folds them away and puts it at the end of the table in the imaginary fourth person's place. She shakes out the fourth person's napkin and puts it on her lap, all in one smooth move.

I will never be able to speak to him. Any romance we might have had is over before it could start because of me. The whole room should be pointing and laughing.

I keep my eyes on the table and tune out my parents while they continue droning on about the cable car. I eat the rest of the cheese balls silently. I drain my juice. I have no idea whether the boy is looking at me because I can't allow my gaze anywhere near him.

After a while I go back up to the buffet to get more juice because the embarrassment has dried my throat right out. There are six different jugs there, but I go straight for the orange because it's delicious. I am pouring it when, behind me, a voice – and I know whose voice it is before I even look round – says: 'I love your hair.'

He has an American accent. His voice is warm and honeyish and it goes right through me. It makes my knees weak. I close my eyes. I don't think it matters now that he saw me spit out a cheese ball.

I turn just a little bit and look at him, and then my face is smiling its biggest smile. This is the smile I have been holding in reserve all my life, just for this moment.

'Thanks.' I manage to stop pouring the juice before it overflows, so that's good. 'It just grew like this.'

'Seriously?'

'No.'

'Oh – right! Are you on vacation with your family?'

'Kind of. Are you on . . . vacation . . . too?'

I've never said 'vacation' before. I feel that if I said 'holiday' I would sound silly. I would sound like Mary Poppins telling him that it was a jolly holiday with you, Bert.

'Yeah. I'm with my friends.'

'I don't normally go away with my mum and dad,' I say quickly. 'It's because of my dad's work.'

'Oh, that's neat.'

'Yes.' I want to keep talking. I want to get us closer, in real life, to the places we have visited in my head. 'I'm Ella.'

'Hey, Ella. It's great to meet you. I'm Christian.'

I want to say something cool. I want him to think I'm funny.

'You're a Christian,' I say, 'or your name's Christian?'

I see at once that he doesn't realize I was attempting a joke. I wish I hadn't said it. The words hang in the air.

'My name,' he says with a grin. 'I'm not really much of a religious person. So what are you guys up to today?'

I stare into his eyes. 'They're talking about going up the Sugar Loaf Mountain,' I say, though my words could be anything. 'But they're worrying about the clouds.'

'Us too. The clouds, I mean. The sun's apparently going to be shining on us tomorrow, and to me and my friends that means "beach". So we're going to get the sightseeing in today before it's too hot. We're doing the Christ statue.'

Our eyes are having a conversation too; and it's a completely different one.

'We did that yesterday,' I say. 'It was cool.'

'Well, we'll maybe run into each other back here later.'

'I hope so.'

Christian's eyes tell me amazing things, and the sun comes out and the walls and the ceiling melt away, and we are standing on a sandy beach in the golden sunshine with those cherubs cavorting around us, serenading us on little harps. I am smiling so hard I probably look deranged.

He turns to pick up a glass, and then turns back. 'Oh, hey. Ella. We're going downtown to Lapa this evening, to catch some music and do a bit of bar hopping. If you'd like to . . . You know. You could come along?'

'Yes!' I answer before he's even finished speaking. 'I'd love to!'

'Cool. Catch up with you later then. Maybe in the lobby, around nine?'

'Perfect.'

As I sit back down I know that my parents are looking at me; they will not be enjoying the fact that I spoke to a boy. In fact they will hate it. It's lucky they don't know that I have just arranged to meet him at nine o'clock to 'catch some music and do a bit of bar hopping' in downtown Rio.

I will find a way to do it.

'All right?' says Dad.

'Ella.' Mum is frowning.

I don't care. I have a date tonight. Our eyes met yesterday. He asked me out today. We're going out tonight. I knew that Rio would be my place.

I wish I could tell Jack. I wish Jack had been able to come to Rio with me, to meet people, to come out dancing. Jack's family are strictly religious in the worst way. They think a woman's place is in the home, that God is a white man who made woman out of Adam's rib. They don't like him being friends with Lily because she's not white. They think homosexuality is deviant and an abomination. The last thing they'd want is a gay son. I hated visiting his house, being approved of by them, particularly when I still had my blonde hair, as the ideal mousy little girlfriend.

I hope Jack feels this lightning bolt too one day. I hope he goes out with someone who makes him feel that he is on fire in a good way. I hope he meets his Christian.

'Yes,' I say to Dad. 'Yes, it's all right. They might be going to Christ the Redeemer today.'

'Well,' says Mum. 'They should have gone yesterday when it was clear. Anyway, we'll have a think about the Sugar Loaf Mountain. Perhaps ask for advice at reception. Maybe we'll leave the trip for this afternoon to give it a chance to clear up.'

'Whatever you think,' I say, and I notice Mum giving me a sharp look.

At nine o'clock I say (my voice both casual and trembling with the importance of getting it right): 'I'm just going to go down to the lobby.'

Mum frowns, because of course she does. 'Are you, darling? Why?'

'I want to pick up some leaflets from reception. I'm sure there are more things we could be doing since we're here and I'd like to see what they are.'

Dad gets up as if to come with me.

'On my own,' I say. I smile and try hard to look casual. 'For once. I'll be back in less than five minutes, and if I'm not then you can come down and find me. I promise I won't leave the building.'

They look at each other. They sigh. I leave the room.

Christian and his two friends are sitting on the sofa in the lobby, waiting for me.

I look at him.

He looks at me.

Time freezes, and I hold my breath, and everything is as glittery and magical as it was this morning.

'Hi, Ella,' he says. They all stand up, ready to go.

'Your hair is so cool,' says the girl.

'This is Susanna, and this is Felix,' Christian says, and he walks up to me and kisses me on the cheek, right next to my mouth. All my skin quivers. It is the strangest thing.

They think I'm coming out with them. I could. I could just follow them and get into their taxi and worry about everything later.

I wish I could.

I can't.

'I can't come now,' I say. 'Sorry. But I'll get away in a couple of hours. Can I come and meet you? Where are you going? And hello. Sorry.'

I think Christian looks a little disappointed. 'Sure you can,' he says. 'You'll need to get a cab. Ask for Lapa. Meet us in a bar called Antonio's. It's on a corner. If you can't find it, ask anyone. I hope you can make it.'

'Eleven o'clock,' I say, and he nods, and they go.

When I know that both parents are properly asleep I slide out of bed. I have changed under the covers, and I did my make-up in the bathroom when the bedroom light was off so they wouldn't see me, and now all I have to do is pick up my shoes and check my pockets (money in one; the spare key card in the other) and open the door as quietly as I can.

It makes a swooshing noise as it crushes the carpet, but the parents don't stir.

I stand on the threshold of the room for a moment, but all is calm and peaceful, and I step out into the corridor and pull the door very gently closed behind me.

It clicks and locks itself. I stand still for a moment, listening, and nothing happens. I walk down the stairs to the floor below, because I know the lift makes a loud *ping* when its doors open. I walk down another floor, just to be sure.

I call the lift to the ninth floor. It arrives. I stand in it and look at my reflection. I pull my hair over one shoulder. I pout as if I was posing for a photo. I look critically at my body, but it looks all right. I am wearing little denim shorts and a light-blue beaded vest.

I'm worried that whoever is working on reception will see me sneaking out and call up to my parents, but the man barely looks up as I cross the lobby. The bright lights glint off the marble everywhere: the whole place is dazzling. I smile at the night doorman, who nods and steps aside to let me out of the automatic door.

'Taxi?' he says.

'*Si*,' I say. '*Por favor*. Yes please.'

He steps on to the warm pavement, and I follow him into the hot night. He holds out his hand, and within half a minute a yellow cab has pulled over. The doorman opens its door for me, and then he slams it and the taxi starts up, and I say: 'Lapa. Antonio's?' as clearly as I can, and we are off.

I have escaped.

I am in a taxi in Rio.

I am on my own for what feels like the first time in my entire life. The world is filled with possibilities. My parents don't know where I am: I'm not sure that has ever been the case before. They have always known approximately what I am doing. I have always been locked in, watched over. And now I'm not.

I hope I find Antonio's. I said eleven and it is now ten fifty, so, depending on how long this journey takes, I should be all right.

I gaze out of the window. I am actually here. This is happening. I am out alone, being my real self for the first time in my life. This is me. This is the real Ella Black. Everything feels hyper-real, and I want to hold on to this feeling and keep it forever.

I stare out of the window. Mostly it's dark, with occasional spots of nightlife. The road is like a motorway and there are not many other cars, and the taxi goes faster and faster, swerving between lanes for fun, edging through red lights when there's nothing coming through the green ones. Bright lights come the other way, speeding closer, flashing past. I might not find Christian when I get to Lapa. I might not find Antonio's. I almost don't care.

I got away from them. Sitting in the back of this cab, I can breathe. Whatever happens next, at least I will have this.

I watch the road as we follow signs to Lapa. Eventually the driver slows and drives under a set of huge white arches. I look out at the scene and gasp.

This is where all the people are. On either side of the road there are tables, and people are sitting at them, and standing around, and drinking and talking and laughing and dancing. It's so packed that I'm not sure I will ever find Christian and his friends, but that is OK. I took two hundred reals from Dad's wallet, so if it comes to it I'll get a taxi straight home again.

The driver pulls over into the forecourt of a closed garage. 'Lapa,' he says with a laugh.

'Antonio's?' I ask, and he shrugs, so I do too, and the meter shows forty reals, so I hand him a fifty note and he gives me change.

I say, '*Gracias*,' and he corrects me.

'*Obrigada*,' he says, and I repeat it as I step out on to the pavement, and am enveloped in noise and music and instant acceptance.

No one comes to rob me. No one threatens me. No one takes much notice of me at all. I walk slowly past all the people, trying to see the names of the bars. There is loud Brazilian music coming at me, clashing, from different directions, and it is heady and joyous and it makes me feel wildly alive.

Even if my parents have woken up they will never find me here. Never. I can stay as long as I like and no one will know where I am. I inhale the night air, the heat, the music, the life.

I find Antonio's down the road, on the other side, on a corner like Christian said. It is frantically busy, with every table taken and hundreds of people standing up between them. The whole bar is open to the street on both sides.

If the boy of my dreams is here, as well as everything else, I will be the happiest girl in the world; the happiest girl there has ever been.

I weave between the tables, looking at each of the people with their bottles of beer and their glasses of the green cocktail Mum likes to drink.

This is nothing like going out at home.

People smile at me as I push my way through. They move aside if they can. Several men say '*Hola*', or 'Hello' (I clearly look foreign), but not in a threatening way, and they don't seem to expect me to reply. I push my way around the whole bar, and I don't see the gorgeous boy, but that barely matters because I am happy. Even if I just walk around here and don't find them and go and get a cab back to the hotel, this outing will have been a massive success.

Someone says, 'Ella!' I look round, but I don't see him. It was his voice – I'm almost sure of it; and anyway it had to be him because no one else here could possibly know my name.

'Ella,' he says again, and this time he taps my shoulder, and when I look he is right there, standing beside me, and I am so happy that I just turn and hug him. He hugs me back, and then he is holding me. My face is pressed against his T-shirt, and I can feel his heart beating against my cheek.

He strokes my hair and keeps a tight hold of me. I don't let go either. He kisses the top of my head. I think we have skipped quite a few stages of getting to know each other.

I feel, just like I did the first moment I saw him, that he's always been there, and that all my life has been leading up to meeting him. I knew him already; I just hadn't been in the right place until now.

'You made it!' he says quietly, just up from my ear.

I pull back far enough to be able to speak. 'Yes,' I say. 'I did. I waited for my parents to fall asleep, and then I crept out and got a taxi.'

'My friends were so sure you wouldn't show. I knew you would and you did.' I nod. 'But, hey, we'd better make sure you get back without your folks finding out. I don't want your dad to freaking kill me.'

'He wouldn't. If they're awake when I get back I'll just say I couldn't sleep and went for a walk. They'll be cross and tell me I'm stupid.' I shrug.

'Hey – you're good at this.'

Briefly I picture them awake now. The doorman would tell them he put me in a cab. He had slammed the car door before I said 'Lapa' and so my trail would go cold right there. They'd probably think I'd gone to the airport.

I look at Christian. His arms are still around me. I want to stay like this, pressed up against his chest, forever. I look at his beautiful face, his cheekbones, his glossy hair; everything about him. I need to keep looking at him for the rest of time.

'Let's get you a drink,' he says, and we disentangle ourselves and he leads me to where his friends are. He reaches a hand behind him and I take it and walk close, attached to him, through the crowds. They have a tiny table, a high round one, and one of his friends (Felix, I remember) gets off his stool to let me sit down. Or, rather, to let me climb up.

Both Felix and Susanna grin and say 'Hey' and things like that. Susanna, who has beautiful long black hair, says: 'You made it! Great to meet you properly, Ella.'

I try to say the right things back. No one seems to mind what actual words come out of my mouth. Christian says he'll get me a drink and would I like a caipirinha? I say 'Yes please' even though I don't know what it means. A waiter appears and the three of them talk to him in Portuguese and I sit back and let things happen. A drink arrives, and it's the pale-green one with the straw in it, and I sip it through the straw and try very hard not to cough or splutter or betray in any way the fact that this is my first one and that it's far stronger than I thought it would be and that I wasn't expecting it to be so sour and to taste of limes. I can't believe Mum has been drinking these, one after the other, right in front of me.

I seem to get away with it; or perhaps nobody is interested in what I think. I'm not the centre of the universe – I am a hanger-on, and I am all Ella with no hint of Bella, which is amazing and makes me feel full of joy and possibility. The alcohol goes straight to my head and I feel so dizzy that I don't think I could stand up. I take another sip. Christian is beside me, his hand between my shoulder blades. I sway towards him, and he steps closer so that we are touching all down the side. His hand is on my shoulder. I lean on him so the side of my face is pressed up against his side.

I don't even know what they are talking about. I piece their story together a bit: they are Cuban Americans and they live in Miami, and when Felix asks where I live I say I'm from close to London, because I am, close enough, and when he asks what I'm doing in Rio, I just say: 'I have no idea.'

They all laugh and Felix says: 'Right?' and raises his glass.

'No,' I say, shouting so they will hear me. 'I literally don't know. My parents came and collected me from school and brought me here and I still don't know why.'

Saying these words is the most liberating thing that has ever happened to me. These thoughts have been going around my head without stopping, and now I can say them. I tell them all about my fears and suppositions, and they listen. They are quite surprised when they realize what I mean when I say 'school'.

'You're still at high school?' Felix is incredulous. 'Hey, Christian. She's at high school.'

Christian shrugs. 'She's not there now. So when do you think they're going to tell you?'

I suck on my straw. That drink vanished quickly. 'Soon, I hope.'

Susanna leans across and kisses my cheek. 'God, that must be strange for you,' she says. She smells lovely.

Some time has passed. Christian and I are walking, his arm around my shoulder, my arm around his waist. The streets are packed with people, and we are walking on the edge of the road. I am woozy and happy and I need to go back to the hotel soon.

A man is standing on something, visible above the crowd, singing into a microphone. The backing track is coming from a speaker somewhere. It is all about the drum beat. It is infectious. My feet want to dance. The people gathered around are dancing. I watch a woman's feet. She is stamping fast, dancing irresistibly, the top of her body calm as her feet do wonderful crazy things. I want to do that too. I pull away from Christian and follow her feet, and try to make my feet do the same. I'm not getting it right, but the movement clears my head and I feel wonderful. I sense Christian watching but I can't look at him because I cannot take my eyes off the woman and her feet. The music vibrates right through me.

I feel amazing.

This lady is a million times better at dancing than I am, and I like it that way. I carry on stamping, feeling the rhythm, trying to get the steps.

Then the music stops.

Christian takes me in his arms.

I know I'm going to kiss him.

I know he is going to kiss me.

I have never kissed a boy before. Everything about this feeling is new. I have never held on to someone who is holding me and pressed my body up against his and felt myself pulled to him as if we were magnets.

This is the only thing in the world, and we are the only people. I never knew this was the way it could be. I never had any idea.

I tip my head back. He leans down. Our lips touch, gently at first. It goes through me: an electric shock that harnesses all the power of the universe. Then we kiss properly, two people joined at the lips, and time stops and I want to stay here, now, in this place with this boy, forever.

At some point the music starts up again but I barely hear it. People are dancing around us but I don't care. We stand in the middle of it all, in the hot Brazilian night, and I kiss the boy.

This is all I have ever wanted, and I never knew it existed. I am on a pavement in Rio on a hot autumn night, and I am a new person. I am happy Ella, dancing Ella. I am Ella In Love.

Later Christian buys us each another caipirinha from a stall under the arches and asks if we can spend some time together tomorrow. I am desperate to see him tomorrow. I never want to be away from him. I want to stare at his perfect face, the little mole on his cheek, forever.

'Yes,' I say. 'I can't tell my parents but I'll work it out.'

'You will? You're sure? I don't want to be the bad guy.'

'You couldn't be the bad guy.' I think about it. My head is clear. 'Maybe I'll pretend to be ill. If I can get them to go out I could meet you at the hotel.'

Those words hang in the air.

'Yes,' he says. 'Yes, that would be awesome. I'll maybe see you at breakfast? You're a fabulous girl, Ella.'

I laugh. No one has called me a fabulous girl before. No one has come close. It is a strange phrase, but I love it because it's Christian who said it.

'And you're a fabulous boy.'

He smiles. 'If you do manage to send your parents out,' he says, 'then maybe you could just come over to my room. You know?' He takes my hand and our fingers interlock.

I am so pleased he said it. I remember, vaguely, Jack and I implying to other people that we were having sex. I never actually wanted to, obviously not with Jack but also with anyone else. It was just not a thing that was on my mind. And now that I have Christian it's the only thing in the world I want to do.

'Yes,' I say. 'Yes. Yes, please.' I will tell him it's my first time. I'll tell him everything. I want Christian to know all of me.

The cocktail from the stall is rough and boozy and I can't drink any more because I know it will make me sick. The first sip is enough to make me see that.

'Can you get me a cab, please?' I ask. 'I need to get back. This has been the best night of my life. Truly it has.'

We stare at each other.

'Of your life?' he says quietly. 'That's quite something. Yes. Let's get you safely back. I'll come with you.'

'No. Don't. If they're looking for me, you can't be a part of it. Put me in a taxi and I'll say I went out on my own and I'll see you in the morning.'

He looks at me, smiling a lopsided smile that makes me want to stay right here and kiss him all night long.

'You fabulous girl.'

And then I am in the back of a yellow cab again, and Christian has told the driver where the hotel is, and he's given me a fifty-real note for the fare even though I have money left since I've spent nothing this evening beyond the cab that brought me here.

I try to sober up as we go, but I am glowing and dancing and I don't want to feel ordinary ever again. I will never be the same. I kissed a fabulous boy. I will have this evening forever. It really is the best night of my life. It has changed everything. I am going to Christian's room tomorrow and I can't wait. I want to tell Jack. I know he'd be delighted for me. I want to tell Lily. I know she would squeal with excitement, then tell me to be careful.

The taxi pulls up outside the hotel. The same doorman comes and opens the car door. I pay the fare and give the man a hefty tip because I love everyone.

My stomach is churning as I step on to the pavement, but there are no police around. I can see into the reception area, and my parents aren't there. No one is behind the desk. The doorman does not look remotely interested in my arrival. I say hello and walk across the deserted, half-dark lobby to the lifts, and as I wait for one to arrive I look at myself in the full-length mirror.

I look like the happiest girl in the universe. I look like a girl who has been dancing in the street and kissing in the street and falling in love.

Falling in love.

I have fallen in love.

I

have

fallen

in

love.

Nothing will ever be the same.

6

32 days

'I've got a headache,' I say, closing my eyes to shut out the sight of her. I feel terrible. I can't get up.

'You poor thing,' says Mum. She sits on the edge of the bed and puts her hand on my forehead, the way she used to when I was small and feeling ill or, later on, when I was trying to get a day off school to avoid Tessa, or because I could feel Bella, and I knew that I would soon need to be in my bedroom, alone.

She is leaning forward with her hair tickling my face, and that means she is close enough to smell the fumes. She drinks those caipirinhas every evening: she must know the smell. I leap out of bed and run dramatically for the bathroom, where I sit on the loo for long enough to make her think there must be some form of illness going on, and then flush it and brush my teeth very thoroughly for a long time.

Last night I crept back into the room, clicked the door closed and slipped into bed. Mum groaned a bit in her sleep, but I got under my sheet and changed into my pyjamas.

I totally got away with it.

While I'm at it, I decide to have a shower. There must be an alcoholic smell coming off me, or a smell of the streets, or grime where there was no grime last night. If I'm going to get away with this I need to be fresh and innocent.

My feet are filthy.

My feet are filthy because I danced in the street in flip-flops.

I danced, with Christian at my side.

I scrub them clean.

'Better?' Mum says when I emerge, back in my pyjamas, with wet hair and clean teeth and an altogether fragrant demeanour.

'Yes, thanks.'

'Were you sick?'

'No. I've just got a bit of a funny tummy.'

'Could you manage breakfast, do you think?'

I have to go to breakfast. I have to see Christian. I hope it's not too late. He and Felix and Susanna will be getting up late, I'm sure.

'Yes. I'll try a bit.'

'Sure?'

'Yes.' I say it weakly, but I am firm too. I am desperate for food. I'm quite sure it will chase away the hangover. I need to eat all the cheese balls there are, and drink lots and lots of coffee and plenty of water.

But the only thing in the world I *really* need to do is see Christian.

I'm glad I came home when I did. My parents are lying to me about something; now I'm lying too.

In the lift down I feel ill, and I can see Mum worrying that I've come down with a terrifying tropical disease (a mutation of the simian flu perhaps). I want to reassure her, but I can't.

Dad gives it his best shot. 'You look all right to me,' he says, sizing me up in the mirror. For a moment I think he suspects the truth, but it passes. The lift stops at floor eight and we shift up to let more people in, but when the door opens it turns out to be Christian, Felix and Susanna.

My legs go weak. My skin is electrified.

I stare at him. He stares back. I smile a little bit. He grins. I sense both parents stiffening, disapproving.

'Hi,' I say, but I address it to Susanna.

'Hi there,' she says, and I really, really hope she remembers that everything has to be kept secret. I hope she doesn't ask if I got home all right, or tell me about the rest of their evening.

No one says anything, and then we are on the ground floor. My stomach is flipping over because all I want to do is kiss Christian again. I want to be alone with him. I hate my parents for being here and stopping me.

I hang back, and Christian does too, pretending to look in his pockets for something. Mum and Dad get out, and so do Felix and Susanna, and Christian and I brush silently past each other, and everything inside me bursts out singing.

Mum and Dad are waiting right outside the lift of course, so we can't kiss or speak, but our bodies touch and I am alive.

I try to convey to Christian the fact that we need to talk and plan, but we all troop into the dining hall and give our separate room numbers to the woman at the desk, who crosses them off her list, and then my parents and I go to sit at one table, and my gorgeous boy and his friends go to another, and every time I look up Christian is looking at me and I gaze back.

'You'd better stay off all that fruit this morning, darling,' says Mum, who didn't notice that I spent the whole of the lift ride down staring at the boy that every molecule of me adores; that I am still staring at him now. 'If you've got diarrhoea. Stick with the carby things.'

I'm glad she didn't say that in the lift.

As it happens, the carby things are exactly what I want. I go straight up to the buffet and fill a plate with cheese balls, a big spoonful of scrambled egg and two white bread rolls. I put that down on the table and go back for a glass of water. When the coffee woman arrives I get her to pour me a black coffee, which she does, though Mum frowns as coffee is bad for upset stomachs. I pretend not to notice, eat everything on my plate, drink the coffee and water and feel much better. So I go back and get the same things all over again.

'Your appetite's all right,' says Dad.

'Yes.'

We sit in silence. I watch the Brazilian news on the screen at the other end of the room. There is footage of a rainforest shot from a helicopter, and thick clouds of smoke. I can hear Christian and Felix and Susanna laughing, and I hope they're not laughing about me, sitting here with my mummy and daddy. My *mommy* and daddy.

'What are we doing today?' I say.

My parents look at each other. 'Well – that rather depends on you, darling, doesn't it?' says Mum.

Dad isn't speaking much. I think the two of them are silently arguing again. He wants to tell me the thing and she doesn't. They have told me that there *is* a thing. They are not remotely remembering to pretend that Dad has to go to work. That was the most half-hearted and pathetic lie ever.

'I feel rubbish,' I say. 'I'm going to stay in bed. But you two should go out. You should just go down to the beach or something. I'll sleep in the room. You can talk about your secret and I won't hear you.'

I say that, just in case it annoys Dad so much that he tells me the secret to get it over with, but he doesn't. He just closes his eyes.

Mum takes a deep breath. 'If you're ill,' she says, 'then I am *not* leaving your side.'

'And if I'm well, you also don't leave my side. I want to spend the morning in the room, resting. Are you *really* going to sit on the edge of my bed and stare at me? Are you going to stay in a darkened room, on a sunny day in Rio, one block away from Copacabana Beach, just because you don't dare leave me in a locked room? Really?'

Neither of them answers. On the television screen a blonde woman wearing a lot of make-up is in conversation with a puppet of a parrot.

Christian is on his feet. When our eyes meet again he inclines his head towards the lifts and arches an eyebrow.

I clutch my stomach. 'I need the room key,' I say. 'Got to get to the loo.'

Dad holds out the key. I take it and walk very quickly out of the room. I press the button to call the lift, and when it arrives I step into it. I hold down the doors-open button, and Christian appears, and I close the doors and press the button for the top floor.

We look at each other and laugh.

'You made it back!' he says as the doors close.

'They have no idea.' Then we are pressed against each other, kissing, kissing, kissing. I push my whole body up against his. He reaches round and feels the contours of my body. I want to go straight to his hotel room, fling off my clothes and stay there all day and all night and all day and all night and all day and all night. I want nothing but Christian.

Instead, the doors open with a *ping*, and we are not on the top floor but on the ninth, and there is a very white couple standing there, all ready to go out for the day, looking annoyed to find that we are already in the lift, and that we are entwined, and that the lift is on its way up rather than down. All the same they get in, and Christian and I stand close together, giggling a little, and then when we arrive at the top of the building we get out and walk down to floor eleven, hand in hand.

'I'll get them to go out,' I say. 'I haven't got my phone, but I'm working on it. So I can't text or anything at the moment.'

'No cellphone?' he says. 'OK. You should maybe call my room when you're ready. Even if they're only out for, like, a half-hour, you could come over. It would be really good to see you. Room 816.'

I grin at him. He's smiling back.

'I'd better go in,' I say, outside my room. 'I know my mum's going to appear here in a few minutes to check I'm OK.'

'Understood.' He smiles and kisses me on the lips, and then I am in the room, and Christian is gone, and I wander around the bathroom a little and make sure I mess things up a bit, and leave the toilet lid down and flush it, and brush my teeth again and stare at myself in the mirror.

My eyes are shining. My cheeks are flushed.

'My boyfriend is called Christian,' I say out loud. 'He's Cuban American.'

I am longing to tell Jack, but I can't. Christian is my real boyfriend; today I'm going to visit him in room 816. I have no idea what has happened to my life, but right now I like it.

Someone is knocking on the door. It will definitely be Mum, and I assume an 'ill' face before I go to open it.

'Oh, darling,' she says. 'Look. Come downstairs and sit on one of those sofas in the lobby and read those leaflets you like, and I'll explain that we need one of the chambermaids to make up the room right away. So you can have lovely fresh sheets. Then we'll get you tucked up in bed. All right?'

I nod, looking as sad as I possibly can. That breakfast certainly washed away my hangover, and I am feeling brilliant. It is important that I don't look brilliant.

'You look a bit feverish,' she says.

I nod. Yes. I am a bit feverish.

The bed is comfy and I do actually fall asleep. First of all Mum is sitting on their bed, reading and looking over at me. Then I nod off and blissfully sleep away the last of the street cocktails, and when I wake up she's not there. The bathroom door is open, and I can see that she's not in there either. I sit up. There might be time for me to visit Christian before she comes back, or there might not. If she comes back and I'm not here, I can just say that I went for a walk down to the ocean to get some fresh air.

She has left a note beside my bed. It is in her fussy calligraphic handwriting, and it says:

Darling Ella,
Dad and I have gone for a
stroll to the beach to get a coffee.
Won't be long! It's lovely to see
you peacefully asleep. Hope
you're feeling better.
Love, Mum xxx

She didn't put a time on it, and I am completely disorientated, and the bedside alarm clock says that it's half past midday.

I pick up the phone and make an internal call to room 816, but it rings and rings. I can't really expect Christian to be sitting in his room staring at the phone for the entire day just in case I managed to call him, but all the same I am disappointed. I'll keep trying. He might be in the shower, or he might come back into the room in a few minutes, or he might be standing right outside this door right now, trying to find a reason for knocking.

I open the door. No one is there.

I sit in bed for a while, but the parents don't come back. I call Christian's room again, but he still doesn't answer. I think about my night out last night. I try to recall every single detail. I relive our ride in the lift this morning. I call his room again. I call again.

Then I realize that I am alone in a room with all my parents' stuff, and I know that the answer to everything must be here, if I can only access it. I am alone in the room with the secret, and if Christian's not in his room I can at least use this opportunity while I wait.

They would definitely have put anything they consider important into the safe. It's locked, and they have set a four-digit code.

I have already tried my birthday, 1711, but I put the numbers in again, just in case. It's not that. If they didn't set it to my birthday, that means they were trying hard to keep me out of it. I try their wedding anniversary: 0606. It's not that either. Mum's birthday is 21 October, and Dad's is 4 May, which enables him to make endless *Star Wars* jokes. It's still neither of their birthdays, and it's not 2104.

Mum hasn't used a number I would guess. If it's something truly random I won't get it. I try 1234, just in case, and then 4321. I try 2468 and then 8642.

The machinery clunks and the doors swing open. She tried to make it impossible for me to guess, but she's never really going to be a superspy.

I snatch up my phone and put it in my pocket. Now I can get my fucking life back. I can't wait to tell Jack and Lily everything that's happened. I take my passport too, on principle, and put it in my other back pocket.

Then there are the official envelopes: my hands tremble as I leaf through them. My head and vision are clear. That's a relief.

I pause. I don't actually *have* to do this. I could put everything back. I might not want to know.

I legitimately have no idea what I'm going to find. Dad told me I'm not ill, but I don't think I believe him. I can't think of any other thing it could be. I wish I could. I would take anything other than that.

I might be better off not knowing.

I bolt the door so that if they come back they won't be able to get in, and tip the contents of both envelopes on to the bed. One of them contains something about travel insurance and a receipt from a currency exchange. The other has a letter from a solicitor on official paper.

I read it. Then I stare at the words. They go fuzzy and blur into one another. I sit on the bed and read it like a small child, running my fingers under the words as I speak them aloud.

Dear Fiona and Graham,

Following our conversation last week, I have made enquiries regarding your understandable concern about Ella and the legal changes that will take place on her upcoming eighteenth birthday.

As you know, an adopted child has the right to look for her birth parents on the Adoption Contact Register when she turns eighteen. However, I have spoken to the caseworkers involved and everyone has assured me that, due to the exceptional circumstances of Ella's adoption, her birth mother will not be eligible to add herself to the register and, although we are all aware that she would like to meet Ella, she will emphatically not be able to do so.

However, due to the fact that she has clearly found your identities and your address, I would recommend that, if you are able to go away for a while, this might be an advisable course of action while Ms Hinchcliffe is made aware that attempts to make direct contact will have extremely serious consequences. I am confident that she can be compelled to stop contacting you, and the law will step in when necessary.

I hope this puts your minds at rest. Don't hesitate to call if I can do anything else for you.

Yours sincerely,
David Vokes

I run to the bathroom and bring up the whole of my breakfast. My eyes are burning. My head is ringing and I gasp for breath. Everything is fading to black and I struggle to make it stay. This is not the time to lose control. It is too important for that.

I breathe in. I breathe out. There is just this moment and nothing else. No past, no future; just now.

My head is ringing. Everything is blurred around the edges.

Hello, Bella, I say.

I KNEW IT!

Do you understand what we just read?

NO.

What shall we do?

WE'LL WORK IT OUT. BUT I KNEW IT.

'The exceptional circumstances of Ella's adoption'.

Ella's adoption.

Adoption.

I am adopted. They have never told me.

People who are adopted *know* that they are adopted. It's not a big shameful secret. It's a good thing to happen. But they never told me.

That woman is not my mother.

That man is not my father.

Other people – people I don't know – are my parents. Not these people. I do not come from them. I do not have any of their genes. They never told me.

We have run away because my birth mother wants to find me.

My

birth

mother.

There were *exceptional circumstances*, and because of them she's not allowed to see me. I don't know what the exceptional circumstances are.

It swirls around. I am just standing in the bathroom.

I am utterly lost.

Time passes.

I have to try to find out more. I sit on the bed and try my very hardest to pull myself together and make a plan. There is only one thing I can think of.

I pick up the hotel phone, work out how to make an international call and ring our house. Michelle might be there, I think, and this could be my only chance to find out more. Michelle is nice. She is always kind to me and she liked my hair when I dyed it.

'Hello?' she says.

I use my mother's voice. Everyone says we sound identical on the phone.

My mother. This is not my mother's voice. It is my *adoptive* mother's voice. We sound the same on the phone because she brought me up.

'Hi, Michelle,' I say. 'It's Fiona. Calling from abroad.'

'Oh, yes,' she says. 'Hello there. Are you all right?'

'Yes, thanks. Is Humphrey OK?'

'Oh, he looks just fine. He's in the living room so I've shut him in there until I've finished. Didn't want to put him in his basket before I have to.'

'Oh, of course. Good idea.' I want her to put Humphrey on the phone even though he would be silent, but I have no idea how to ask that. I want to hear him breathing.

'Michelle,' I say instead. 'Could you do something for me? A little favour?'

'Of course, love,' she says.

'Right. Well, you'll need to go to the study. Is that OK?'

'I'm on my way.'

'There's a filing cabinet. Could you open the top drawer?'

'What am I looking for?'

'Ella's birth certificate.' My voice shakes.

'Right you are. Putting you on speakerphone. Hold on.'

I don't say anything because I have no idea how the filing cabinet is organized. I just leave it to her to look.

'Here we go,' she says after a few minutes. 'You *are* organized, aren't you? I've got yours and Graham's, Fiona. Would this be Ella's? It's an envelope that says Ella on the front?'

'Yes. That's right. That's the one. Could you open it?'

Oddly, I am managing to talk in Fiona Black's composed manner while tears course down my cheeks.

'Right. Oh. It's an adoption certificate . . . I didn't know Ella was adopted.'

'No. It's not something we ever talk about.'

My voice cracks at that, and I have to hold the phone away from my face for a few seconds until I regain control.

'But it's not a secret,' I say. It's not a secret now. 'Is there a birth certificate with it? Or just the adoption certificate?'

'Just the adoption certificate that I can see, love.'

'Could you read it? I just need to check something.'

'If you like, dear.' I'm pushing my luck. I know I am. I don't care. 'It says: *Ella Charlotte Black, female, born 17*

November 1999, in Birmingham. Adopters Graham and Fiona Black . . . and it gives your address. Let's see. *Date of adoption order: 8 January 2000.* I had no idea. I won't go shouting it out. Are you all right, my love?'

I cannot speak, and so I drop the phone on the floor. I curl up on the bed and hug my knees. I never knew. I never had the faintest idea. They never told me. It's *my* life, and they never told me. It was in the filing cabinet all along, easily found, and I never looked.

I was born in Birmingham.

Not Kent.

I was born in 1999 and adopted in 2000. The millennium passed and they never told me.

Everything I thought I knew about my life is a lie.

Someone is outside the door. I stare at it. I can hear sounds out there, and then they are pressing the door handle down and it isn't opening because I bolted it. One of them knocks on the door, and my so-called mother's voice says: 'Ella?'

My world has fallen to pieces. My world has always been in pieces. The pretence has fallen away and my real life stands there, looking completely different.

I hate them. I hate them completely. I hate everything about them. I hate them for lying to me. They knew that, one day, I would find this out. My birth mother is looking for me, according to that letter. She's not allowed to find me so I am going to find *her*. I try to breathe.

I need my dark side.

GET AWAY FROM THEM.

I know. I can't see them. But they're here.

TELL THEM TO FUCK OFF.

I need to focus. I have to do this right.

I know that I do have to get away from them. This is too much. I pick the phone up off the floor and put it back in its place.

I take my passport, my phone, all the cash I can find, and some clothes, and I shove everything into my bag. I take the credit card that is in the safe, hoping that I will be able to crack the PIN as easily as I did the safe code. I take my toothbrush, toothpaste and deodorant. I push it all in, and only then do I unlock the door and stand and stare at them; at these people who pretended to be my birth parents.

'How are you . . . ?'

Mum's voice tails off as she looks at my face. Then she stares into my eyes for a long time and I stare right back. Tears are pouring down my cheeks, but I don't say a word because I need *them* to say it. Only Dad – or not-Dad; the man I thought was my father – seems to be functioning. He looks past me at the open safe. He closes his eyes, breathes a few times and opens them again.

'Right, Ella,' he says, and he puts an arm round my shoulder.

I flinch and push it off.

'OK. Let's go and get a coffee at the café over the road. Or something stronger. And we'll talk this through. I'm sorry. We never meant it to be like this. You had to find out some day and we should have told you.'

I don't speak. I don't think I am ever going to be able to

speak to either of them again. I watch him put paperwork back into envelopes, and envelopes into the safe. The letter from Mr Vokes is in my bag but I don't tell him that. He doesn't seem to notice that my passport isn't with the others. I watch him close the door and lock it. His hands are shaking.

I take a piece of hotel notepaper and a hotel pen and write my mobile number on it, with a +44 at the start. I fold that and put it in my pocket. Neither of them seems to notice.

Mum is a statue. There is no colour in her face. She looks like an old lady. She looks, in fact, as if she's had a stroke. I hope she *does* have a stroke. I hope she dies.

I pick up my bag and follow them out of the door. When either of them tries to touch me, I flinch and pull away. I don't look them in the eye. I don't care if they're looking at each other over my head because I'm not part of their family and I never was.

I was a charity project

an experiment

and I think I failed.

I can't hear anything but the swooshing of my blood and the ringing noise, which is now so loud it sounds like a fire alarm. The fire is my whole life. I stand waiting for the lift, having an internal conversation with Bella that is different from any we have ever had before.

KILL THEM.

Shall I?

YOU KNOW IT.

I can't. How and what with?

134

COULD YOU PUSH THEM DOWN THE LIFT SHAFT?

There's a lift in the lift shaft.

I stumble because I can't see very well, and my dad reaches out to steady me, and I walk away and stand on the other side of the landing, leaning against the wall, until the lift arrives.

I am on fire. Everything that is in me, that is part of me, my whole self, is going up in flames. I am like someone's house on the news: at the moment the flames are leaping, the drama is going on, the change from what used to be there and the blackened ruins is underway. Soon I will just be charred remnants; a wasteland; nothing. Right now, however, Bella and I are burning.

I have no idea who I am. These people are not related to me. I have no family.

I want to stop the lift at floor eight. I try to remember Christian's room number, but everything from before-the-safe has gone fuzzy and blurred. It began with an 8. I think it had a 6 in it. I can't slide my number under the wrong door. I will give my piece of paper in at reception.

However, as we walk out of the lift on the ground floor Christian is standing right there in the lobby, and his face lights up when he sees me, and I look at him. He is all I want. I want to tell him this, to tell him about me, to make a new life away from these parents who lied to me all my life.

I was born in 1999. I went to live with the Blacks in 2000. I lived with my birth mother across millennia. That feels important.

Maybe she was young. Perhaps she was ill. It probably wasn't her fault that she couldn't manage a baby.

I want to be grown up now. I want to be with Christian. I walk up to him, hand him the piece of paper with my number on it and kiss him on the lips. I feel his surprise, and then I feel his smile.

'Call me,' I say. 'I've got my phone back.'

My parents don't say a word as we leave the hotel. I don't think they are really focused on anything.

It is warm and sunny, and this is the first time I have been out today. The clouds have gone. This would be a perfect time to take a cable car up a mountain. There would be no clouds there at all.

The man I thought was my father puts a hand on my shoulder and guides me down the road to the traffic lights. I push his hand away without looking at him. The woman who is not my mother walks on the other side of me, but she's not looking at me either. We are both looking straight ahead.

I know I have asked her about her pregnancy, about my birth, about what I was like as a tiny baby, about how they celebrated the arrival of the year 2000. In fact they didn't have me then. They didn't sit up with a tiny me to welcome in the millennium. All those stories were lies. The story of my birth (a dream birth, apparently, in a water pool with no pain relief) was a fantasy. Breastfeeding cannot have happened. All that was made up, just to stop me suspecting. And of course I didn't suspect. You believe your parents when they tell you that you're their baby.

We cross the road. The sun is hot. I know why they

brought me to Rio. They brought me here because my real mother was looking for me as I'm nearly eighteen. Boring Mr Vokes told them to go away and assured them she wouldn't find me. I would like to assure him that *I* will find *her*. I want to look at the woman who gave birth to me. I want to meet my real family, whoever they are, whatever has happened.

'Come on, Ella,' says not-Dad, and he ushers me to a table on the pavement, on the other side of the road from the hotel. I sit on a chair because I don't know what else to do. Not-Mum sits on one side of me, him on the other. They still think they can keep me under control. I hold my bag between my feet.

'Coffee?' he asks. 'Or a beer or something?'

I would like to get drunk enough to obliterate everything. However, I won't: I can't let the parents think they can win me round by buying 'medicinal brandy' or whatever they are thinking of, and trying to pretend we're all in this scrape together.

'Coffee would be fine,' I say. 'I got drunk last night, by the way. I sneaked out of the room and got a taxi to Lapa and met the Americans from the hotel. That's why I was ill. I kissed Christian in the street.'

'You didn't.'

I shrug. I don't need to pretend any more because nothing they do or say can affect me. They can believe what they like. I had the best night of my life, and I am glad I did it, just before everything collapsed.

I stop to check the inside of my head again for Bella.

She's right there, but she's not fighting me. *We* are fighting *them*. It's a strange feeling, being complete.

Not-Dad goes in to find the waiter. I see Christian coming out of the hotel with Felix and Susanna. He stands on the other side of the road and looks at me. I raise a hand. I can see from the way he is standing that he is worried. I make a 'phone' sign with my hand, and he nods and walks away, looking back over his shoulder.

The woman who did not give birth to me wants to say something. She keeps opening her mouth and closing it without speaking, and I don't do or say anything to help her. I can see her out of the corner of my eye, but I won't look at her.

'We always . . .' she says, but then she tails off.

I don't respond at all. I act as if she hasn't said a word.

Dad comes back and sits down. He takes a deep breath and begins talking.

'Your mother and I were desperate to have a big family,' he says, and every word is a sharp little knife, so much so that I think he must be doing it on purpose to hurt me. 'But it didn't happen. There were plenty of pregnancies, but they never made it beyond the first few weeks. Every time we hoped it would be different, but every time it wasn't. And after it had happened seven times –'

'Eight,' Mum says, very quietly.

'– eight times, then we agreed that it wasn't meant to be, and that perhaps we were meant to find our family somewhere else.'

'Second best.'

'Not second best. Best. Best and only. So we were assessed for adoption. Jumped through a lot of hoops.'

He stops. This is the bit I need to hear them say. It cannot be real until they say it.

'And then a baby turned up.' I say it because somebody has to.

'Yes. Then a baby turned up, and it was a baby girl, and she was the most perfect and adorable baby that had ever lived, and we both knew from the moment we set eyes on her that this was the reason why it had never happened before: because this baby was always going to be out there, and you were always going to be needing a home, and we were the people who were going to give it to you. We were able to take you away from the . . . difficult . . . start you'd had and give you the closest thing to a perfect life that we possibly could.'

I shiver. He is talking about a baby, and it's me.

'That's worked out well,' I manage to say.

'It *has*!' Mum is whispering through tears, staring down at the table, barely audible. 'Ella – you have no idea how much we love you. I've loved you from the very moment I saw you. I'm your mum and I always will be. We've always adored you.'

'Well, it was kind of you to save me from a difficult start in life.'

'Ella,' says Dad. 'We did try to tell you you were adopted, starting when you were three. You refused to hear it. We took you to psychiatrists and tried to work out what to do. This is complicated and hard to explain, but you found it so difficult and distressing that we ended up deciding it was better not to try. We decided that because the circumstances were so ... unusual you'd be better off thinking that you were our biological daughter, for the time being at least. It's not the standard way of doing it, but it made you so happy and secure, and that was the only thing that seemed to matter. Because as far as we're concerned, you are our birth daughter anyway.'

'So I'm not ill?'

Dad looks confused. 'Do you feel ill?'

'I thought I was here on a bucket-list thing. I can remember those appointments, a bit. I said so the other day. I thought I had some genetic illness and that we were here because I was going to die.'

'Oh, darling,' says Mum. I see her start to move towards me, but I lean away and she stops.

'You're our little girl,' she says. 'Our precious, wonderful girl. I'm so sorry. Everything we've ever done has been because we love you.'

'You've lied. All my life. Ever since I can remember, you've lied to me. It's not such a big deal being adopted, but it is if no one bothers to tell you.'

I cannot look at their faces. I am on fire. They don't know it, but I am gone. I am still here in body, right now, but I've gone. Everything I thought I was, I am not. Everything. I have never felt like this before. I knew I had a dark side and I gave her a name and she is in me now. She *is* me now. I pushed her away because I didn't want to be like that, but now I welcome her back.

HURT THEM, says Bella.

I don't try to push her away. I don't reach for the mantra about the universe.

How?

IT'S EASY OUT HERE. LOOK. HE'S GOT A BOTTLE, RIGHT THERE.

I am shaking all over. My jaw is clenched. I need to get away from these people.

I shouldn't hurt them. That wouldn't help.

YES IT WOULD.

It wouldn't really. Would it?

Mum reaches across and runs her hand down my arm. It's a stupid feathery touch and I hate it, and so I give Bella an internal nod and she grabs Dad's beer bottle and smashes it on the edge of the table, and Bella and I are lunging at her – at the only mother I have ever known – with a broken bottle. Dad grabs my arm.

There is all sorts of shouting going on. I don't care. I am Bella, and Ella has gone, and I want to hurt this woman, and I don't care what else happens.

I spin round to shake the hand off my arm, and the waiter is standing behind me. I need him to go away so I turn and swipe the broken bottle at him. I want to hurt him too. It cuts across his face and a line of red springs up. My vision is clouded and I have to run.

I grab the bag from the pavement and drop the bottle, and I am gone.

I am running.
I run and run and run.

My feet pound the pavement. One foot. The other foot. One foot. The other foot. I can't stop. I can't think.

I swing round the corner so they won't see me, and sprint faster than I have ever sprinted before. I run down the middle of the road. Cars can hit me if they like but they don't.

I run to the beach without any thought other than *Get away*. On the road beside the beach the cars are coming from the wrong direction – they are going in the opposite direction to the arrows. I dodge between yellow cabs and buses and cars, and they honk their horns and I don't care. Again, they don't actually run me over, and if they did that would be fine too.

The other side of the huge road is closed off, and then there is a lot of shouting and whistles are blowing but the police can't have caught up with me this quickly. Can they? When I stop to look in the direction of the commotion I see that there has been a zombie apocalypse, and a crowd of zombies is making its way towards me.

It is possible. Anything could happen now. The zombies have come.

I run over to the beach side of the road, straight into the crowd. It's not really a zombie apocalypse. It can't be. These are *people* dressed as zombies. It must be a Rio thing, and anyway, whatever it is, I'm in the middle of it and it engulfs me, and perhaps they won't find me here. I walk up to a zombie who is covered in blood and gore; I want that blood and gore so I hold her face and kiss her on each cheek, and she is laughing so I press my cheeks against hers and she kisses me on the mouth. All the old rules have gone: they were never really there in the first place. I rub my face on the zombie's until the make-up is all over me, and I know I can be a part of this crowd. I can be a zombie. I can become Bella full time. I am Bella: I look like her on the outside already. I am myself – Ella/Bella – and that is as frightening as any creature in the world.

I smear the goo over my face with my fingers, and then I rub my fingers down my T-shirt and hold my arms out like other people and walk like a zombie.

No one cares. Zombies and spectators smile at me. No one knows I just slashed a man's face with a broken bottle. People are watching with cameras, and I don't care if by some freaky chance the parents or the police see me on the internet or the news because by the time they see it I will be gone. I don't know where, but I will be gone. I don't care what I'm walking towards.

I have enough money to keep me going for a few days, and that is all I need right now.

WE'RE NEVER GOING HOME. Bella is triumphant.

I know we're not, I tell her. *We should get some water though.*

WHO CARES ABOUT WATER?

I hope I see Lily and Jack one day.

YOU WILL. NEVER MIND ABOUT THEM NOW.

There is a drum beat somewhere at the back of the march. The sun is heavy on my head. I know I should be drinking water but Bella stops me caring. Now I am myself for the first time since I was a tiny baby, when they took me away from my real mother and gave me to the Blacks.

A pregnant woman is walking beside me, with a plastic baby's head and arms, covered in fake blood, bursting out of her real baby bump. A little child in a Snow White outfit is covered in gore; she holds a doll with a severed head. Two small twin boys are both dressed as zombies from the old movies, lurching along in ragged clothes with their hands out in front of them, laughing helplessly. I keep walking, up the beach and up the beach, and when I am far enough from the hotel I will dart away and be lost.

I keep walking. I snarl at photographers. I take my hair in both hands and twist it around itself, tying it in a knot on its long side to get it off the back of my neck. I try to smear my make-up more, but the gore has dried, and after a while a boy passes me a pot of some kind of green greasepaint and I cover myself with it, rubbing it all over my face to make me as unrecognizable as I can, though I know my hair will give me away instantly if they see me.

I wait for a hand on my shoulder any moment. I knew that Bella would attack somebody one day, and now it's happened. I am Bella, and I went after my mother with a broken bottle, and I slashed a man across the face, and now the police will be after me.

Every now and then the procession pauses and there is a staged battle between zombies and people dressed as police and soldiers. Zombies grab bystanders and pretend to bite them, and *they* turn into zombies too, either joining the parade or melting back into the crowd. At one of these performances a monster zombie grabs me and pretends to bite my shoulder, even though I'm already a zombie, and I scream as loudly as I can, and then I find that everything I am feeling – all the feelings I cannot put names to and all the horror and all the fury – is coming out in that scream. I scream so long and so loud that people begin to gather around me. They are laughing. They are admiring me for getting so fully in character, and I realize that this is a place of extremes and I can do anything here, anything at all. I can be anybody. I don't have to be Ella Black because I didn't come into the world as Ella Black.

I don't know my own name.

I keep on screaming.

After a while I know that I need to go. The waiter will have called the police, and my parents will be mobilizing everyone they can to look for me, even though they're clueless in Brazil.

I need to find a place with an internet connection and start the process of discovering who my real mother is. This Mr Vokes is weirdly determined to keep her away from me, which doesn't make sense, and anyway it's not going to happen because I'm going to find her myself. No one asked me what *I* wanted, but I'm going to do it anyway.

If I hadn't just attacked two people I would go to the airport and fly home and wait for my real mother there: she knows where we live and is supposedly coming to look for me. I could just sit in our house and hope she arrives. But I can't do that because I hurt a man with a piece of glass and there was blood all over his face, and I knew that

Bella would do that one day and she has, and I don't want to go to prison.

As the parade reaches the top of Copacabana Beach I duck out and cross the road, dodging between cars, turning and giving them a zombie snarl if they beep at me. I run down a street and then I am back on the road where our hotel is – Avenida Nossa Senhora de Copacabana. This road is the worst place to be. I need to get off it as quickly as I can. There's a bus, so I get straight on. I find some coins in my pocket and give them to the driver and push through a metal turnstile and sit down by a window and stare at everything. I wish I had a hat. Everyone will be looking for a white girl with purple hair.

After a couple of minutes the bus passes the hotel. As we bump past I look out, then quickly lean down to fiddle with my shoe. In that fraction of a second I saw a police car parked outside, in the space where taxis stop. Inside the hotel reception I glimpsed two police officers, and a crying woman, and a man who I think caught my eye before I ducked out of sight.

Then I am past, and they are gone.

I want to get off at the next bus stop and run back to them.

THE POLICE WILL ARREST YOU.

I know, but I want to go back anyway.

YOU'RE A CRIMINAL. DO YOU KNOW WHAT BRAZILIAN PRISONS ARE LIKE?

No. Do you?

SHALL WE FIND OUT? WOULD YOU LIKE THAT?

I hold my breath and try to imagine it. Much as I have always been sheltered and treated like a baby, I'm pretty sure the Brazilian justice system would consider me an adult, responsible for her own violent actions.

No, I tell Bella. *No, let's not.*

I hold my bag on my lap and look through it. I seem to have packed reasonably well for going on the run. I have some clothes and a toothbrush. I have my passport and what I think is quite a lot of money. I have a credit card without a PIN. I have the letter from boring Mr Vokes, who knows a lot more about me than I do myself. I have nowhere to go and nobody to talk to. I have no friend in the world. I'd give anything to have Lily here. To have Jack.

All I can do is find a place to hide and track down my birth parents so they can tell me who I actually am. I am going to look into the eyes of the woman who gave birth to me and tell her that it's OK that she gave me up, because there must have been a good reason, and at least she was honest about the fact that she couldn't look after me. At least she's never lied to me. At least she wants me back.

When I've done that I will happily hand myself over to the police.

Will I?

I don't want to go to Brazilian prison.

I gave Christian my phone number. I hope he calls me. I switch on my phone, making sure the volume is off. I ignore all voicemails for now and look at the texts. There are loads of them from my parents, of course, and I don't read any of them. There are messages from Lily, Jack, Mollie and even Tessa. There is nothing from Christian.

When I am sure there is nothing I turn off the phone. If they trace it to this spot they won't know I was on a bus, or where it was going.

Tears are running down my face, and when I wipe them away with the back of my hand they leave green and black trails on my skin. I must look like a mess, but there's a zombie apocalypse and I look undead and nobody cares because that is the point. I stay on the bus, staring out of the window, feeling my heart pounding and seeing nothing until it stops and everyone gets off. After a while I do too.

I am on the pavement in the hot sun, in some suburb of Rio. The air is very still and nothing is happening. I have no idea where I am. Everyone who got off the bus has gone.

Everything I thought I was has melted away.

Every bit of me is a lie.

I should be feeling a lot of things, but all I am is numb.

There is nothing much around. Cranes poke into the air nearby. The buildings are big and warehousey, and there are no cafés, no houses and no people. I start to walk.

I walk and walk, and I would really like some water and some sunscreen. I follow all the touristy-looking signs, and after a long time I find myself on a huge road with cars and buses travelling in each direction. This road seems to be lined with banks and things, and they are all empty and deserted. I am the only person walking, and I am very, very tired and very hot and the most thirsty I have ever been in my life.

I feel like a character in a computer game, on a quest, knowing where I'm trying to get to (my real parents) but not having a clue how to pass this level. Sometimes everything goes blurry and I tell myself that if I just press the right part of a wall or the pavement, a new level will open up and I'll be closer, but when I try it, that doesn't work because I am an actual human girl and this is really happening.

I pull myself back from that. This isn't the time to let things go weird. I can't look around for some magical solution that might work in a dream. I can't indulge in anything. I need to focus and find a way to walk into the next stage of my life.

I keep walking and I try to do it normally. One foot in front of the other. I am in a part of the city with more people around now, and then there is a shop and it is open, and so I buy a huge bottle of water and drink it in one go. I buy a little bottle of sun cream and smear it on my pink arms and legs and face.

Then I need to go to the loo. There are no cafés anywhere nearby and, as far as I can see, no public toilets either. It suddenly feels so urgent that I contemplate finding a corner and just doing it right there.

Across the road is a square surrounded by huge buildings, and at the far end I can see a kiosk selling tickets of some sort. There are pictures of boats so I walk towards it. If I got on a ferry it would probably have a loo. I ask for a ticket on the next boat, in English, and the woman frowns and tries to work out what I mean. I think she is trying to ask which boat I want, where I want to go and I try to convey that I just want the next boat and I don't care about the destination.

She passes me a plastic ticket shaped like a credit card, and I slide a large bill under the security screen. She sighs and pushes lots of change back, and points to a set of turnstiles, off to my left.

I manage to say, '*Obrigada*,' and she says, '*De nada*,' and then I push my ticket into the turnstile, but I'm doing it wrong, and a man comes and does it for me, and I push through the barrier and walk straight on to the back of a huge metal boat, and I see a sign for the ladies' loo and follow it, because that is all I can think about right now.

I open the metal door, and at first all I see is that there is indeed a bathroom in there and that I will be able to pee. Then I smell it and note that I am very definitely not the first person to use it. I can hardly get near the toilet because the smell is making me retch, but I have to because I need to use it more than I need anything else in the world. I want it, right now, more than I want my real mother, and that is a lot.

I have to breathe through my mouth – I cannot bear the smell. But I know that breathing through my mouth means that I am gulping down particles of sewage, and that makes me retch even more. I hover over the metal toilet, which is of course blocked and clogged and full almost to the top with strangers' shit, and I pee because I have to,

150

and of course the flush doesn't work, and then I stumble to the basin and stare at myself in the tiny mirror that is nailed to the wall.

My face is covered in blotches of green and black. My eyes are so bloodshot that the whites are actually pink, and I truly *do* look like a zombie. My hair – my lovely purple hair – is slicked back with sweat and grime, tied at the side of my neck in a knot. I'm wearing a dark red T-shirt and a pair of small denim shorts, and I could be anybody.

I breathe deeply. There is something calming about that because it's true.

I could be anybody.

I

could

be

anybody.

That means I can be whoever I like.

Though the only thing I've done since I found out that I could be anybody is lunge with a bottle and cut someone's face.

There is a jolt and a small crash and the boat begins to move. I hope we're going somewhere far away. If it's a place that has somewhere to sleep, then I will sleep there. If it has internet I'll try to track down my birth mother. When I can't stay away any longer I will go back and hand myself in to whoever wants me.

I step out of the bathroom, smiling apologetically at the girl who's waiting (hoping she doesn't think its rancid state is entirely my fault), and find a small deck at the back of the boat. I stand there and fill my lungs with gorgeous fresh air as I stare at the water. The engine is roaring, and there is land receding behind us. I don't care what happens now; I only care about putting water between me and everything else. They can't come after me because they don't know where I am. The air is hot on my face. The boat is moving slowly, noisily, and the stretch of water between me and the land grows as I stare at it.

I am leaving. I am running away.

My legs feel weak. I walk back down to the inside of the boat and find a place to sit beside a window. Up ahead there is a huge bridge, with arch after arch after arch. We are going to go under it. It looks like a bridge from a story; a bridge that spans the whole ocean.

I close my eyes; the movement of the boat rocks me and, although I know that I will never actually sleep again, I find myself yawning. I will just close my eyes for a moment. I will just shut it all out. I will just rest for a few seconds.

Waking on a random boat that is taking me, made up as a zombie, to an unknown destination feels like it's part of a strange and horrible dream. Then I remember.

My parents are not actually my parents.

I attacked my adoptive mother with a broken bottle.

I cut a man across his face, on purpose.

Those things are real. That is my new truth.

They brought me to Rio because my mother was trying to find me. My mum. My birth mum; the unknown woman who grew me.

She wants me back.

She could be anyone.

I could be anyone too.

I have paid no attention to the people on this boat, and they in turn have left me completely alone. It's about half full. There are families with young children. There are young and old men, on their own and in groups. There are women, with babies, with children, alone. People are walking around offering things for sale, but they're not pushy about it and it's easy to shake my head. A woman sitting nearby spends ages looking at big pieces of jewellery. The man with her drapes them over his arm and she fingers each in turn, holding the big fake rubies on cheap metal chains.

If I can sit still like this and watch the world going on without having to interact with anybody ever again, then I might be all right. I could live on a boat and go nowhere forever.

Of course, even though I am willing it not to, the boat stops. We are at our destination, wherever that may be. I stand up when everyone else does and file off. A man grins at me, and I know I look ridiculous with my face covered in smeared zombie gunk and my eyes red and a cloud of desperation and running-away all around me.

'*Hola*,' I say to him, just to see if my voice is still working.

He says something back in Portuguese, but there are too many words and I don't understand them, and so I smile and shake my head and walk off the boat behind a family with two children – a girl and a boy who are fighting and bickering until their mother tells them to stop.

They are a family. That woman is their mother, and they are brother and sister; and I bet none of those facts are lies. Though they might be. Most people don't think to question the basic foundations of their existence.

A crowd of people are waiting for the boat but there are no police. A young man walks up and hands me a flyer, and I force a smile and keep walking. Another man, an elderly one, does the same. He laughs and points to his own face, and says something and puts on a scary expression. I think he's saying that his face is scarier than mine even without any make-up, and so I laugh too and keep going. I push both flyers into my back pocket and keep walking because I don't want to look lost or vulnerable. I don't want anyone to talk to me, to ask if I'm all right, to report me to the police as a teenage runaway or as the criminal they saw on the news. I look fierce right now and I want to stay fierce.

I will never blend into a crowd with purple hair. I need to change that.

I don't know what to do. I don't belong here, or anywhere. I feel Bella laughing inside me. She is crowing. She is telling me that she always knew it.

She doesn't blur my vision or make my ears ring any more. She doesn't need to.

The ground under my feet is sandy and stony. I walk over to a display board and look at a map. This place seems to be an island: according to the map it is called Ilha de Paquetá.

I walk down the street in front of me, breathing the warm air, walking on the stony road. I pass restaurants and cafés and souvenir shops, and step aside to let a horse and cart go by.

I am not the real Ella Black. I try to process that fact, now that I have escaped. The child I thought I was actually died in the womb eight times over, and I'm the imposter, the changeling, the next best thing. I thought I had come into the world as someone, but I actually arrived as somebody else, and I don't know who that person is, who I would be if I had stayed where I started.

I wished for this. I wanted to be anyone but myself. Only the other day, just after I killed the bird with the hammer, I wished to be a different girl. I've got my wish. There is someone else out there who wants to find me and to be my mum.

I want to find my mum. I want my real mother.

It's not straightforward. I have done the terrible thing I knew I would do one day, and I don't know what I can do except hope that the poor man is all right.

There is a bike-hire shop on my right. I stop.

'*Hola*,' says a boy sitting behind a desk. He has little round glasses and curly black hair, and if he had a scar he would look like Harry Potter.

I take a deep breath and say, '*Hola*.' That is pretty much all my Portuguese used up already.

'Hi. You speak English?' he says.

'Yes.' I smile my relief. 'Yes, I do.'

'Are you interested in hiring a bike? Special rates for zombies.'

'Yes, please.'

'Good call. No cars here so it's the best way to see the island.'

His English is fluent. He speaks like an American, with the very smallest of accents. His voice is a bit like Christian's.

'No cars?'

'That's right. Didn't you notice? That's what makes it cool.'

I am thinking of Christian now, and I have to stop for a moment and pull myself together. Christian will have told my parents about our night out in Lapa. I'm sure he will. It was only last night. I told them and they didn't believe me. They'll believe Christian when he's saying exactly what I said.

'Is there a place to stay?' I manage to say.

'Sure there is. You backpacking?' He looks dubiously at my little bag.

I look at it too. 'I left my backpack with a friend in Rio.' That sounds convincing, and anyway he won't care.

'Sure,' he says. 'Well, there are a few hotels. Are you looking for a hostel?'

'I'm looking for a place that's cheap. I don't care how basic.'

'Right. Look, take the bike and go explore. One of my friends rents out rooms, and I'm sure she'll have a bed for you. I'll give her a call while you're out, OK? There are many places to sleep here. It's a touristy place. It's totally easy.'

'Thank you!'

'How long do you want the bike? It's ten for an hour.'

I shrug. 'Two hours?'

'Sure.' We both look at the clock on the wall, and I realize I have no concept of the time at all. It is nearly five o'clock.

'Seven,' I say. I hand him twenty reals.

'We close around seven,' he says. 'So that's perfect.'

He asks my name so I say Chrissy because I am thinking of Christian, and he writes it down, and then he shouts to his colleague, and they both look at my legs in an objective way, and then a bike is produced that is approximately the right size.

'We got you one with a basket,' he says, 'so you can carry your bag.'

I stare at him, this wizard boy who is making everything all right. I don't know what to say to his kindness.

'What's your name?' I say.

'Alex.' He extends a hand, mock-formally, and shakes mine.

I wheel my new bike into the dusty road, and turn and wave, and get on and start to ride towards the sea at the end of the street. I am wobbly at first, and the road is a bit stony, and the sun is harsh on the top of my head even though it's late in the afternoon. There are people riding huge tricycles – two people side by side, usually laughing – but those things look like gimmicks for the tourists. I am glad I'm on a real bike, the sort you could ride in Rio or London or Hong Kong. A bike is a proper piece of independent transportation and I am on my own now. I pedal hard, making my legs burn. I have always loved cycling.

At the end of the road I turn right and ride alongside the sea. I take a path leading inland, and then I ride furiously around the island, to different beaches and past huge crumbling houses, past trees with drooping vines and plants with massive tropical leaves. The breeze makes my hair stream out behind me and blasts warm air into my face. People watch me pass, and sometimes they say, '*Hola*.' I ride and ride and focus on the details – on the caterpillars and the tiny birds and the flowers and the peeling paintwork. All the time, though, I am thinking about my biological parents.

She was young when she had me.

She was forced to put me up for adoption.

She has missed me every day, and she's looking for me now because she knows I'm nearly eighteen.

She wants to find me. I know that this part is true.

I want to find her. I want to know where I came from.

The real mother who takes shape in my head as I ride is someone like me (of course, because I am her daughter). She was young, she got pregnant, she had no family support, and she gave me up for adoption because she had no other option. I forgive her. Over and over again I forgive her.

After some time I stop and push the bike on to a beach and lean it against a tree. I kick off my flip-flops which,

I realize, have rubbed between my toes and given me a blister, and I walk to the shoreline and step into the water. It is brown, which I wasn't expecting, but there are some girls further down the beach who are splashing and swimming, so I am sure it's fine. I paddle into the water, and then I reach down and scoop it up and wash my face in dark, possibly polluted, Brazilian sea water from a strange corner of the edge of the Atlantic.

I have no idea if the green and black and the crusted zombie blood have actually come off, but I probably look a bit more human. The water is cool on my feet, and I stand in it for a long time. When I stare out to sea I realize there is some land, but I don't know whether it's another island, or this island curving around, or the Brazilian mainland. I could probably work it out if I tried.

I try to feel things, but I'm really just numb.

The sun is as hot as ever and the rules don't apply any more. There are no grown-ups to tell me what to do. I don't want to be arrested. I sit in the shade of a tree and look at the sand that is glued to my feet.

I take out my phone, take a deep breath and switch it on.

It has full reception. I watch as more texts drop in, as the number of voicemails goes up and up as it counts them. I don't want to look at any of the communications from the Blacks, so I skim past them. I only want to hear from one person, and he still hasn't texted me.

I need to listen to the voicemails, and I do it, deleting them as soon as I hear '*Ella, it's Mum,*' or '*Ella, it's your dad'*. I am cold with horror when I imagine what those messages might be saying.

Then it is there.

'Hi. Ella. It's Christian. I'm really worried about you as your parents say you've run away and the place is swarming with police. I know everyone is trying to find you. I hope you're OK. Um. Thanks for giving me your number. I guess you got your cellphone. So. You'll need to do the plus one for the States, and then it's 555 849 5923. I hope you're safe, Ella. I miss you.'

I draw the number in the wet sand by the shore, with the +1 in front. I take a photograph of it, then put it into my phone. I call it without stopping to think whether or not it's a good idea.

'Ella?'

It is his voice. It is Christian's voice.

'Hi.' My voice barely comes out at all.

'Jesus. Ella, are you OK? Where are you? They're going insane looking for you.'

'Would you ...? Could you come and meet me tomorrow?'

'Could I? Yes, sure. Of course.' I close my eyes and make myself breathe deeply. He said *of course*. He didn't have to stop and think about it. He has no idea what I did. 'You have to tell your parents you're OK though, Ella. You really do. They've been talking to the police. They're insanely worried.'

I cannot tell him.

'I'll tell you what it's about tomorrow.'

'OK. Where are you?'

I hesitate. I can't tell him I'm on this island. If he realizes that the police aren't looking for me because they're worried about my safety, but because I've hurt someone's face, he might tell everyone I'm here. If he doesn't know he can't say anything.

'I'll text you in the morning at nine. Promise you'll come without telling anyone. Until I've told you what's going on.'

I listen to him thinking.

'Sure,' he says in the end. 'Sure. OK.'

I am back at the bicycle place at seven. The boy looks up from an old-fashioned laptop.

'Right on time,' he says. 'So, Chrissy, I've got you a bed at the Hostel Paquetá. It's not far away. You can easily walk there. You can rent a bike for a couple of days if you like. I'll draw you a map of how to get there. The lady who runs it, Ana-Paula, is expecting you.' He pats his stomach when he says her name, as if her main attribute is being fat.

'Thank you, Alex.' I beam at him. I have a bed, and in the morning Christian is coming and I will tell him everything, even the bad things.

The hostel is actually a big house with crumbling plaster and yellow windowsills. A huge tree in the garden trails vines over my head as I walk down the path. I can hear insects making wild little noises from all directions. The grass is short, and the plants have huge leaves. I watch a beetle walking along one. The air is perfectly still.

When I feel ready I knock on the door, first softly, then, when nothing happens, a bit louder, and eventually, when that still doesn't work, as loudly as I can. The silence is oppressive and I can smell ripe things beginning to rot. Even though I know that the sea is all around us and that literally just across it is a huge wonderful city, this could be anywhere. It could be in the middle of any tropical place. It could be any spot in Latin America.

It couldn't, of course. I know nothing about Latin America. But this place reminds me of Gabriel García Márquez, of the stories of weird things happening in strange fertile places. Anything could happen here. Strange things do happen. I know that.

Nobody answers the door. It doesn't matter. I have nowhere to go, so I sit on the stone doorstep, which is warm and cracked, and put my bag down next to me, and lean back. It's starting to get dark. My parents might find me here. The police could track me down easily enough, thanks to my hair. Christian might tell them I'm here the moment I text him.

While I've been riding around the island my plans have been forming. Tomorrow I will see Christian (I hope he comes I hope he comes I hope he comes). And unless anything else changes I will stay here and be Chrissy for a few days. When I find an internet connection I will do everything I can to help my real mother find me, and then I will show myself.

I will go back to the Blacks so they know I'm all right, and I'll hand myself in to the police. If they let me, I'll go home. I have no idea what might happen then.

A woman comes round the side of the house and I see what the Harry Potter boy meant when he patted his stomach. She is heavily pregnant, and I think of the zombie woman in the parade earlier today, with the bloody baby doll bursting out of her bump. This woman has very long black hair and she is wearing a little vest and a long skirt that she has pulled down to go under her belly. She looks exhausted, but she smiles when she sees me and says, 'Oi,' and then some things in Portuguese.

I stare at her baby bump. I try to imagine what it would be like to grow a baby like that, inside your actual body, and then give it to someone else to look after. No one would choose to do that. It would only happen if someone was forced into it. I feel sad for my mother: she has probably missed her baby for nearly eighteen years.

I wish I spoke Portuguese. For now, the pregnant woman and I manage to communicate by speaking our own languages while miming, and she says her name is Ana-Paula and I remember that mine is Chrissy so I say that, and I follow her round the house and in through a side door.

It is dark in there after the outside world, and the floor is covered in cool tiles. I seem to be the only person staying here: Ana-Paula opens a squeaky door and shows me into a dark room with trees outside the window: there are four bunk beds in it and no sign of anyone else. I put my bag on a top bunk, because why would you choose to sleep on the bottom when you can sleep up in the air? Until a year ago I slept on a top bunk of my very own; or rather in a 'high sleeper', which meant that, in the absence of a sibling, I had a desk under my bed. I think high sleepers are supposed to be for rooms that don't have much space, but there was plenty of space in my bedroom at home. I just wanted to go up a ladder to get into bed.

I have a little wooden ladder to climb to go to bed tonight, and I am so exhausted and so confused that I want to go to sleep right away. The last thing I want is to have to go out and find something to eat, but I cannot ignore the fact that I haven't had anything since the hotel breakfast, back in my other life, and that all ended up being puked down the toilet. I am absolutely starving.

Ana-Paula looks at me and asks something, miming eating.

Some time later I am sitting in the kitchen with her, eating rice and beans. The beans are in a gorgeous brown meaty sauce, and this is definitely the best thing I have eaten in my life. I smile at Ana-Paula and she smiles back and says things to me. I want to ask about her baby but I can't, and anyway if I think too much about her baby I will fall apart. A woman was this heavily pregnant with me eighteen years ago, and I don't know her. I don't know her face or her voice. I don't know anything beyond the fact that she was forced to give me up. That is not a good only-fact to know about your mum.

She must have looked at me. I must have looked at her. We must have been each other's worlds for a moment.

I blink back tears. Ana-Paula pats my arm. I know she would let me sob on her shoulder but I can't do it. I need to control myself.

I wake up in the middle of the night and stare at the ceiling. I lie awake, certain that I will never sleep again.

7

31 days

At nine in the morning I send Christian a text.

Ilha de Paqueta, I write. You can get a boat here from Rio. PLEASE DON'T tell my parents I'm here. And particularly don't tell the police. Come and talk to me first at least. I promise I'll contact them all if you think I should, after you've heard the story.

I stare at the words 'my parents'. I don't like writing that, but I have to if I don't want to tell Christian what's wrong just yet.

I will tell him everything when he gets here. It will be a relief to say it out loud, to have someone here who knew me before I found out the truth about myself, even if it was only for a day.

A magical day.

I stare at the phone until he replies. It takes an agonizing seven minutes, but then there is a text from him that says the words I most want to hear:

On my way.

I stand at the ferry terminal and just stare at every person who gets off each boat, waiting for Christian to arrive and hoping the police won't turn up. In between boats I get a bottle of water and drink it. Other than that I just stare. I shut off my brain and look at the sun glittering on the sea, and try to think of nothing at all.

He might be bringing my parents with him, or worse. If the Blacks arrive I will tell them I don't want to see them yet. If they bring the police I'll admit what I did. I can do that, I think.

I run through things in my mind. I must have needed my birth certificate sometimes, because people do, but I've never seen it. My parents – my adoptive parents – must have made sure of that. It never occurred to me to look. But I'm about to be eighteen, and to leave school. They wouldn't have been able to keep this a secret much longer, no matter what. It was always a time bomb.

I'm sure if you grew up being told that you were adopted it would be perfectly all right. Adoption is a brilliant thing. There are two girls at my old school who were adopted from China, so they could never not have known. At least then you'd know approximately who you were. You would have the right feelings about your adoptive parents: you would know all along that they weren't the people who gave birth to you, but the people who rescued you and gave you a family and a better life. Adoptive parents are wonderful, in theory. Other ones are; mine are not, because they deferred to me when I refused to hear them say that I was adopted. They let me have my own way, when actually they *did* know better than me: I was only a tiny child and they should have told me.

I feel second best. Actually I'm ninth best. The real Ella Black, the one they told me I was, actually died in the womb many times over. I am her shoddy replacement, the best (the only) one they could get.

They told me I was her because that was who they wanted. They didn't want someone else's cast-off baby; they wanted me to be their own child come to life. And so they bought me everything I needed, and sent me to a posh school, and got me a kitten, and made me eat healthily and go to ballet lessons, and did all the things they would have done for their real child, if they'd been able to have one.

By the time Christian steps off the boat I am determined to move out of the Blacks' house and get a job, if I manage to get home. Phrases like 'actual bodily harm' and 'aggravated assault' chase each other around my brain, and I have no idea what is in store for me when the authorities catch up. Luckily Christian is on his own, and even more luckily he walks straight over to me, takes me in his arms and kisses me properly.

I allow it all to drift away for a few minutes. I relax into his arms. I feel his mouth on mine. I smell his smell. He knows me for who I am; or, rather, he doesn't actually know me very well at all. I can be any Ella I want with him. He doesn't care who gave birth to me.

I love him, even though I hardly know him. I love him.

I nuzzle in as close as I can, wishing we could merge into the same person. In the end we have to break apart just a little so we can talk.

'So,' he says. 'Ella. It's so great to see you. I cannot tell you how relieved I am. Want to tell me about it?'

'Yes.'

'Should we get lunch?'

'Lunch?'

'It's midday. That's good enough for me. Lunch and a beer. How did you find this place?'

I smile as we start to walk down the sandy street. 'I think it found me. Literally. I needed the bathroom, and I saw a boat and thought there'd be a toilet on it so I got on.'

'That's it? That's what brought you here?'

'That's it.'

'*Was* there a bathroom on the boat? I didn't look for one.'

'Yes, but it was disgusting. It was, like, the most disgusting bathroom you could possibly imagine. I was desperate.'

I said 'bathroom' like an American and I like that. This is not the romantic conversation I was imagining; but we're both giggling, and that makes it better than anything that happened in my head. Laughing feels strange and wonderful. I wish I deserved this.

Christian sits opposite me at a rickety metal table, and I stare at him. I gaze at his cheekbones and his jaw, at the lovely shiny hair that frames his face so perfectly. I stare at his huge dark eyes, and he looks back at me. We both smile.

Sometimes you don't need to say anything.

'So,' I say. I pick up my beer bottle and he takes his, and we clink them and take a sip. I wish I didn't have to tell him what I did.

'So,' he says as we put them down.

'So,' I say. 'Thank you for coming here. I'd better tell you some stuff.'

He nods, and I take a deep breath and start talking.

I thought it wouldn't take long: after all I have only two actual facts to relate. However, for some reason I talk for hours and hours. I tell him everything. I have never done that before. I've never told the truth about myself. I tell him all of it because there is nothing to lose, and because I want him to know the truth about me.

We order fish and potatoes, and it arrives and we both eat it and I barely notice because I am so busy talking. I find myself telling Christian about Bella, and am horrified to hear the words coming out of my mouth. He reaches across the table and grips my hand as I talk, because the words make me shaky. I have never spoken about her to any human being, not even Lily; not even when Lily came into the room and saw Bella killing a bird.

'She's made me do awful things.' I stop, wipe my eyes on the napkin he passes me and take a deep breath. 'I've thought for a while that it was building up to something terrible. And then it happened. Yesterday.'

I talk him through yesterday, and I don't leave anything out. I tell him about the letter and about my phone call to Michelle, and about the café and the thing inside me that smashed the bottle and would have slashed my mother's throat with it. I tell him about my dad catching my hand, and the man being right there, and the line of blood across his face.

'It's the worst thing I've ever done,' I say, and I'm not hungry any more. I want to be sick. I expect Christian to get up and walk away from me. He looks at me and I see uncertainty on his face. Then he nods.

'And you can make sure it's the worst thing you'll ever do,' he says. 'Look – I don't know what's going on back there but your parents didn't tell me any of that. They just said you'd had a fight and run away. There were police around but they probably weren't . . .' I see that he doesn't know what to say. He wants to reassure me that I'm not in trouble but he can't. 'I don't know,' he says in the end. 'I don't know what would happen if you went back right now. Maybe you should stay here a while. I can go back and find out for you.'

'Will you?'

'Can I tell your parents – your adoptive parents – that you're safe?'

He is so kind. He is gentle and lovely. I had no idea.

'Yes, but – please don't tell them I'm here. Find out if I'm going to prison and then I'll work out a plan. In fact I'll write them a note and you can just give them that when you get back, so they'll know you really have seen me.'

Christian nods. He looks more worried than ever now. 'Look. I have to be in Rio this evening because it's Felix's birthday and he's booked a show and shit like that. I'll talk to your parents. I'll give them a note. I promise I won't tell them you're here, and I'll find out everything you need to know. Right?'

'Yes. Thank you. Anyway. You know everything about me now and I don't know anything about you. But you seem to be so together. Your life isn't falling apart like this.'

He laughs, though he doesn't sound as though he thinks it's funny. 'Are you kidding?'

'No.'

'Yeah. There's a bunch of stuff you don't know. Let's pay the check. Let's not talk about Bella or anything that happened yesterday. Let's take your mind off it a bit. So, this island has no cars? Are there bikes?'

'Yes. I hired one yesterday. I'll take you to the rental place. The owner's nice. He speaks perfect English, luckily for me.'

Christian pays the bill even though I try to make him split it with me. We walk down the road hand in hand, and when we reach the bike rental place I rent mine again and introduce Christian to Alex.

Alex says: 'Oh, the friend in Rio! I knew it would be a boyfriend.'

I feel too shy to look at Christian's face. I want him to be my boyfriend. I wish he could be. I could do anything as long as he was standing where he is now, holding my hand. He knows everything, and yet he's still holding my hand.

Christian doesn't correct him. In fact he squeezes my hand and gives me a secret glance, as if we are in this together, which we are, and my heart fills up and overflows with sparkles and joy and love.

'It's ten an hour,' says Alex.

Christian takes out his wallet. He says, 'Three hours?'

He takes out thirty reals, and I watch him do it, and I see, because it's in front of my face, that in his wallet there is a picture of a girl.

She is a beautiful girl.

She has long black hair.

She is smiling.

You only have a picture of a girl in your wallet if she's your girlfriend. So Christian *does* have a girlfriend.

It's not me.

I've just told him everything. I told him all my secrets and he never told me that he had a girlfriend. He never said he *didn't* have one, and I never asked.

He pays and puts his wallet away and gets on his bike, and I get on mine too, and we pedal down to the end of the road. Except that now I don't know what to say because, having seen that picture, I can't really carry on as normal.

Christian doesn't say anything either. There are other bikes and the funny trike things and then a horse and cart, so we don't really have the chance to chat anyway. Then we turn off down a stony path, past those peaceful houses, and the world is silent except for the buzz of insects, and no one is here but us.

'Ella,' he says, slowing down so we are riding side by side. 'I know you saw the photograph back there.'

I look at him and then look back at the road. 'Oh?' I try to pretend to be surprised, but there's actually no point. 'So I guess you have a girlfriend back home?'

'No,' he says. 'No, I don't. I really don't. I was happy when that guy called me your boyfriend.'

'Were you?'

'I was. Look. Ella. That was Vittoria. My sister.'

Immediately I'm relieved, but then I sense something. It's in the tone of his voice, and the fact that no one carries a photo of their sister in their wallet.

'Shall we go and sit on the beach?' I say, and we keep going until we reach a stretch of sand. Then we push our bikes across it and lean them against a palm tree, and we kick off our shoes and sit down at the edge of the water, looking out.

Christian reaches for my hand. 'So let me tell you why, in spite of what you might think, I am not at all *together*.'

We sit there, and he tells me all about his life, beginning from his earliest childhood memory of himself and his twin sister, Vittoria, sharing a cot. He tells me how they did everything together; how everyone called them 'the twins' instead of using their names. They grew up in a nice part of Miami and went to good schools and had their own groups of friends, but they were so close that they felt like 'two halves of the same person', he says. He talks about the big house, the emotionally distant parents, the sense he always had that it was the two of them against the world.

'And then she got sick,' he says. 'I knew it at the same time she did. She got sick, and we knew it was serious, and it was. It was a very rare cancer. Anaplastic thyroid cancer. If you get it, the chances are you'll be dead soon. You can fight it, but it's not one you beat. Our friends and family tried to be positive, and I did too – she was my fucking twin sister, and if positive thinking might help, then I was going to do some positive thinking. But it didn't help. I knew it wasn't going to and Vicky knew it too. So.'

'Oh God. I'm so sorry.'

'Yeah. Me too. It sucks.'

I can't think of the right thing to say, so I just hold on to his hand.

'You would have liked her. She'd have told me you were too young for me. I can hear her saying it. But she would have loved your hair.'

'How long ago . . . ?'

'A year. One whole year. It's a lifetime, and no time at all. Felix and Susanna came over here with me for the anniversary. Or, rather, to get away from the anniversary. My parents would have preferred to have me home with them, and I feel bad about that. But I couldn't do it. Vicky would want me to be here with you, sitting on this beach, right now. She would.'

Christian is holding my hand, playing with my fingers.

'It's not today?'

'No. You know what? It was two days ago. The night we met up in Lapa. You said it was the best night of your life, and that meant the world to me. It really did. When you said that I felt like, actually, *Life can go on. I can be happy. People can be happy.* I felt good.'

I stare out at the water. 'I've just spent, like, four hours telling you all my problems, and they're just nothing next to yours. I'm sorry. I feel like a dick.'

He shakes his head. 'Your problems are very much not nothing, Ella. My problem is boring. It's about getting through the rest of my life when there's only half of me here. It's about living Vicky's life for her too. It's something I have to work out just through living. Yours, Ella ... yours is immediate, because you're *here* and your parents – the people who have always acted as your parents, whatever – are a few miles away over *there*, and I seem to be the only one who can move between you and them and try to help you work it out.'

I try to digest everything Christian just said. There is a lot to process.

'What did Vicky like to do?' I feel self-conscious saying Vicky instead of Vittoria, but he doesn't seem to mind.

He looks at me. 'She was much smarter than me. She wanted to be a doctor. And she loved to dance. She would have been doing the samba in the street with you.'

I nod. I want to have a sense of her in my head.

'She sounds brilliant.'

'She was. Always. But I didn't plan to come here and talk about her. I really didn't. Like I said, I've got to go back to Rio tonight. And I'll do everything we said. Can I come back tomorrow? I'll come in the morning. Could I ... Could I stay the night with you? Tomorrow? Depending on everything else.'

I turn and look into his eyes. We stare at each other for a long time. Then I answer his question by kissing him.

I see his ferry off, and he stands at the back and leans on the rail and waves to me until he blurs into nothing and the boat carries him over the horizon. The boat, huge and white and made of metal, carries my Christian away from me, but only until tomorrow.

He is coming back. I thought I loved him before, but I had no idea because I didn't know that it was possible for another person to make you want to open up. I have never been open with anyone. I always hold things back because I'm scared of them, but I told it all to Christian. I told him my horrors and he told me his, and we sat on the beach in the sun and kissed and kissed and kissed.

He's coming back tomorrow and he's going to spend the night with me, and then I hope the next two nights after that too. I'll ask Ana-Paula whether she has a double room, and if she doesn't we can go somewhere else.

I left school a few days ago thinking I was Ella Black, but now I know I'm someone different.

Maybe that is a huge opportunity.

I am invigorated, and the only thing I want to do right now, since Christian is gone, is find my real mother. Life is short. Weird things can happen. I don't know who I am and that feels fundamental. Christian and his twin sister were united against the world, but I have no one to unite with. I know no one with whom I share genes, and I need to find them. Even if I just look into her eyes and see parts of myself there and walk away – that would be enough. I don't want to be anyone's baby girl any more. My birth mum doesn't have to look after me.

I need to find a place to use the internet and a computer – I have a phone but no charger, and although I've been keeping it switched off most of the time it won't survive a long search for a birth mother. I guess I might be able to buy a charger here. I'll try to find a shop in the morning.

Until then I'll see if Alex can help me.

'Could I borrow your laptop?' I say.

He barely looks up from his magazine. 'You can try. It's older than you are. You might as well communicate with the world by carrier pigeon.'

'Oh. Well, do you know anywhere I could use one? I've got my phone but I have to do some stuff on the internet for a family thing and it'd be much easier on a computer. I'll, like, pay or whatever.'

Alex puts down his magazine and looks at me over the top of his little glasses.

'Most people just use Wi-Fi on their phone,' he says. 'On the island, I mean. If they need to. I'll give you the Wi-Fi code for this place if you want to use it. Or you're welcome to have a go on this old thing. I just about manage to keep the bike-hire website updated but it's not easy. I could bring my MacBook along tomorrow if you like.'

'Thank you. That would be amazing.'

'Your boyfriend's a nice guy.'

'He's wonderful.' I know that I am glowing. I can't believe Alex brought up the subject of Christian. Now I get to talk about him and I didn't even make it happen. 'He's coming back tomorrow, to stay.'

'Hey. That's great. Did you two have a fight? Is that why you showed up all jittery yesterday? You do . . . Well, you seem much happier now.'

'It wasn't a fight.' I can tell he's not that interested, but I decide to keep it as close to the truth as I can. The new me is going to try to be upfront with people. 'It was family stuff,' I say. 'The same stuff I need to use a laptop for now.'

'Take it, and good luck.' Alex grins and pushes it towards me along his little desk, then picks up his magazine again.

I sit at the back of the bike rental place, on a step beside a load of bikes, and open the laptop. It is dark here: the front of the shop is open to the street and there are no lights on. It smells of bikes and wooden floors and walls.

It takes a long time to connect but I don't mind waiting. When it's working, and connected to the Wi-Fi, I start googling.

I begin with my old name, Ella Black.

My fingers are trembling.

I need to know who I am.

I
don't
know
who
I
am.

My adoptive parents haven't told the papers that I'm missing, and the police aren't searching for me. I guess they're probably working on bigger crimes than mine. I shelve that for now.

I look up how to go about finding your birth parents, and fill in a form to join the Adoption Contact Register. I know, from the adoption certificate that Michelle read out, that I have the right birthday, and I'm glad about that because it would be very strange to have been celebrating on the wrong day all these years. I navigate slowly through the internet and do everything I can to help my birth mother to find me in two weeks' time, on my eighteenth birthday.

Then I take Mr Vokes's letter out of my bag and uncrumple it. I realize I know the name on it, I just haven't let myself think about it for a while. I read that part again.

It says: *Ms Hinchcliffe*. That is her surname. That is my real last name. Ella Hinchcliffe. She must have had a name for me that wasn't Ella. I wonder what my first name was.

I want to find *Ms Hinchcliffe*. Mum. I want to tell her that I'm all right, that the baby she had to give away because she was too young or too poor or too ill has grown up. I want to tell her that they lied to me all my life, but that I know now and I forgive her. I want to tell her that I have been Ella and Bella, that I always knew something was wrong. In my head Ms Hinchcliffe was not to blame for what happened. She was young and she couldn't handle a baby. Maybe her family wouldn't let her keep me. If I was pregnant (which is not actually a possibility, but it could be after tomorrow – that thought makes me shiver with excitement) I might not be able to handle it. I might have to give the baby to someone else so that it could have some proper parenting. I imagine her looking like me, being young and scared, struggling with the idea of motherhood, knowing she had to give her baby to some grown-ups. I want to tell her that, although I've had all the material things in life, I've missed her every single day without knowing what it was that I didn't have.

I take a deep breath and type the words *Hinchcliffe baby 1999 UK*. It seems unlikely, but you never know.

The computer works slowly. I squint through the darkness at the sunlight outside. Alex is talking to some tourists who want to hire bikes. I can't understand a word any of them are saying, but I can vaguely follow what's going on through their gestures and the tones of their voices. One of them is very tall and is looking for a particularly big bike, but Alex isn't sure where he put it.

I look back at the laptop. It's still thinking. The Google search comes up but the rest of the page is blank. I am only half hoping for a birth announcement or something, and you probably don't really put them in the paper or online if you're about to give your baby up for adoption. Nineteen ninety-nine is a long time ago and the internet was different then. I am sure there won't be anything, but I have to try because that name is the only fact I have.

The results start to appear, but they are irrelevant, as I thought they would be. All the Google hits are about a recent court thing which has nothing to do with me. That's annoying. I add the word *adoption* to the search, and they keep coming, the same results, about some boring other thing.

The first image to come up is an ancient photo of a woman being arrested. She's called someone Hinchcliffe. I look at the picture just in case, but she looks nothing like me: she has a tiny, skinny face and thick black hair and she's not my mum. I scroll down the page to the bottom, but all the results are about her.

That is irritating. I want to find my birth mother and I'm not interested in this woman who has . . . I click on one of the results to see what she has done.

'I'm going to close up in a minute.' Alex is standing beside me. 'But you're welcome to borrow my MacBook tomorrow, like I said.'

'Sure. Thanks. I'll just be a second.'

'Ten minutes?'

'Great.'

The news story has loaded and I look at it out of curiosity. This woman is called Amanda Hinchcliffe, and she has just been released from prison. That sounds familiar: I've heard her name before. I discover that she has been in prison for being an accessory to murder: she found young women in the street and took them back to her boyfriend's flat, where he tortured and killed them, long ago.

She has been in prison since 2000. There are no photos of her now, but there are several of her when she was arrested.

I look at them all, just in case.

I look at them.

I look at her.

I look at her stomach.

She was pregnant.

She

was

pregnant.

She was arrested in October 1999, and she was pregnant.

My ears are ringing.

My vision is closing in. I thought I was Bella already, but more Bella is coming in.

I stare at the screen.

I am looking for the words.

Finally I see them.

Her baby, they say.

Her baby was taken into care.

Into care.

The baby was born.

It was taken into care.

It doesn't say if it was a boy or a girl baby. It just says that it was taken away from her.

I heard her name on the car radio. It comes back to me in a flash. Driving away from school. The news. *Amanda Hinchcliffe released*. My mother jabbing the button, stopping the words.

It's not easy to adopt a baby. I have no idea how many babies were born in November 1999 and taken away for adoption, but I know that not many of them would have been taken from mothers with the last name Hinchcliffe, at that exact time.

There is an old photo of her boyfriend, the murderer. His name is William Carr. I hadn't thought about my birth father at all, and I don't want to. I push the man away. I see his picture out of the corner of my eye and I don't want to focus on it. I can't look at it. I know why not: it's because even out of the corner of my eye I can see one thing about it, and it is a thing I do not want to see. I want to hide. I want none of this to have ever happened. I can't handle it.

I'LL TAKE OVER.

We can't do anything. It already happened.

WE CAN ALWAYS DO SOMETHING. I KNEW IT. I KNEW WE CAME FROM BADNESS.

I suppose I knew it too.

NOW WE CAN BE BAD. NOTHING MATTERS NOW.

The world has faded away. I am not in it. I can't tell what I can't see, because I'm sitting in the dark anyway. I struggle for a while and then I succumb.

THIS IS WHAT I KNEW ALL ALONG.

IT IS WHAT I AM.

IT IS WHAT I HAVE ALWAYS BEEN.

I KNEW IT.

I

KNEW

IT.

I am Bella. I am my Hinchcliffe self. I read the news report, every word of it, and I look at the man who murdered five women eighteen years ago, and who would have killed more if he hadn't been caught.

The man in that photograph is young. It's a mug shot. He looks at the camera, and he looks sideways.

The man has my cheekbones. He has my mouth. He has my original fair hair and I think he has my eyes.

I am their daughter.

I am a demon.

It's nearly dark and I am on the beach, sitting on the sand staring out to sea. I don't know what has happened. I don't know how I got here. I pick up a little stone and throw it into the water. This is the time when the sun has gone but its light is lingering.

I want to walk into the water and keep going. That would be the best thing. It would be so easy. I could just walk. The water is brown and nasty and it would come into my mouth and nose and stop me breathing.

She should have had an abortion. I have been going for eighteen years too long already.

I thought I wanted to find my birth mother.

I had her last name and I found her easily. I didn't have to wait until my birthday because she is famous. My parents are infamous.

I cannot meet my real mother.

I cannot meet my real father.

I could go back to my old life and face whatever's waiting for me in Rio. I could pretend I never found out any of this and go back to being Ella Black and be grateful for it. For a moment I picture myself doing that. I could go back to school, do my university application and take my A levels. I could grab hold of the stupid orange lifebelt and let myself be pulled back on to the boat and pretend I never fell off.

That is impossible.

The Blacks know who I really am and I never want to look them in the eye again. I cannot pretend I don't know, and I cannot pretend to be the baby they never managed to have. No one else can ever know where I came from. Yesterday I thought I could tell Christian everything, but I cannot tell him this. I am absolutely on my own. This was the Blacks' shameful secret, and now it is mine. I know they tried to tell me I was adopted, but I also know they would never have told me who my biological parents were. No wonder they backed down gratefully when I refused to hear the truth.

I feel a twinge of sympathy for them. Their lies were better than the truth. They did a good thing; it's impossible to argue with that. They did a good thing, but I can't go home to them.

I need to go back online and see the details of the crimes. I was clearly conceived right in the middle of it, and I can't even say that William Carr might not be my dad because you only have to look at him to see that he is.

This, finally, is real. I am Ella Hinchcliffe-Carr, child of murderers, and my dark side, my demonic Bella, is my truth. Bella Carr. That would be my birth name.

I lean back against a tree and close my eyes.

I had only vaguely heard of Amanda Hinchcliffe and William Carr. I can summon it up in little flashes of newspaper coverage: a sidebar of *other famous serial killers* when something happens; a link on the internet; a mention here or there. But that's all. I suppose the Blacks must have shielded me from it, and I try to revisit my childhood to see them distracting me with cookies and kittens when anything came on the news. I suppose that, if something is in the news when you're a baby, it's faded from the headlines by the time you're old enough to notice it.

My school knows who I am.

I see that in a flash. Not all the teachers, but Mrs Austen knew. I remember her tearing a piece of paper to shreds as she told me that I had to go with my parents whether I wanted to or not. She knew who I was all along.

It must have been strange for her.

She knew, and maybe some other teachers did too, but I don't think the students had any more idea than I did. They'd better not have. The idea of my friends knowing that about me makes me shudder.

I made most of the teachers like me by ruthlessly controlling my bad side and pretending to be quiet and nice (if you pretend to be something it's almost the same as being it), but at my heart I am bad. I have always known that. Now I know that I was made from badness and born into badness. I have bad genes, and no amount of education, healthy food and ballet lessons was ever going to make me good. I tried to be nice, but more and more I had to fight against my real self to do it.

Fiona and Graham Black are, on the face of it, the nicest people in the world. They are never mean to anyone. Those new parents gave me everything I ever needed or wanted or asked for, and yet I still smashed a bird to pieces with a hammer and slashed a stranger across the face with a broken bottle; and that is easily explained by the fact that I am the product of a famous criminal partnership. We are up there, us Hinchcliffe/Carrs, with Hindley and Brady and the Wests. You don't mess with us.

I cannot live with this. I stand up, stretch and walk to the edge of the sea. No one is around. It's nearly dark. I can hear the sound of drumming from a house nearby. I step into the water. I don't have a bike with me so I suppose I must have walked here. I cannot remember a thing between surrendering myself to a gleeful Bella and finding that I was sitting on the beach. I know why I came here. I know what I have to do.

I walk out in a straight line, up to my knees. I'm wearing the same little shorts so I can get thigh deep before they get wet. I pause with the water just below them. I can walk on, keep walking, and die, and they will find my body easily because this water doesn't seem to be the sort that moves around.

I want to. I desperately want to. I want to walk out and find a lovely blankness. Everything would go away. All of it. I have the power to extinguish myself.

But

I can't.

I want to but I can't.

I

want

to

but

I

can't.

My feet won't take the steps. My body is refusing to choose to die. Bella is screaming at me to turn round and walk back to the world. I can't push myself under the water: if I did that I wouldn't be able to breathe, and I need to be able to breathe even though I don't want to be alive any more. I can't get past that.

I can't conquer my need to breathe.

I can't die. I don't seem to be strong enough to take those last few steps.

I've failed at dying.

I knew this would happen. The one time I tried to harm myself in my old life, I took a craft knife into the loos at school and tried to get rid of the demon like that. I'd read about self-harm and I thought it might be the best way for me to deal with Bella without hurting anyone else, even though the idea made me feel so sick I couldn't stand up and had to slump against the partition wall. I put the blade against my arm and waited.

I couldn't do it. I couldn't override my instincts. That's why I just have two silvery lines on my left arm that no one sees. That was all I could manage. I couldn't do it then and I can't do it now.

I turn and walk slowly out of the water. I am a different person, just the way I wished in that other lifetime. If only I'd had the faintest idea. I seem to have decided to live, but I can't stay here. I can't tell anyone who I am. I need to start again. I need to leave everything behind – every single thing – and find a new life.

I pick up my bag and walk back to the hostel. I can't see Christian tomorrow. I need to get away.

I see from Ana-Paula's face that something has happened to make her worry about me. I don't know how much time passed between my seeing the face on the screen and finding I was on the beach. I might have smashed up the whole town, striding through it like Godzilla. I have no idea.

'Are you OK?' she says in careful English.

I nod, even though it's a lie. She talks in Portuguese, and I don't understand a word so we can't communicate, and that's all right by me. However, she is not giving up. She takes a pencil and a piece of paper, sits at the table in her warm kitchen and draws a picture of a girl who looks enough like me, with tears on her face. She adds a laptop and some primitive bikes. As she draws she talks, adding arrows to show me leaving the bike shop in tears and running away.

She mimes flinging the laptop on the floor.

She draws a boy like Harry Potter, his mouth open in shock.

I try not to cry, but I know I've failed when she puts an arm round me and hugs me tight. She smells of coconuts. Her huge baby bump is pressed up against me and I feel the baby squirming around.

That makes it worse.

8

30 days

I sit up all night thinking. I spend an hour reading about my real parents on my phone, watching the battery dip. Then I tiptoe into Ana-Paula's kitchen and write her a note saying: *Sorry I had to leave. THANK YOU.* I put it on the table with some money.

I write a much more difficult note too. It says:

Dear Christian,

I love you. I fell in love with you completely. I love you with all my heart. I know I've only known you a few days but I feel I know you better than I've ever known anyone, ever, and I love you.

I'm sorry I can't stop saying that.

I'm sorry I'm not here.

I'm sorry.

This is nothing to do with you and everything to do with me.

I'll always love you. Thank you for everything. I can't stay.

Ella xxxxxxx

I fold it in quarters and write *CHRISTIAN* on the outside. I don't even know his last name. I hope that it will get to him.

According to the timetable the first ferry leaves at half past five. Quite a few other people are waiting for it, but I avoid their eyes and wrap myself in a cloak of misery. I hope I can get away before Christian arrives. I need him to keep the best Ella in his head, the one he loved. That me – the one who was between Ella Black and Bella Hinchcliffe-Carr – only existed for a few days.

She was the one with possibilities.

The engine starts and the ferry moves off with a jolt. I stare out of the window. This boat is much emptier than the one I arrived on two days ago. I lean my forehead against the glass and watch the island disappear in the dawn.

I know now what my parents were doing for the year before I was born. Amanda, my mother, would go to a carefully selected public place and cry. When a kind woman stopped to ask whether she was all right she would say yes, but ask the woman to walk her home, just round the corner. She would lead her directly to the flat in which Billy, my father, was waiting. He would keep her there for days, doing things that I have forced myself to read about and will never erase from my brain, and then, at night, he and Amanda would go and throw the body in the canal, because of course I'm not from a privileged little town in Kent, but from a city far away from there that has canals running through it.

They got away with it for a long time because Amanda chose a place without CCTV and without witnesses, a short walk from their home. The women would be reported missing, but nobody linked them to Amanda and Billy because they had no connection.

Until, one day, they did. One of their victims was less of a loner than the others; her family made a huge and immediate noise when she went missing, and there was a sighting of her walking with a young woman. When the police dredged the canal they found not just the body they were looking for but the other ones too. Everything unravelled, and in the middle of the unravelling I was born.

Amanda was eighteen and heavily pregnant when she was arrested. The newspaper reports barely mentioned the fact that the baby (name and sex never given) was removed as soon as it was born and taken into care. That is where my public story ends.

I was *in care*. I was adopted by people who couldn't have their own baby and were reduced to rescuing one from murderers, and I was named Ella Black and brought up for seventeen years thinking this was who I was.

My adoptive dad claims they tried to tell me I was adopted. They clearly didn't try very hard, or I would have known. I can see why they decided not to tell me though. *I* wouldn't have told me if I was them. All they did was the best they could.

I was 'given a new identity', it says, in one of the brief mentions of my existence. Ella Black: a new identity. I have a new identity, like Jason Bourne. I was brought up oblivious to the fact that there was a fundamental truth about me that they never told me, like Harry Potter or Luke Skywalker.

I have enlarged the photos of Amanda Hinchcliffe pregnant at her trial until they are as big as I can get them, and I stare and stare at them and I know that this was where I began. I imagine a creature growing under the fabric of her baggy sweater, inside the waistband of her stretched leggings. I grew inside her, and before I was big enough to breathe she was caught tricking kind passers-by into coming home with her to be tortured and murdered.

I stare at her face. She was only a tiny bit older then than I am now. She has a nose like mine. It is a completely ordinary nose, but it's the same as *my* ordinary nose. Perhaps all noses are the same shape, but my nose, like hers, is neither big nor small. It doesn't turn up at the end. It has no lumps or bumps in it.

I study her eyes. I would like a mirror to check, but I think there's something about our chins that is the same. Her hair, in these pictures, is thick and dark, and no amount of looking at it can change that. Mine is straight and fine and currently purple, but otherwise blondish.

I want to look like her because I don't want to look like *him*.

This phone is almost out of battery. It has my old life on it. It has my friends from school and my enemies from school, and all my photos and texts and emails. In its search history it has the truth about my birth. I was going to throw it into the sea, but I can't do it because the entire truth of Ella Black is on it.

The boat arrives in Rio, and everything is quiet. There is no sign of Christian: of course he wouldn't be coming back to the island at half past six in the morning. I step into the pale sunlight and smile as my ears start to ring and my vision blurs. I welcome it.

I'VE GOT THIS.

Thanks.

I walk across the square in the cool sunshine and I feel my strength surging as I go. The old me drowned in the sea last night. This me has feet that barely touch the ground. This me has nothing to be afraid of because nothing can touch her.

NOTHING
CAN
TOUCH
ME.
BRING
IT
ON.
I'VE GOT THIS.

I am Bella through and through, and I am strong. I feel the violence beneath the surface, and I know that I could do anything to anyone now. I'm not sorry about the man's face any more. I'm not sorry about anything. I miss Christian with a terrible nagging ache, but I know I can't see him again because he is too good for me. I am walking away from the love of my life because I have to, because he loves Ella and I am Bella.

I flag down a yellow taxi, and the driver starts driving before I say where I want to go, and then I say the only word I can think of that will lead me to a place where Christian and the Blacks will not think to look for me.

They won't look for me because it's too dangerous.

Everything is dangerous.

Bring it on.

I say: 'Favela.'

The driver wants me to clarify. There are lots of favelas.

'The biggest one,' I say.

He speaks enough English for us to have a basic conversation. He says a word that sounds like *Hosseenya*.

'Yes,' I say. 'There.' Whatever that means, it will do.

This is what I know about favelas: they are shanty towns dotted around the city and they are terrifyingly dangerous. I know that Fiona and Graham Black would never venture there. I know that it would never occur to them to try. Ella Black would have run horrified from such a place. Bella Hinchcliffe-Carr, on the other hand, will walk straight in.

Right now I need money and I need a place to go. It feels ridiculous to get the taxi to stop at an ATM so that I can get out lots and lots of cash to take into a dangerous, lawless area of a South American city; but I know I need to do it. Even if they trace me to the ATM, they would have to be very quick to catch me before I got back into the waiting cab, and then they still won't be able to follow me to my brutal destination.

The driver stops outside a bank which is red all over. Although it's still early in the morning I am able to open

196

its lobby door and get blasted with freezing cold air-conditioning. I put the card into a machine. It asks what language I would like it to speak, and I press the button next to the word ENGLISH. I put in 1711, my birthday, knowing that it will work, knowing that they use that number for everything even though they didn't meet me on that day at all. It works. I half expect the shutters to come down and trap me in this room, but nothing happens. When it asks which account I would like the money to come out of, I tap the button next to CHECKING because it's the first on the list of options, and then it grinds into action and gives me 1,500 reals, which feels like a lot of money.

I get right back into the taxi and we are on our way again. My heart is pounding. I need to stash most of this cash somewhere secret. I can't put it in my shoe because I'm wearing flip-flops. I can't put it all in my bag in case the bag is stolen. I end up separating it out and, when I think the driver isn't looking, I put most of it into my bra, some of it into my shorts pockets and a bit more into my bag. Whatever happens to me next, I should still have some cash.

The streets are getting busier and I stare out of the window. Christian will go back to the island to meet me, like we agreed, and he won't find me. He'll go to Alex, and Alex will tell him where I was staying, and all about my meltdown, and then he will find my note.

I stare at a lagoon which has busy roads and traffic jams around it although it's still early. I know that I can only live from one moment to the next right now. I cannot stop and consider the bigger picture, or even begin to imagine what I will be doing tomorrow. This should be overwhelming, but it isn't. I don't know where I am going, but my dark side has taken control and she will deal with this. I am made from badness and I come from criminals and I will survive.

I am never going back to my old life. I will try to live in the favela. The adrenalin throbs through my whole body. This is madness. It's probably an elaborate way of killing myself, and that's why I don't care.

The cab follows lines of traffic into a massive tunnel. All the noise is amplified and the sun is gone and everything is tinged with red from the queue of tail lights in front of us.

Then we are out, in bright sunshine, and the taxi swerves across a lane of traffic and stops.

'*Hosseenya*,' says the driver, grinning, and I take a deep breath and step out of the cab. I pay him through the window, and he smiles and waves and says, 'Good luck to you.' He drives away, and I am alone.

I am alone in a slum in Rio and I should be terrified

but

I'm

not.

Five days ago I was at school.

A day ago I was falling in love.

An hour ago I was on a boat.

Although I am heartbroken in a million different ways, the energy of running away is carrying me through. Ella is hiding inside me, sobbing. Bella is going to get on with things, and there's one thing she needs to do before all others.

Shops and stalls are beginning to open up, and there are people and motorbikes everywhere and I don't speak the language. I hold my bag tightly, half expecting someone to snatch it.

I know people are noticing my hair. It makes me stand out.

In front of me is a stall selling cooked chickens that are lined up under a glass counter. There is a barber working nearby. I walk over to his shop and sit on the bench outside. I smile a hello to the other people waiting, and they don't actually seem that interested so I just sit there and wait my turn, and while I wait I literally think of nothing. I just stare at the people going by, and I feel nothing and I think nothing. No one robs me or talks to me, and then a barber calls to me and I tell him I don't speak Portuguese, but I pick up a strand of my hair and make a face, and he laughs. I mime shaving it all off because he doesn't look like someone who is going to dye it black for me. He checks a few times that it's what I really want, and then he takes some clippers and runs them over my head, and locks of purple fall on to the ground, and he does it again, and then it's finished.

I look in the little mirror and run my hand over the top of my head.

Just like that, I have no hair.

I have no name. I have no family. I have no boyfriend. I have no hair.

Actually I have a little bit of hair. I have a few millimetres of the stuff, and it's blonde and fuzzy. It feels nice to stroke it. I must look as if I'm having chemo. The man sweeps the purple strands into a pile of everyone else's dark hair and I pay him a tiny bit of money and walk over to the café that is right there. On the way I pass a bin, and I put my phone down on the ground and stamp on it before dropping it in. I really can't have it any more.

I wish I had a guidebook, or any kind of information at all. Right now I am thirsty and bald. I am in a slum, but I can put one foot in front of the other and make my way towards a place to sit, and although it feels hallucinatory that I am even here, it works.

The café is called Super Sucos. It's a juice bar so I order a juice by pointing at a picture of a pink one on the menu, and the woman motions for me to sit down. I sit, and am ignored even though I am strange and foreign and have just had my purple hair shaved off. After a while a plastic cup with a lid and a straw arrives in front of me.

'*Obrigada*,' I say.

'*De nada*,' says the woman.

The Blacks felt sorry for me because I was the offspring of murderers, and so they wanted me to have a nice life. That was kind of them. I needed parents and they needed a baby. I still managed to grow up demonic.

Maybe they wanted me to like them so I wouldn't kill them. Now I hate them. Perhaps I *will* kill them. Perhaps they are expecting it.

*

The juice tastes like strawberries and watermelon. I drink it as slowly as I can, and order another, a green one this time. I sit and sip at it and keep my eyes on the table in front of me and wait for time to pass in the hope that half an hour from now I might know where to go.

The buildings are made of concrete rather than corrugated iron and cardboard. It's not how I thought a shanty town would look. This actually feels like the kind of place that might have somewhere for travellers to stay.

It is less terrifying than it should be.

I pay for my juice and say to the woman: 'Do you speak English?'

She speaks enough English to know that I am asking whether she speaks English, and shakes her head.

'Hotel?' I say.

She calls a man over. They talk, and look at me, and talk about me, and I don't like it because I might have been on the news and they might be going to call the police. They might have seen me getting out of the taxi with my purple hair.

'Actually don't worry,' I say quickly, and shake my head and make a *forget-it* gesture with my hands. I will just walk up the hill on my own and see what happens. I try to leave the café, but the man stands in my way. I am breathing too fast. My legs tremble.

'You,' he says. I look for a way past him. 'You want hotel?'

I swallow. 'Yes?' It comes out as a whisper so I say it again, more bravely: 'Yes.'

I am Bella Black and I am keeping us alive. I am a monster and I can do anything. I'm not going to get this far and then crumble. 'Yes,' I say again. 'I want a hotel. *Por favor.*'

'You come.'

I follow him over to one of the men with the motorbikes. He speaks to him while I attempt to follow their gestures and catch an occasional word. When he motions for me to get on to the back of the bike I do it immediately, and the guy revs his engine and we are off. The bike vibrates under me, the engine roaring as it climbs the steep hill.

My life is in his hands.

Fuck it. Fuck it all.

We swerve in between people because they are walking in the street. They are everywhere: the place is busier than I would have thought possible. A tiny child perches on the handlebars of a bicycle as her mother pedals uphill (I assume it is her mother, though of course you never know). Other motorbikes buzz around the place. People sit at plastic tables on the pavement drinking coffee and Coke and beer. A man carries a huge bag with something with white plastic edges in it. A group of young men walk, laughing, down the street. Every type of thing is for sale. There is more meat, electrical appliances, a man doing some welding with sparks flying through the air, another barber. Every corner has a trader on it.

As we get off the main street it stops being commercial and becomes houses. I stare at them, packed together, painted in bright colours. Children are messing around with a football, and they stop to watch me pass. A young man sits on a doorstep having a shouted conversation with someone I can't see. Two girls in white T-shirts and blue shorts, dressed identically, are doing handstands.

I pass it all, glad to be removed from it, to be on this motorbike, even though I am entirely in the hands of a stranger in a Brazilian slum and have no idea where he is taking me.

The roads become smaller, and then we are in an alleyway so narrow that I could put an arm out on either side and touch the walls as we pass. When the bike stops I am ready. If the man mugs me I'll hand over the cash from my front right-hand pocket and run away. I should be able to find my way back to the place with the buses and the taxis and the juice bar, just by running down the hill.

However, he bangs on a door and calls something. A woman comes out. She is tiny like a little bird, and looks young, and when she sees me she smiles and nods and talks at me. The driver says something to her, and she says: 'Hello. I speak English very bad.'

'I speak Portuguese very bad too,' I say, amazed at how brave I feel. 'But I'm going to learn.'

'My name is Julia.'

I pause, unsure of who I am. I can't be Ella. I can't be Chrissy, much as I'd like to remind myself of Christian, because I used that name on the island.

'Lily,' I say. As soon as the word is out of my mouth I wish I'd said something different, but it's too late. I should say things that have no association with my old life. I am not Ella Black. Lily is Ella Black's best friend, so that was stupid, and now it's too late. I can't say that I actually meant Jessica, for example. That would be crazy, and my bald head and everything else about me is already crazy enough.

I pay the motorbike driver the small amount of money he asks for by holding up fingers, and add a tip to show that I'm grateful for the lack of kidnap and robbery. He nods, turns his bike round and drives off. Then I am just here, deep in the slum, following the woman called Julia into her house.

It really is a guest house. The room is nicer than I expected it to be, like the whole favela so far. It's small, with white-tiled floor and walls, and the single bed has a green nylon cover. The only window, high up in the wall, doesn't let in much light. This feels like a place to hide. I put my bag down on the bed and ask how much it costs.

'How much time?' Julia asks.

I take a deep breath. 'Could I stay for a month?' I ask.

'One month? Yes, of course. You work? Teaching English?'

'Yes.' It is much easier to agree with this than it would be to attempt to explain myself in any other way, and I'm grateful I don't have to make something up.

We agree on a rate for a month's rent and I don't bother to convert it because I know I have enough money just in my bra. I insist on paying up front because that means I will have less cash for anyone to steal. I have money on me now, so I'm not going to use the credit card again for a long time. This is it. I am hiding, and I have a place to live until December.

The bathroom is next door. Julia shows me that there is one other guest room, currently empty, and tells me that she and her husband, Anderson, live in another bedroom. The kitchen, with a table in it, is completely available to me, and there is a little sitting room with two comfy chairs. All the floors are tiled in white, and everything is faded but spotless.

'I go out to work,' she says. 'I work here, in Rocinha. Anderson works many hours in a hotel in Ipanema.'

It didn't occur to me that people who work in hotels live in places like this; but of course they do. Everything I know about slums and shanty towns comes from geography lessons and *City of God*, and the overriding idea I had is wrong. In the school version, a slum or shanty town or favela is chaotic and desperate, with houses made from cardboard and corrugated iron, stuck together any old way. No one has a job: they are beggars, or root through bins and rubbish heaps, or sell drugs. They are different from me.

I had to be brave to come here, but in fact it's just a place like other places, and so far the people here have helped me out in every way I've asked them to. They have cut off all my hair and sold me juice and taken me on a motorbike to the exact right place and given me a bedroom.

I remember how, a million years and also four days ago, my pretend father said that 'they' did tours of the favela, and the three of us winced at how horrible that would be. Actually this neighbourhood is alive. It is scary because it's different from anything I've ever known, but really it's just a place like any other, with people living in it.

My fake parents would never have imagined that. Because they're comfortably off they are scared of people who have nothing. They wouldn't look for me here; and if they tried, they would struggle to find me. They'll be looking for a girl with purple hair: I need to keep my bald head down and stay away from everyone who knows me, and also from anybody who might like the cash I'm carrying. For now, at this moment, I am all right. In fact I am bursting with adrenalin and I feel like I could fight anyone and anything.

However, even though I have all the energy in the world, I don't have a plan beyond hiding out. I'll have to find some analogue entertainment. I wonder if there is a book in English anywhere nearby. If I could find a sketchbook and some pencils I would like to do some drawing. I wonder whether a bald girl sketching would be a curiosity or just ignored.

I know I can't really sit around reading and drawing for a month, even if I did have the materials. I would still need to eat, and so I would spend money, and eventually my money would be gone. Then I would have nothing to do and nowhere to live. I'll try it out for a few days while I get used to being here, and then I'll see.

Julia gives me a glass of water and I close my door and sit on my bed. Even though I'm so wired, the moment I lie down

I fall asleep, and when I wake up it's the middle of the afternoon. I have absolutely no idea what to do and I'm scared to go out, now that my energy has been snoozed away. I look at the wall for a while and nothing happens. Then I go to find Julia, and sit with her watching the telly in the sitting room. I want to check that there's nothing about me on the news; but actually she's watching *Seinfeld*, dubbed, and I manage to concentrate on it and not think about anything else at all for several minutes. I pick up a newspaper and stare at it, and flick through the pages, trying to use my GCSE French and logic to work out the words. It's a lot easier written down than when it's spoken, that's for sure.

When I turn a page and find my face staring back at me, my head starts to ring and I think I'm going to be sick. There are blotches all over my vision. I can't remember how to breathe.

It's me. I am in the paper.

I am on page fifteen, buried but very much there, on display to anyone who picks up this newspaper and flicks through the pages. I want to translate the words, but I can't ask Julia to help. I pick out my old name, Ella Black, and the adoptive parents' names, Graham and Fiona Black. There is no Amanda Hinchcliffe in there, no grainy photographs, no notorious murderers. There is no waiter with a mutilated face, though he might feature in the article.

The headline says: O MEDO AUMENTA SOBRE O DESTINO DO ADOLESCENTE DESAPARECIDA. *Adolescente desaparecida*. Disappeared adolescent? Desperate adolescent? Despicable adolescent? Whatever it says, this is about me and my *destino*. I've seen stories like this in the papers at home. They usually end with the discovery of a body. This one won't. Not yet.

The photograph is one that Dad – Graham – took on the beach three days ago, just after I did the sketch of Copacabana. In the black-and-white photo my hair looks light grey and it is long and loose. I touch the stubble on my head and wonder whether Julia thinks I have been terribly ill. In the picture I am squinting a bit because the sun is in my eyes. I'm wearing my halter top, the one I have in my bag, so I need to get rid of that. The flat line of the ocean horizon is behind me. I look happy. I am actually smiling. I attempt it now, but it feels like a strange thing to do with my mouth. The Ella in that photograph is the same as the Ella I am in my earliest memory, in which I am held up to stroke a horse's nose. I am two. When I was two I believed what I was told about the world. Last week, although I was suspicious, I essentially believed that the world was the way I'd always known it to be.

Now I know better.

Julia looks over at me, and I force a smile and turn the page. The newspaper is called *O Globo* and I don't know if it's local or national. Not that it makes any difference, as I know no one outside Rio could possibly have seen me. My hands tremble as I turn another page, and it shakes in an invisible wind.

I have to find a way to stay here. I don't even speak the language. The first thing I need to do is learn it.

'Will you teach me Portuguese?' I ask Julia.

'Yes,' she says. 'You help me with English?'

'Deal.'

After a while she offers me some of her food but I say no. I go to bed early but I can't sleep.

I miss Humphrey. It's ridiculous, but I am thinking about my cat.

I miss Lily. I miss my friend, the one who kept me on track. The one who helped me try to be good without even knowing it.

I miss Jack, my gay boyfriend, the boy who told me his secrets and helped me out.

I miss having a place to go every day.

I miss my life.

As a baby I must have missed my mother. Before I was born she was my whole world. I wonder whether they let her cuddle me before they took me away. I think I have been craving her smell all my life. I am a part of her, and I always have been.

I wipe away the tears. I cannot cry for that woman.

I think about my adoptive mother instead. I wish I could say, *She's my mum, no matter what, and I love her,* because that would make everything easy, but I just can't. Not now. She has probably spent the past eighteen years feeling sad about the babies she couldn't have. That must have been complicated, when she actually had a baby but it came from murderers.

I am second hand. I come from killers. She has done her best all this time, but she must have known that I had a bad thing inside me. She must have known all along.

She tried too hard to be perfect. She made sure I ate lots of vegetables. She painted my bedroom exactly the way I wanted it. She got me into the best school, encouraged me to work hard and drove me everywhere I wanted to go. She was driving me to school last week, while everyone else walked or cycled or even drove their own car. She cooked dinner for me and Dad every night, and picked at a salad herself.

The other mothers were different; mine worked harder at it than any of them. Even Jack's mum dashed around taking his little brothers to Scouts and to church things, and made a point of saying how lovely it was to see me, and that we should help ourselves to juice and always leave the bedroom door open. We laughed about that when she was gone.

All the other mothers were different from each other, and all were interesting. All seemed like human beings who happened to be temporarily responsible for some children. Mine was the mother who was terrified of everything, who quadruple-locked the door, who would never have to drop everything to help me out because she was never, ever doing anything that she might need to drop.

I wonder now whether she was on Valium like women used to be in the fifties. I bet she fantasized about the imaginary biological family. The real Ella died in the womb again and again, and they had to put up with me.

I was the demon all along.

Real Ella would have had a brother – they would definitely have gone for a nuclear family. He would have been called something unexceptional like Tom. Tom Black would have been a cheeky blond poppet who climbed trees and whom everyone loved even though he was 'spirited'. In time he would have calmed down and ended up working in the financial sector like his dad.

But they couldn't have any of that. My adoptive mother must be devastated that I tried to stab her and I bet she's a tiny bit pleased that I've run away. My so-called parents raised me almost to adulthood, so they did their job. It's finished. Soon I will write to them and tell them that I'm fine, that I've got a job, that I'll see them again one day. Now she can become whoever Fiona Black really is. She can do her own thing and blossom. Her burden is lifted. I can never trust myself to go near her again: I would probably fly at her again, and this time I might succeed.

So all I have to do is become fine and get a job.

I have no idea how you get a job.

I live in the favela.

I need a job.

I will need money. I have never not had money.

I didn't have money in the first part of my life.

I had nothing.

I was taken

into

care.

*

I stay awake all night. I don't seem to need sleep in the way I used to any more.

I hear Anderson coming home. Julia talks to him, and I know she must be telling him about me. As soon as I hear the low rumble of his voice something changes. I know I should be worrying about him.

He works at a tourist hotel.

I realize that I cannot hide in his house. He works at a tourist hotel, and I am in the paper because the police are looking for me. It must say in the paper that I have purple hair. Now I have no hair. A person with distinctive hair, hiding, would cut it off. My baldness is not really much of a disguise.

I can't even get a wig now because Julia will have told him about me; she will have said that I have no hair, because that is the most remarkable thing about me.

And I have the same face as the girl in the paper because the girl in the paper is me.

And he works at a hotel in tourist Rio, and that is where people are looking for me.

After a while they go to bed. It is quiet. Sometimes there are voices outside, but there is no gunfire and nothing that sounds like trouble. For a shanty town it seems very peaceful.

I wish I hadn't told Julia my name was Lily. My best friend Lily might have been in the papers herself, worrying about me. Julia will have told her husband that I am Lily. At the hotel he will tell everyone that there is an English girl here called Lily. Since people are looking for an

English girl, word could get back to the Blacks that there is a bald English girl here, and when they hear the name Lily they will know.

I can't stay here.

I realize it with horror. If I want to stay hidden, then I cannot stay in this lovely little room buried in the favela with the friendly landlady who lets me watch *Seinfeld* with her and is going to teach me Portuguese.

I stumbled upon a nice place and I paid for a month's rent, but I have to leave. I need to be on my own. If I stay here the police will come and arrest me for hurting that poor man.

I desperately want to stay, but I have to go.

I am terrified. I remember thinking about applying to university or art college. I thought those were the kinds of decisions I was going to have to make. Instead my decisions are: drown myself or run to the favela? Stay here and risk being arrested for hurting someone, or run away into the unknown?

I stare at the wall and try to make myself strong enough to go out and find a way to live.

I cannot stay.

I cannot stay.

I cannot stay.

9

28 days

For the second morning in a row I get up early and creep away. I walk out into the favela with no plans and less money than I would like. It is dawn and the light is pale. The door clicks shut behind me.

That is it: I cannot go back to Julia's house. The early-morning sun is tickling my face, and I am standing on the hard earth of the alley. Then I am walking away, my few possessions and all my money in a bag over my shoulder.

The only creature I see is a chicken. She fixes me with a glare and struts away. When I get back to the tarmacked road, however, I see that there are plenty of people around. Across the road a woman in a black-and-white uniform with a name badge is climbing on to the back of a motorbike, and then the bike speeds away down the hill, taking her to work at, judging by her clothes, a tourist hotel.

A man in a green jumpsuit walks past so closely that I step back in surprise, but he turns and grins and waves a hand in greeting or apology. He too is going to work somewhere in the city; somewhere outside the favela. All the way down the hill I see people walking down to where the buses stop or getting on to the backs of motorbikes.

There is a police car driving slowly up the hill, and I turn away and walk up a bit and duck down the first alley I see. I go on to the end, turning sharp right and then left, wondering whether I am in someone's garden but always finding a small gap to squeeze through to the next place. At least no car can follow me here. All I can do is keep walking and hope that I don't stroll into something terrible and get shot.

I take a step, and then another. I can only live from one step to the next. A teenage boy, younger than me, is fixing a bike, and he stares as I pass but says nothing. I don't smile but I don't not-smile either. We make eye contact, and I keep going.

When I come to a wider road I follow it uphill because I know that downhill leads to buses and cars and people who might have seen me in the paper. I keep walking, knowing that I am hungry, knowing that I am going to have to make a plan, and then I come to a stretch of grass that, as I get closer, becomes a little football field. It has a view of the entire city and the sea and the mountains.

I walk across the grass and stand and stare. Below, the water is glinting and gleaming in the sunshine. The mountains are the same ones I painted at school, but they are a million times more beautiful in real life, and now I am standing on one of them. There is a cool breeze blowing into my face, and although it is early it's warm. In spite of everything – in spite of the fact that I have gone into exile in a Brazilian shanty town and have no particular future in sight – I must be in the most beautiful place on the planet.

I am homeless in paradise. I cannot hear anything except the buzz of distant engines somewhere behind me. The air is fresh and smells of the sea. A cluster of chickens peck at the ground in the distance.

I am thankful that it's early. I have a day to find myself a new place to stay.

I can't last until night time without sleep, so I end up on a beach, dozing while trying to look like a tourist. If I curled up on someone's doorstep and dozed, the police would find me. However, if I sleep on the beach behind a pair of cheap sunglasses, with a cotton scarf wrapped around my head, I look enough like everyone else to get away with it. I hope I do, anyway.

I bought the glasses and the scarf at a little stall on my way down the hill. They are my disguise and my protection. My head was burning, and now it is covered in factor 30 and the stubble has gone all weird, and it's covered with my scarf anyway.

I'm at the end of a beach I found by walking in the opposite direction to the city. I should stay away from tourist places. This beach is busy enough to make me feel I can blend in a little, but it's different from the glossy beaches in the city. There aren't as many people selling things. It feels very different from the favela, and very different from Copacabana too.

I don't have a bikini with me, but I think I could go into the water in my underwear without anyone particularly noticing. My underwear needs a wash anyway.

My mind races, even as I lie flat on the beach, but I can't decide anything. I go round in circles. I could find another guest house and hide out for a week or so, and then go back to the Blacks and face whatever is coming to me because I can't really avoid it forever. I could find out where people learn English, like Julia said, and try to become a teacher, even though I should be at school myself. I could take the credit card back into the city and get more money out. I think I'll try that, and ask at Super Sucos for another hotel. I try to stop thinking; I try to empty my head of all its stuff. I won't be able to think straight without some sleep. I'll end up making a mad, hallucinatory plan that makes no sense.

I lie so still that I must look like yet another person soaking up the sunshine without a care in the world. Nobody can tell that I'm the child of murderers, brought up by liars. They can't tell that I met the love of my life and had to walk away so he would never know what I am. They can't tell that I cut a man's face when I was trying to hurt my adoptive mother.

That fact is worse now that I know the truth about myself. I hurt someone like my birth parents did. I could have killed that man. Perhaps I did. I have bad blood. I was showered with every material thing; and I still grew up violent. I kill little creatures. I have tried to hurt myself on occasion, to stop me hurting anyone else.

I told Christian about Bella and he didn't hate me. I thought I could tell him everything, until I found out the worst thing of all. I cannot tell him that. I just can't.

The thoughts make me too agitated to sleep. I gather my stuff into my arms and carry it to the water's edge. I leave it there, on the last bit of dry sand, and take off my T-shirt and shorts and scarf and run into the sea in my underwear. The water is murkier than it is round the corner on the big showpiece beaches, but I don't care. It's cleaner than it was on the island. I wade in and sink down so it covers my shoulders. I swim out, even though I'm swimming into murk. I hold my head underwater and rinse the place where my hair used to be. I spring back up and check my clothes are where I left them, with my bag underneath them. They are. No one is looking at me. People are probably fighting their own battles.

I swim along parallel to the beach, and it makes me remember how tired I am, so I head out of the water to pick up my things. The sand is hot under my feet.

I go back to the spot I left, further up the sand. There are more people around now, but I don't pay them any attention because if I did I would become paranoid about them looking at my bald head and recognizing my face from the paper. I quickly pull my T-shirt on over my wet body and squeeze into my shorts, and I lie back and close my eyes.

When I wake up I am lying on the powdery sand of a beach whose name I don't know, in the glare of a perfect sun, sweating and overdressed in shorts and a T-shirt. I have no hair. I am in Brazil. I am alone. It comes back to me in a rush.

The loneliness hits me in the face for the first time because I'm not running any more. I am just here, in a random place, on my own. The excitement of the running-away has gone. I don't know if I'm Ella or Bella or someone completely new. I'm limp and exhausted and I try to list the things that are important.

1. I need a place to sleep tonight. So I have to go and ask for another guest house.
2. I don't want to go back to the Blacks or to Julia and I don't want the police to find me, so I must find somewhere else to stay round here, even if it's just for a bit.
3. I'm going to be eighteen soon so I need to make my own decisions.

I could go somewhere else in Brazil, or I could fly home. If I got through the airport without being arrested and thrown into scary Brazilian prison, I could go home and find a job and a flat. But I don't have any qualifications and I know that Britain will absolutely not hand me such things. I don't want to go back there.

I could go to the Amazon, up in the north of Brazil. I'd be impossible to find up there. Someone would want to learn English, or I could just clean out the Blacks' credit card and go off and see what happens. I will need to learn Portuguese and keep my head down.

I reach for my bag to check how much money I have left.

I feel around. I have cash and the credit card in here. I can get a bus to the north; that feels like the best plan. I feel into the corners. It is in here. I put it here. It has been right next to me the entire time. I checked it was all there when I came out of the sea.

I sit up and look around. There are a few groups of people nearby. No one is looking. No one is holding up my money and card and laughing. I turn my attention back to the bag, noticing that my scarf has gone. I pile my things on the sand and turn it inside out and shake it, but there is no money in there.

There is definitely no money.

I have lost all my money.

Lost my money.

I

have

nothing.

Someone stole my money and my credit card while I was asleep.

I should have put some money in my pockets again. It was so much less money than yesterday but I was wet from the sea and I didn't even think of it.

I try to imagine a human being creeping right up to me while my eyes were closed, and picking up my bag, and taking every last real out of it, as well as the card, which I had already stolen.

I stand at the edge of the water and scream as loudly as I can out to sea. I scream and scream and scream. I cry. I shout. I swear. My voice is carried away on the breeze.

This is as far as I can go. I cannot carry on without money. I need to find a police station and hand myself in and see what happens. I need to get a police car to take me away.

I can't. I can't go to prison. I'm too scared. I can't look Fiona Black in the eye, knowing that I tried to attack her with a broken bottle. I can't look at the man I wish was my real dad, knowing that he grabbed my arm to stop me slashing at his wife. I can't. That is a bare fact.

It takes me ages to walk to Leblon, which is the name of

Ipanema Beach at the favela end. I get there, sweaty and smelly, hungry and desperately thirsty, and I know that this is it. I will either flag down a police car and give myself up, or I'll dodge the police and do something else. I have no idea, at the moment, which it is going to be. I walk along the edge of a different favela, which goes up the hillside, and then I head down into the smart, shiny, tourist part of the city.

I don't look like Ella Black. I look like Bella Carr. I don't bother about being recognized because either I will be or I won't and there is nothing I can do to change it. The beach is busy, and the water is crystal clear, so the first thing I do is go for another swim. I wash my head in salt water and kick around listlessly with tired legs. This time I don't worry about anyone stealing my stuff because I haven't got anything worth stealing. For a moment this feels like freedom.

I stand on the sand and look around. A man catches my eye and smiles and mimes stroking my head but I frown and he looks away. I walk along the beach, looking at the people.

DO IT, says Bella.

I don't even make her ask again. I know exactly what she means, and I do it because I want to do it too. I pick up the bag casually, in passing. I don't pause. The people beside it are asleep, just as I was when my stuff was stolen. I am shaking all over as I carry on walking, and when I reach the wide pavement I run. I run through crowds of people, back in the direction I came from. I wish there was a zombie parade now. I know that by running while looking what Fiona Black would have called 'a fright' and holding what is probably an expensive bag (I hardly looked), I am drawing so much attention to myself that I might as well have THIEF written on my forehead in Portuguese.

I take a deep breath and slow down. I pull the bag up over my shoulder and try not to look suspicious. The last thing I want is the Rio police picking me up now that I have chosen this path. I cross the main road, running between cars that hoot at me and slam on their brakes, and head up a side street, and down another. This is tourist Rio; I would be better off in the alleys of the favela.

I stop and edge over to a building and let my legs give way so I'm sitting on its marble doorstep, because I've just realized something that changes everything. I have lost my passport too.

It was in my bag, and now it is not in my bag.

I can hardly do a thing now. Not officially.

DOESN'T MATTER.

YOU WEREN'T GOING TO USE IT TODAY.

WORRY ABOUT IT LATER.

I stand up and force my legs to walk down the road. In a tiny park I sit on a bench and try to look casual as I open this new bag. It's a stripy canvas one, bright pink and bright blue, with a gold clasp. It is distinctive, and I need to lose it. I take all the things out of it and drop them straight into my old bag, stuff the new bag into a nearby bin and walk off.

I keep walking in the direction of the favela, and when I find another bench I sit on it and open my old bag to have a proper look at what I have stolen.

There is a purse, but it only contains a small amount of cash. I have a credit card in the name of Jens Bierhoff, but I don't have a clue how to get money from that because its PIN almost certainly won't be my birthday. I have an iPhone, and a book that I think is in German. There are a few other cards in the purse, but they will be no good to me. If I was nice I would just take the cash and leave everything else on the steps of a police station, but I have committed two crimes now, so I am not nice at all. I keep the purse, put all the cards in the trash except the credit card, just in case, and count the money as quickly and surreptitiously as I can.

On the other side of the street a group of boys with skateboards are staring at me. They know what I'm doing. I start to walk away but they follow, and so I walk faster and they call things out at me. I don't think they like my skinhead look. It's impossible to tell what kind of things they are saying: they could be yelling at me for being a thief, or they could be inviting me to join their gang. When they start to hiss I speed up, running back to the main road and getting on the first bus I see. I grab some coins from kind Herr Jens Bierhoff to pay my fare.

The bus takes me away. I don't care where it's going. I stay on to the end of the line, and then I get off in a random suburb and sit on a bench to wait for another bus to take me somewhere else.

I look at the German's iPhone.

I STOLE FROM A STRANGER.

I STOLE.

I

AM

A

CRIMINAL.

I

AM

AMAZING.

I'm not amazing.

It all crashes quickly. At home Bella was separate from me, compartmentalized. Now I need her strength but I cannot bear the badness. I crumple as I stare at the phone. My strength and excitement drain away.

My catalogue of bad things is growing.

I tried to hurt Fiona Black, and in fact I wanted to kill her.

I hurt that café man, and I did it on purpose.

I stole a bag from a beach so I didn't have to ask anyone for help.

I want to say it was Bella, and not me, who did those three things, but it wasn't, because Bella is me.

No one will find me here. The phone doesn't have a passcode. Before I know what my fingers are doing, they have called Fiona Black's mobile number, with a 0044 country code at the start.

I only want to hear her voice. I tried to kill her, and she knows that, and I want to hear, from her voice, whether or not she can forgive me.

I struggle to breathe as it starts to ring. It rings with an international tone, and then the woman I always thought was my mother actually answers.

'Hello?' she says, sounding fast and desperate. I don't say a word because I tried to hurt her, and I really meant it and she knows I did, and that fact will be there forever.

I form the shapes of the words I cannot say with my mouth.

Hello.

Mum.

Seconds pass. This is the voice I heard from babyhood, the one I believed when it told me who I was. It is not, however, the first voice I ever heard. She used to say she had given birth to me, but she never did. She is not my mother.

But she *is* my mother. She took me in and cared for me and I hate her and I love her.

I'm hungry. I want to go home. I don't know where that is.

'Hello?' she says again. 'Ella? Is that . . . Ella?'

I cannot bear to listen and yet I cannot hang up. I take a deep gasping breath and she hears it. A weird animal sound comes from the back of my throat.

'Ella,' she says. 'Ella, darling. If it's you, then don't –'

I press the button. I cannot hear what she was going to say. I throw the phone into a bin and find a bus that's going to Rocinha, which seems to be the way you spell the favela I slept in last night. I get on, and I stay there until it goes through the tunnel, and then I get off by the juice shop, and this time I walk up the hill myself.

I haven't had anything to eat or drink for a long time, and that doesn't help anything, and I have nowhere to sleep. Still, for some reason it feels better to be here than it does to be anywhere else. I buy a bottle of water and a bar of chocolate and I eat and drink as I walk. I see a sign for a guest house and knock on the door, but the man who answers it says they are fully booked.

I need to find a place to go and I don't know what to do.

10

27 days

I am dozing and then alert.

I am asleep and then awake. I am awake because something bad is happening. I am awake and my heart is pounding and there is something around my ankle and it's someone's hand. It is someone's hand around my ankle, and it's gripping me and pulling me hard towards it.

I was asleep in a corner of an alley, and then this happened. A man I can't see has grabbed me by the ankle, and my back scrapes along the ground as he pulls me towards him. Bella is yelling *FIGHT!* at me, and I scream and scream and scream, but then he puts his hand over my mouth. I struggle and try to bite him, but it doesn't work because I can't get my teeth around his hand. I kick and kick and flail around with my arms. I wish I had that broken bottle in my hand right now.

I can't scream, but someone else is yelling. Another voice says: 'Get off her, you bastard! Get off her now!'

Then the man is gone. I hear his feet running off down the alley. He was chased away by a woman shouting in

English, but that can't have happened and it must have been me, even though his hand was over my mouth.

I don't know what happened, but the man has gone and there is no one else around and it is still night and I know I can't go back to sleep, and I can't sleep on the streets any more and that means I am finished.

I sit in the same place, the sheet of plastic I was using as bedclothes wrapped around my shoulders like a blanket, and wait, jumping at every sound, for it to be morning. I am so, so, so fucking bored and scared. I have broken myself and I'm hungry and I need water, and all I have is my little bag with sunscreen and a few clothes in it.

I get through to sunrise by thinking of lists and telling them to Lily. I send them to her in my head and hope she finds them popping into her brain and knows where they came from. That is all I can do: I can't tell her who I am or the things I've done.

The top three worst things about sleeping in the street, Lily, are:

1. Danger. It's dangerous: specifically with regard to rape and murder. So that makes it difficult to sleep.
2. Sleep. It's truly impossible to sleep because it's not comfortable. Remember how hard it is getting to sleep when you're camping, like when we did our D of E. Then at least you have a soft mat. Now I would give anything for a soft mat.
3. Food. You're so hungry all the time. And thirsty. And a bottle of water a day may be what you've decided

you're allowed, but it's not actually enough. Food and water become impossible luxuries: you can't decide you're a bit hungry and go and get a piece of toast or a cookie. We used to withhold food from ourselves to make ourselves thin. That feels like a joke now. When you're hungry it's the only thing you can think about.

Then I make another list.

The top three people I miss so much it hurts:

1. Christian. I wish you could meet him, Lily. I fell in love at first sight – I love everything about him.
2. You. Lily. My best friend. I asked you to be my best friend forever and I wish you were here now because you'd know what to do. You would help me out of this. If I had to go to prison, you would come to visit me.
3. Jack. I never told even you the truth about my relationship with Jack. I miss him. I miss our secrets. I hope he's happy. I wish him all the light and joy in the world.

I watch the sky becoming lighter, and as soon as it's daylight I get up and fold my square of plastic and walk down to the beach so I can try to sleep there. The beach is out of bounds during the night: I know because I stood in the shadows and looked at it, and there were groups of men, and I don't know what was going on but I knew it was no place for me.

In the light of day I can see that I am filthy. I must smell terrible. I have no idea how Bella and I fended off that man, but we did. I guess you do strange things when your life is at stake.

I walk down to the clean end of the beach, leave my bag on the sand, then take off my shorts and top and walk into the sea. I lie on my back and let the dirt wash away. My skin is terrible: it's gone all dry down my legs. I won't sleep outside again. I found the best spot I could, in the shadows away from the road, and it was no good.

Today I need to steal another bag, hoping that this one will have enough money in it for me to sleep in a bed for a few nights, and to eat something that will fill me up. I wish I could go back. If I had my passport I could try to leave the country, but as it is I'm stuck.

I get out of the water and pull my clothes on to my wet body and lie on the beach. A man comes over to me. I make a point of not looking but I sense him there, tall and muscular. I feel his gaze.

'*Hola*,' he says. I look up and he runs his hand over his head and smiles. I thought not having hair would stop me being interesting to men, but it doesn't seem to work like that. They seem to want to touch my head. I thought that my skinny body with its horrible skin would put men off too, but it doesn't.

I shake my head. I want to shout and scream at him to go away, but I don't want him to know that I'm foreign because that would make me more vulnerable and he might have seen me in the news, so I keep my mouth closed. He shrugs and goes away.

I feel the hand around my ankle again and again. The fingers that gripped me are still there. Someone saw my body and wanted to take it.

I put on some sun cream and lie down because I can't do anything until I have slept.

When I wake up I have no idea how much time has passed. I sit up and stare out at the paradise sea, the gorgeousness of Brazil, and I know that I have to decide whether to give myself up.

There is something lying next to me that wasn't there before. It's a paper bag with words written on it. I pick it up to look at the writing.

It says:

Something to help you Jo. From a friend.

It's written in English, but not, I think, by someone who speaks English fluently: the letters are too carefully formed. This, though, is from someone who knows I am English.

They think I'm someone else. They think I am Jo, but I'm not. This is meant for her, whoever she is, and they've given it to me. I open the package and find cheese balls, a little bottle of water and some money. It's enough money to buy a coffee and more food. I drink the water quickly in one gulp and pause, breathing deeply, hoping that it's not going to make me sick.

When my stomach has settled I take a bite from a cheese ball. It has ham in it, and that is one thing I was not expecting. I have to run into the sea, my legs wobbling, so that I can be sick without anyone seeing. My stomach heaves and empties itself into the water with a surprising amount of vomit considering how little I have eaten; it disperses and a shoal of little fish appear and start to eat it.

I get myself under control and walk back across the beach. All the water I drank has gone, and I am dehydrated again. I now know that this food has ham in it and I eat the balls slowly, one by one. They fill me up, and I feel stronger, better.

A stranger left food beside me. That is actually scary. Someone has seen me and helped me, and quite possibly saved my life. I wish I knew who it was, and why, and who they think I am and who Jo is. I imagine a second homeless girl, a Jo. I wouldn't be alone if I met her.

I will go and buy more water because I am so thirsty I can hardly think. I will drag myself back to Rocinha and get water and coffee. Whoever just helped me is the opposite of the stranger who took my money yesterday when I was sleeping at the other end of this same beach. I get up and start walking, imaginary Jo at my side, keeping me going.

I get there in the end, hot and with my head pounding and my legs screaming. I stop at the first café I see, and force a smile while I ask for a white coffee in the hope that milk will give me extra sustenance. I drink my water as slowly as I can. I order two cheese balls, which feels like a luxury when I have already had several ham ones. I don't think about the spoiled girl who piled up food on her hotel breakfast plate without being hungry. However, I do remember Ana-Paula handing me a plate of rice and bean stew on Paquetá Island. Perhaps one day I could try to go back there. I could live with her and help her with the baby. Even Bella would be nice to that baby because Ana-Paula was so kind to us.

Baby. That thought cracks me open, and I push it away.

When I feel I can loiter no longer I go to the counter to pay. There is a woman at another table, a fat middle-aged woman, and she is looking at me with far too much interest. I keep my head down and turn my back. I know I look weird. I look homeless, and white and bald. Of course everyone stares. There is another woman with long tangled hair at her table, and she stares too for a while.

'Do you speak English?' I say to the café woman, just in case, because why not?

'Speak English?' She nods, and shouts behind her. I am expecting her to produce another adult, but instead a tiny little girl emerges. The girl has shiny chocolate-button eyes and she looks away from me, shy.

I realize that the woman is pointing at the girl's T-shirt, which is white and clean and uncreased. It says: FAVELA ENGLISH SCHOOL in red capitals in a circular logo.

'Favela English School,' I say aloud. I try to get the girl to look at me.

'Do *you* speak English?' I ask her, though I know she

can't because she's only about three, or maybe five. I don't really know much about children.

Favela English School.

'*Twinkle, twinkle, little star,*' she sings, and I laugh and join in, and she looks me in the eye and laughs too.

'What is your name?' I say. I crouch down so that I'm looking right into her face. This is the closest I have been to anyone for days, apart from the man who grabbed my ankle.

'My name is Ana,' she says clearly, and everything about her is perfect and gorgeous. I want to cry. I was a perfect little girl once too. I thought I was. I didn't know I was damaged and second-hand, even then.

I point to myself. 'My name is . . .' I pause. Not Ella. Not Lily. I need a new name, and it needs to be bland. I need a name that could be Latin American so I don't stand out. I have no idea what to call myself, and when I realize that the silence has gone on too long, even for a tiny child, I say the first thing that comes into my head. 'Paula.' I pronounce it *Powla*, the way Ana-Paula did on the island. The girl nods. She is called Ana and I am called Paula.

'Hello, Paula,' she says. 'I am pleased to meet you.'

'And I am pleased to meet you too.'

She reaches out and strokes my head, and I let her. I am having a conversation, in English, with a toddler. I have food and coffee inside me and everything feels a tiny bit better.

People who say that money isn't everything have never tried to live without it. Money is literally *everything*. I sometimes used to give money to homeless people. I would fish out fifty pence and feel awkward and bad. Fiona Black donated money and food to food banks and said that was better than giving someone money when they would only be tempted to spend it on alcohol or drugs.

Of course they want alcohol or drugs. I would love something that blotted out reality, even just for a few minutes. If I ever managed to go back to my old world, I would give money to every homeless person I saw. I would give them food. I would give them hot drinks filled with sugar, and I would give them alcohol too.

'Where is your English class?' I ask the girl, and her perfect forehead wrinkles as she doesn't understand.

'English school?' I shrug. I look around, pantomiming a search for something. I point up the hill. I point at the house opposite, raising my eyebrows. I have to make this work. I hope I'm not too close to her because I know I must smell disgusting.

She giggles and points up the hill. In the squeaky voice of someone who hasn't known how to talk for very long, she explains at great length, in Portuguese, how to get to her English class, showing right and left turns with her hands, talking me through it all in words I don't understand.

I turn to her mother, and soon I have a map, drawn with a stubby pencil on a thin napkin.

I want to hug little Ana, but I don't know if that's allowed, so I pat her head instead, as she did to me. I pay for my coffee and cheese balls, and I get a tiny amount of change which I put carefully in my pocket. I thank them and wave, and thank them again and wave again, and ignore the fat woman who is still watching, and do my best to follow the map to the place that teaches English to tiny children. My language feels like the only skill I have.

'Hello?'

My voice is strange. I haven't used it much lately and I'm not used to the way it sounds. I sound like Fiona Black trying to see if there's a shop assistant in the back room. In fact I am no one and entitled to nothing.

I am standing at the end of an alley, on ground that is made of compacted earth, and I have no idea whether this is the right place. There is a strong smell of cooking which came from a doorway further back. I cannot walk any further because the building in front of me is the last in the alley. There is just a door, which is closed, and I knocked on it and nothing has happened.

I think I followed the map. It took me ages to get here – I have constantly gone back on myself, tried different turnings, interpreted the woman's scribbled pictures and clues about what would be on the corner by the turning I should take, jumped out of the paths of motorbikes, and tried, at all times, to look as if I knew what I was doing. Also I am not very good at walking today.

I can't get here, find it all closed and give up.

'*Hola?*' I shout, wondering why I didn't do that in the first place. I am in a corner of Rio. Here, we say *Hola*. Or we say *Oi*.

I am in the shade and it is just cool enough. My clothes are stiff with salt, and I know they have white tide marks on them.

'Hello?' Someone is looking down from an upstairs window. I step back. It's a girl of about my age, as far as I can tell. Her black hair is hanging down and she seems friendly. She is Asian and she looks like the girls from my sixth form, with creamy skin and a healthy glow. I wonder how different from that I am now.

I think I am very different.

'Hi there,' I say. I take a deep breath. I have to do this properly. I have to be Ella Black, but with Bella's confidence. 'Hi – I was just wondering. Do you give English lessons here?'

'Sure. Hang on. I'll come down.'

As I wait I try to line up the words I need. This girl cannot be in charge: she is too young. I need to get her to take me to the person who is, and then I need to beg them to give me a job as an English teacher. I cannot give my real name or a passport or spend any money at all. I'll also need a place to sleep.

It doesn't seem likely; and yet I have to make it happen.

I hear a key turn, a bolt being pulled back, and then the girl is standing in front of me. I see myself through her eyes, and then I try hard not to.

'Hi,' I say. 'I'm Jo. I'm wondering if you need an English teacher here at all . . .'

If I manage to make anything happen today it will be thanks to the person who left food and drink and money for Jo. That makes me Jo, I think.

'Oh, hi,' she says. 'Hi, Jo. Normally people come out as part of the programme. Ben said someone just dropped out, but I don't think . . .'

She doesn't look at me with disgust, and I love her for that. She is talking to me like an equal even though I am a massive horrible mess.

'I'd be happy to do anything,' I say, knowing that I sound desperate.

'Great. OK. Well . . .' I see her hesitate. I watch her internal struggle as she tries to work out whether she's allowed to invite me into the building.

I'm not sure where her accent is from, but it's not the south-east of England. I think she might be Irish, but accents are not my strong point.

'I'm Jasmine,' she says. 'You'll need to speak to Ben or Maria. I'll see if I can get one of them on the phone. We've no children in until later this morning. Would you . . .?' She looks at me. 'Can I get you a coffee or something?'

The sympathy in her eyes is going to make me fall apart. I have to hold on. 'I would absolutely love a coffee and a glass of water if you've got one.' I speak fast, desperately trying to be the person I need to be. 'Sorry. I'm sorry if I'm being weird.'

'Hey, no problem. Sure. Come and have a sit-down and I'll get your drink. Your drinks.'

This room is a schoolroom, with murals of Rio all over the walls. The skies are pink, the sea yellow, and everything is painted in chunks of brightness. I look at the painted Cristo Redentor statue, who has a happy smile daubed on his pale blue face by a child.

'Thank you,' I tell Christ the Redeemer. When I visited him I had no idea what was about to happen. He probably knew. I could use some redemption right now.

There are laminated posters of colours and numbers, with the words in English. There are finger paintings pegged to a washing line going across the ceiling. The seats are child-sized plastic chairs with little desks clipped across the front of them, and I squeeze my body into one. Although my knees are up by my shoulders and I am not remotely comfortable, I decide I will lean my head down on my arms just for a moment.

'Hello? Excuse me?'

I hear the words but I can't move. When I dozed on the beach and down the alley I woke up knowing exactly where I was and what I needed to do. This time I am deeply unconscious, and I have to ascend slowly, through thinking I'm Ella Black, to remembering that we came to Rio, that my parents lied about everything, that my money was stolen, that I stole someone else's money, that I'm in a favela, that Bella is part of me, that I'm homeless. I came to the place that teaches English and I have to make a good impression.

'I'm so sorry.' It is a man's voice and he doesn't sound sorry at all: even in my befuddled state I can tell that he is deeply pissed off. I am squeezed into a tiny chair. My back, my arms, my neck all scream in protest as I stretch, and I don't dare to try to stand because I would definitely fall over.

The man is smiling but there is steel behind the smile. He is a black man, dressed casually in blue shorts and a Favela English School T-shirt, and he has long dreadlocks and his face is open, but his manner is formal and I think he is angry. I need to make him like me. I need to charm him, even though I am not charming at all and he doesn't look like someone who is ready to be charmed. I have to do what I used to do: I need to pretend to be normal, and hope that this will actually make me normal.

He passes me a glass of water and I drink it in one go.

'Hi. I'm so sorry.' I echo his phrase back at him and shake my head to try to make some words of my own come. I beg Bella to lend me her bravery while withholding her nastiness, although I'm not sure where I end and she begins any more. I reach across to Bella's side of my brain and take some courage. 'I'm so sorry,' I say again. 'I didn't mean to fall asleep.' He might have seen me in the paper. I know I invented a cover story and used a different name but I can't remember what any of it was right now. 'I was really tired.'

'I can see that. So you're looking for work? I'm Ben. I'm sorry but we don't have anything and we don't work like that. Jasmine should have said that at the start.'

I'm pretty sure he's Brazilian: his English is American-accented and fluent.

Jasmine shouldn't have let me in. He doesn't need to say that because everything about him is saying it wordlessly. He wants to shove me out and close the door behind me.

'I could help out. I can teach English, but I can do anything else too. I'll do anything. I met one of your little children today. Ana.'

Ben's eyes are noting everything about me. I can see every detail being transformed into data and filed away. He is like Mr Richards, the teacher we had in Year Ten. Once he saw me holding the point of a compass against my arm to try to appease Bella, and I saw it in his eyes every time he looked at me. I hated that. I wanted to tell him that I would never have done anything with it.

'Forgive me,' says Ben, 'but you are clearly down on your luck and you've plainly been extremely ill. In fact you look like someone who should be in hospital. Our volunteers pay to be here. They pay up front before they arrive – that's how we keep running – and everything is arranged before they leave home. It's highly unusual for anyone to locate us like this. We run a programme that's staffed by gap-year volunteers, mainly from Europe, the US, Canada and Australia, not by casual workers who drop in, and also not by EFL teachers. And if I may say so, you don't look like someone who's recovered enough to hold down a job.'

I take a deep breath and try to sound believable. I summon Bella, and she comes. My dark side steps in and actually helps.

'I'm not ill,' she says. He thinks I've had cancer. I look so shit that this man is assuming I'm terminally ill. 'What happened, right, is this. I was travelling and it went wrong. I was robbed, so I've got almost nothing right now, as you can tell, but I will soon have access to money from home. It's a long story how I've ended up here, but I haven't done anything remotely illegal. I've been sleeping out of doors while I wait for the money, and I need to stop that. I promise you I'm not ill and I don't want any charity or anything like that. I haven't got any money to pay you today, but I can get some, and that's a promise. I've taught English before and I know a lot about art and books.'

'Have you? Where have you taught?'

Bella plucks a word at random. 'Venezuela.'

It was written on a man's cap on the train up the mountain. The picture of Christ the Redeemer in this room has taken me back there. Luckily Ben doesn't follow up on Bella's bold claim, since I wouldn't even be able to tell him the name of Venezuela's capital city.

He is sizing me up. 'The thing is, Jo,' he says, 'I really can't take you on as a volunteer. For one thing it's our volunteers who fund what we do. I know everyone has an opinion about gap-year children coming into poor places to do good works, but we've made it function properly here. We're not an orphanage – you met Ana, so you know they're kids with families. We teach English to the local children because it improves their life chances. We have a relatively high turnover of teachers, but my partner Maria and I make sure there's enough consistency for the kids. It's a carefully run business and I cannot act as a charity for sick Westerners who need a bolthole. Sorry. It sounds harsh, but you have options. You can go to your embassy and they'll get you home.'

I can't go to my embassy because I cut a man's face.

'Can I do anything at all?' I say. 'Sweep the floors. Cook. Clean the toilets?'

'You can go home and let us concentrate our efforts on the kids. With respect, Jo, we don't owe you anything. And you know you can get home if you go to the British consulate. They'll take care of you. That's what they're there for.'

'Someone just dropped out though.' Why not? I have nothing to lose. 'Jasmine said so.'

'Did she?' He doesn't look amused. 'Well, people often get scared and pull out. It doesn't mean anything.'

'Give me a chance. A temporary one. Give me a day.'

Something in Ben changes, as if his refusals have been a test. He sighs and rolls his eyes.

'You're persistent. Jesus. Look, for God's sake, have a shower. Then we'll see, but it would be a couple of days' boring work at most, and then you're done. You would of course be welcome to apply for the programme while you're sitting right here, if you can get hold of the money – and by the way it's a lot, and every penny of it goes on our day-to-day running costs. But if you can shower and smarten up a bit, I might be able to let you fill in a very short gap. If you can teach like you say you can. You'll need to work with Jasmine this morning so I can have a look at you.'

I smile at him with every atom of my being. It's a tiny lifeline, but it feels enormous. I am dizzy and confused. He's going to let me do something. I have to do this brilliantly. *Pretend to be brilliant and then you* will *be brilliant*. I wish I could ask him for food. I could ask Jasmine but not this man.

Jasmine leads me out of the room, and I follow her through a door and up a dark staircase to a corridor with a concrete floor. She doesn't speak because she doesn't know what to say, but she emanates sympathy and niceness. When she pushes a door on our left it swings open to reveal a tiny, concrete-floored bathroom with a shower and a basin and a loo.

'Here you go. This is our stately bathroom. Just a sec.' She leaves, reappearing almost instantly with a threadbare towel, which she hands to me. 'Would you, y'know, like some clothes? We've a few that Kate left behind. She just went, a few days ago. Off to Argentina. I'd say they'd fit you. They'll perhaps be a bit baggy.'

I look at Jasmine's wide eyes and lovely face. 'Thanks. Thank you. Thank you, Jasmine. Thank you so much. I've got to work with you this morning. I think Ben just said that because he was pissed off with you for letting me in. What are you doing this morning?'

'Cleaning. Doing the admin. The first class is at eleven. They're the older children, the eleven-year-olds.'

When I have the clothes as well as the towel I lock the door and turn on the shower. Running warm water is an impossible luxury, and I stare in wonder at the fact that people harnessed an element, made it run through pipes and invented taps. I think I'm delirious. I scrub the salt off my body and rinse my fuzzy scalp.

I mustn't mess this up. As the water pounds me I want to lie on the floor and cry, but I need to help Jasmine teach some eleven-year-olds English instead. It'll take far more strength than I have to get through this; but I have to do it somehow.

I dimly remember that there used to be different moisturizers for face and body, and make-up and perfume and all kinds of expensive things, but I know for certain that I have never had a better shower than this and I hope I never will. I hope I never will because a shower that was better than this could only come after something worse than my past few days and I can't let myself picture such a thing in my future.

The clothes Jasmine gave me are a pair of shorts that are PE style, almost reaching my knees, and a T-shirt with FAVELA ENGLISH SCHOOL written on it. It is a big version of the one tiny Ana wore; a smaller version of Ben's. She has even given me underwear. I don't hesitate to put on another woman's knickers and bra, and they fit well enough. Everything is clean. It smells of basic washing powder, and that is the best perfume in the world.

I brush my teeth with toothpaste on a finger and allow myself only the quickest glance in the tarnished mirror. I really *do* look ill. My skin has gone darker, but blotchily. Without hair I look weird and ugly. I still see myself in my eyes.

I try to remember French lessons at school. How do you teach a language to a class of children when they're too old for nursery rhymes? I have no idea. I will do whatever Jasmine does and try to be confident.

I push everything else aside. This is the only thing that matters. My whole life depends on getting this right: if I can do this, and get a couple of days' work, then maybe somehow I can find the money and end up living here like Jasmine and the invisible other volunteers. That would give me a chance.

'What stage are they at?' I am sipping the second coffee that Jasmine has made me, since I fell asleep before the first one arrived. It is instant, the kind of thing they would scoff at in the sixth-form common room, and it is the best drink ever. Everything about this place is the best thing ever. Even being able to say *What stage are they at?* like a grown-up teacher makes me go warm inside. I feel like I'm hanging off a cliff, clinging on by my fingernails. Jasmine has no idea that she's reaching down, hauling me up.

'Oh, it's a tricky age,' she says. 'It's much easier with the little ones. This is actually art class, so just do an art class in English. Can you do art? It doesn't matter if you can't. I certainly can't.'

'I'm –' I stop myself. The rest of that sentence would have gone: *I'm doing it for A level.* Instead I say, 'I love art. I might not be brilliant at it, but I like it.'

'Oh, I was useless at it at school too. I just let the kids get on with it. Some of them are good. So. You'll be fine actually. I was terrified the first time I did this.' She looks around, clearly checking that no one in authority is nearby.

'I messed it up completely, but it was different because I was already in the programme. Ben likes to check everyone out when they get here. He's very particular. But I'll be with you, Jo. We never do this on our own. I'll make sure you're OK.'

I grin at her. 'Oh my God, Jasmine. I love you. So what do we do?'

She has blushed pink. 'Oh, we just start it off by talking, and then let them get paper and pencils. Today they're sketching whatever they like. They're cool. If you get stuck, just ask them about football.'

Twenty minutes later I am running on adrenalin. I'm leaning over a skinny boy's bony shoulder, admiring his picture, which shows a footballer in action, his leg pulled back to kick the ball, an open goal in front of him, a rudimentary goalkeeper diving in what is clearly going to be the wrong direction.

'Goooooooooaaaaall!' I say.

He replies in Portuguese, so I tap his shoulder and say, 'In English.'

'The peoples.' He gestures to the blank space around the edges of his sheet of paper. I take his pencil and look at the sheet. It would be wrong to do his picture for him, but I can do what Miss Cook, who in a different lifetime taught me art, would have done. I'm sure that would be all right. I look around, and no one is watching, so I do my best to fill in some spectators for him. I draw the structure of some seating, roughly sketch in the top row of a sea of faces, and hand the pencil back to the boy.

I like this. I can actually help someone. I can help him with his picture, and I can help him with his English. Everything I have is focused on him right now. Not being focused on myself makes the whole world feel lighter.

I look around again and see that Ben is watching me now.

The boy grins broadly. He has a white birthmark down the side of his face, and it changes shape when he smiles.

'Thank you, Teacher Jo,' he says. His smile vanishes as he turns his attention back to his work, frowning, using my sketch as a basis and filling in every face, every expression. His spectators are happy, shocked, sad, bored. They become real people – rudimentary ones, but real.

I leave him to it and wander around the room. Dark heads are bent over work, and I look at a cluster of houses all crammed in beside each other, an empty beach, a family holding hands. I stop beside each child in turn and show them how to use perspective to make a house look more realistic, how to sketch out a face, how to fill the rest of a blank page. I do something different for every child. I concentrate completely on each of them in turn.

'Talk in English,' says Jasmine. She is walking around helping people too.

A girl raises her hand and I go over and look at her picture, which shows a girl sitting on a doorstep with her chin in her hands, looking grumpy.

'She's not happy,' I say. 'Is she you?'

The girl nods. 'Yes,' she says, and she giggles, looking at my head.

I smile back and stroke it with my hand. I help her out with the rest of the picture, showing her with rough lines where she can put other houses, the rest of the street, any other people. I add light perspective lines. She nods and starts drawing in a shop next door.

If I was properly in charge here, I would teach them how to actually draw. Today they are doing what they like, and no one is ever going to critique these pictures properly because, I imagine, the point is that they are sitting in a room working hard, speaking in English, and concentrating on a task. I think they might as well learn to draw while they're at it.

I would get them to draw an object that was in front of them, or draw each other. I would show them a Frida Kahlo self-portrait and encourage them to do something like it. I would show them how to shade and, if possible, give them the right sorts of pencils. I would teach perspective and vanishing points. We would do silhouettes, and clay pots, and Jackson Pollocks. I would get brightly coloured paints and show them abstract art. I would take them up the hill to paint the view. I would do everything I could to inspire them, to get them to express themselves, to let them lose themselves in art. Art makes life exciting.

For now, however, I walk around the room helping them out one by one. I show a girl shedding tears of frustration how she can draw a face that won't look so childish, and she nods and gets down to work.

I would quite like Mrs Browning to see me now.

They are only here for an hour, and when Jasmine claps her hands to bring the class to an end I want to cancel the rules, to make them stay all day, to carry on and on with it. I'd managed to put Ben out of my mind, but he has been lurking there the whole time. Now, as Jasmine gets them to chant, 'Goodbye, Teacher Jasmine. Goodbye, Teacher Jo,' he stands up. The moment the children start to leave the room, chatting in Portuguese and showing each other their pictures, he is at my side.

'That was interesting,' he says, and I cannot interpret his tone. 'You're an artist?'

'Not a professional one.' I feel stupid immediately. He didn't suggest I was a professional artist. Of course I'm not. I am filled with excitement now. I loved that class. I'm longing to do it again.

'A capable one. How would you teach art class, if it were up to you?'

'I know they're here for English, but I'd teach them art too. I'd rearrange the desks into a semicircle and get the group working on the same things, and show them techniques. If you could get other types of pencils I'd give them softer ones. If there was paint we'd be able to do all kinds of things. If there was clay we could do sculpture and pots.' I keep talking, surprised by the words that are coming out, surprised at Bella for making me strong without making me mean. I am also aware that while I'm speaking Ben cannot tell me to go away. In the end, however, I have to stop because it is not an infinite topic.

'Thanks, Jo,' he says. 'Look, I'll need to think about this and talk it over with Maria. You can stick around and help the girls clean the place up if you like, but that's it; we have to safeguard the kids and I can't let you stay until I've talked it over. Come back tomorrow at twelve.'

'Can I stay now? Please? I'll do anything. I'll clean your floors. I'll cook. I'll do ... anything. Just anything. Absolutely anything at all.'

The hand on my ankle, pulling my body.

I need a door.

I need a roof.

Ben is unmoved.

11

26 days

I wake up to someone shaking my shoulder. My hand is in a fist, ready to fight and scream and hurt and run.

Jasmine steps back.

I stare into her face. 'Sorry,' I say. 'Sorry, Jasmine. I didn't mean to –'

'Oh, you're OK,' she says quickly. 'I *thought* it was you. Jo. Look, you can't be sleeping out here. You've been here all night? Come on inside, for goodness' sake. You should have said. I'd have got you in.'

I stretch my legs out and stand with difficulty. Jasmine helps me up and I grasp her hand tightly. I like the feeling of her hand in mine.

The sky is light and drizzle is still falling. It is early. I can hear engines on the main street. People are heading off to work. I stretch as many muscles as I can, reaching up for the sky. My back is not happy. Neither are my arms. I wonder whether Jasmine would let me lie on her bed for a while.

'Ben told me to come at midday,' I say. 'He wouldn't want you bringing me inside now.'

'Well, he's not here so he won't know, will he? Come on.'

I wonder whether Jasmine knows that I chose that spot because I knew she could be summoned with a scream. I wonder if she knows that she is my only friend in the southern hemisphere. I think of Lily and Jack, longing for them both with all my heart.

It's a quarter past six. Jasmine makes me coffee and gives me a glass of water, and I am spectacularly grateful. We sit in a little kitchen that I didn't see before, and she hands me two bananas and a piece of bread and jam. I do my best to eat them slowly.

'You're up early,' I say.

She smiles. 'I always am. What can I say? I just like the early morning. But, Jo – you've been sleeping rough?'

'Oh, Jasmine. It's so awful. I can't begin to tell you –' I stop. I can't break down.

'What is it that . . . ?' Her voice tails off. Jasmine is a nice teenager, and I can see that she doesn't quite want to ask me for my story in case I don't want to tell her. I am grateful for that. All the same I don't want her trying to look me up online so I'd better say something.

'I was travelling –' I try to tell it in a way that will be compatible with the version I gave Ben – 'and it went wrong. I've done some teaching in Venezuela. I know I look like I'm ill but I'm not. I shaved my head because I dyed my hair and it looked awful. Then my stuff got stolen, and my relationship broke down.' That is true at least. My relationship with my adoptive parents has definitely

252

broken down. My relationship with Christian burned brightly, and then I ran away. 'I can't go home because things aren't good for me there. It would be worse. So I've been here for a while, and all I need is to get back on my feet by doing . . . the kind of thing you're doing really.'

I cannot tell her what I did to the café man. I will carry that secret with me until it catches up.

'You're so strong.'

I don't feel strong; however, now that I'm telling another human that I've been sleeping on the streets I can see that it makes me sound tough.

'I'm not,' I say. 'Or if I am, it's because I've had to be.'

'Jo, you were an amazing teacher yesterday. I was, like, totally in awe of you. You're so good at talking to the kids. I feel a bit shy when it's not the little tiny ones. You really were far better than any of the rest of us. Ben kind of despairs because we're a bit shit, but he says he just has to train us on the job. He knows he's taking most of us straight out of school and we're paying him to be here and getting a tiny salary back, and that's just how it works. Professional teachers won't pay to work, and the people we teach can't pay for lessons, and we're all native English speakers and we have to get on with it. You should have seen him watching you. He thought you were epic. That's why he's changing his mind.'

I smile at her. 'That is the nicest thing anyone's ever said to me.' I replay her words in my mind: *You're so good at talking to the kids. He thought you were epic.* I've never done anything like that before, and I did it and it worked.

I use the shower again, and by the time the other volunteers get up for breakfast I am in Jasmine's bed, hiding until midday. Her room is basic, with a metal-framed bed, a shelf for clothes and a little table which has a pile of books on it.

I gaze at them. Books are a luxury; another world for when you need to lose yourself. If I had a supply of books, living rough wouldn't be quite so bad. I'd be able to shut reality out much more effectively.

I pick one up. It's a children's book, *A Little Princess*, and it has clearly been read many times. I remember it from when I was little. I start to read.

At midday I am still woozy from the mingled sleep and tiredness, but I am standing in front of Ben, wearing my own clothes, which I've washed in non-salt water and dried on the windowsill in the strong sun. The doors and windows are open, and the schoolroom smells of hot earth after rain.

'You came back,' he says.

'Yeah. I did.'

'Have a seat, Jo.'

I follow him, and we both sit on little tables in a smaller classroom. His face gives nothing away. My plan B is casual theft on tourist beaches. I will try to amass enough money that way to buy myself a ticket to the north of Brazil and a new life. Someone in northern Brazil might want me to teach them English. It seems to be the only skill I have, and as I don't have a passport I can't leave the country.

'I've been talking to Maria,' Ben says. 'She wanted to come and meet you but she's teaching all day over in Vidigal, so she can't. Look, Jo. This is unorthodox, and you must understand why we're hesitant.'

I close my eyes. *He's going to tell me to go away. I know he is.*

'However, you did a good job yesterday, and we'd like you to try teaching art with us, just temporarily, one day at a time. You can also help with the other classes.' He takes a few pieces of paper out of his bag and pushes them towards me. 'I'll need you to fill all this in – passport number and references and so on – and then we need to talk about money.'

I want to hug him. I want to kiss him. I manage not to.

'Of course,' I say, trying to be prim, trying not to allow my feelings into my voice. My emotions escape as tears fill my eyes, and I blink them away though I know he sees.

'We can't pay you – as you know, *you* need to pay *us*. However, we can feed you with the rest of the volunteers. You clearly need shelter, and I've just spoken to Jasmine and she's happy to share with you, so we'll put a mattress on her floor. I'm sensing that would be acceptable to you.'

'That would be amazing. I mean it. The most –'

I have to stop talking because I am choked up. I screw my eyes shut for a moment and try to take deep breaths. I must not fall apart now that I have a lifeline. I must not. I could ruin it all. I take the pieces of paper. I'll fill them in with rubbish and hope for the best.

A roof over my head. A place to sleep. Food. I am swaying, and there is a ringing sound in my ears, but it's not Bella. Bella has kept me going through the past few days. Bella has been working with me, not against me, and the ringing in my ears is just exhaustion and relief.

'Take a moment.' I feel Ben's hand on my shoulder and keep my eyes closed as he holds me steady. I don't speak for a long time. I can't.

'I'll do anything,' I say when I pull myself together. 'I'll do everything. I'm a terrible cook, but I'll learn. I'll clean. I'm just so grateful. I'll be the best teacher you've ever had.'

He nods and stands up. 'I hope so.'

I fill the paperwork in carefully, calling myself Josephine Marsh and inventing a passport number, and help with every class for the rest of the day. I make drinks for everyone. I want to cook, but they won't let me because some volunteers called Scott and Clara are on the rota, and I can see I'm annoying them by asking for something to do.

In the end I go for a walk because I don't want them to get sick of me before I've properly arrived. I expect they need space to talk about me, as there are ten volunteers living there, and nine of them have only just met me. I walk to the main street, the Estrada de Gávea, and spend an hour wandering the pathways. It feels different now that I have a purpose, a home, a job.

I end up in the juice bar at the bottom of the hill, the first place I ever visited in Rocinha. I want to go back to the me who stepped out of that taxi with her cash concealed all around her body, and tell her to do it differently. I want to send her straight to the English school, to hand her cash directly to Ben and apply to join the programme properly.

I have enough money for a juice, and so I order the first one I had here before, the pink one with strawberries and watermelon. I sit at a table and prepare to make it last.

While I drink, I watch people coming and going. There is a man selling goat carcasses, hung up around a doorway. Another is the same street barber who shaved off my hair: he sees me looking and raises a hand in greeting. I can see someone welding, someone selling brightly coloured clothes. Buses pull in, and people get on and off them. Power lines cluster overhead. Taxis pull up. Motorbikes buzz around. A family at the next table are having an argument, but they don't seem to be properly angry. I like sitting and observing. I like sipping my juice through its straw, and knowing that it is full of vitamins, that it will sustain me.

I like knowing that I have a place to sleep tonight, that I have work to do, that I will be part of a community. The relief is so overwhelming that I have to make a conscious effort not to collapse.

I watch a taxi pulling up. A man gets out. He is wearing a suit even though he must be hot, and he is half bald, with black hair combed over. He pays the driver through the window and strides off up the hill, clearly with a place to be.

A police car goes slowly by. I look down at the table. They might still be looking for me and I still don't want to be seen. I don't think I look like my old self at all: I have lost weight and I feel utterly different with my bare head. All the same, I am the person they've been looking for.

The next taxi to pull in disgorges a white woman with long tangled hair. She is wearing a lime-green dress and sandals. I watch her pay her driver and set off up the hill, swinging a small backpack. I've seen her before. A little way up she meets another woman – the fat one, who is definitely local – and they walk together, deep in conversation.

The next taxi brings three men in their twenties, who pile out laughing and come in here and sit at a nearby table, pushing each other and talking loudly. I shrink away: the last thing I want now is attention from anyone at all.

I finish the juice quickly and walk back towards the English school. *Home*. It feels odd to call it that, but it is my home more than anywhere else is at the moment.

Home is a strange concept. I wonder if I actually need one.

12

20 days

I wake up early (I cannot imagine sleeping in ever again) and make my bed quietly so I don't disturb Jasmine, who is fast asleep with her hair fanned out all over the pillow. My bed is a mattress on the floor, and it's the best thing ever. I've been here six days now, and while Jasmine gets up early and does stretches and writes her diary with a coffee at her side, I tend to get up earlier still.

Before I went to sleep I was reading *To Kill a Mockingbird*. Ben is right: the books collection here is random, but there are some legitimate classics and I'm going to make my way through them one by one. When I leave the room I take the book with me and creep downstairs, where I unlock the door and sit on the doorstep looking out at the alley. I slept out here six nights ago, and now I sleep just a few metres away, but it's a different universe.

This is the only part of my day that's not busy. The sun shines down on the alleyway, and although it doesn't reach my face I stretch my bare feet out into its warmth. Today I am going to be teaching some classes of kids; cooking; showing some of the other volunteers how to do some art things; sorting through a box of picture books that have arrived from a former volunteer. I like my quiet dawn coffees, but I like the packed days more. I need to be such a part of life here that no one will ever be able to manage without me. I've told Ben and Maria, who has long grey hair and a kind face, that I don't want any time off.

'I want to work all day every day until I can pay you what I owe,' I told her. I will get the money from home at some point, when I dare. I will have to.

'You have to have at least one day off a week, sweetie,' she said, but I work through it anyway.

Life is Technicolor and I appreciate every single moment. When there is food I eat slowly and savour it. That is a habit I want to hold on to. When I get into my bed on Jasmine's floor I stretch out and close my eyes and feel intensely thankful for the luxury of a place to sleep, and walls and a roof and a door.

I see now why people go to church, why they pray. You don't have to believe in any god to feel the need to stop from time to time and thank the universe for the fact that you are all right. Life is fragile, and to be safe and fed and busy is an incredible piece of luck. I stare down the quiet alley, where a feral cat is pacing about looking for scraps, and take a deep breath. I thank the world for sending me here. I feel safe. *No doubt the universe is unfolding as it should.*

I wonder whether my adoptive parents are still at the hotel, a few miles from here. As soon as they come into my head I try to force them away because I'm not ready for it.

I know that I need to tell them I'm all right but I can't see them yet. I dither, staring up the alley, knowing there is a payphone just up the hill, but then Bella steps in.

NOT YET, she says, and she keeps my bottom planted firmly on the doorstep.

I never feel in danger here because I rarely step out of doors. I'm done with wandering the streets, even just to get somewhere. When I do go out I am wearing my Favela English School T-shirt and everyone is friendly because I represent the organization, and the local people, I now see, are happy to have a free English school for their children in the area.

I have stopped eating meat completely; it turns out that if you say 'I'm vegetarian', no one questions it or considers it momentous or even interesting. I remember looking at the poor battery-farmed chicken on the plane out here. I don't need to use the corpses of animals to fuel my body. I don't want to damage any creature. I have done quite enough damage. It's actually easy not to eat meat because there are the always-wonderful cheese balls and there is rice and there are beans. We cook on a rota, and the menu often features the bean stew that saved me when I needed it. Last night it was my turn, and I tried to cook it without meat, and it came out just about edible, which was a triumph. Bella and I rejoiced together. She is always with me now, and I'm beginning to think that Brazil and this crisis have tamed her.

It turns out I don't even know how to chop an onion properly. Last night I started by plunging my knife into one and trying not to let it slide out of control.

'That's an interesting technique,' said Jasmine, who was cooking with me, laughing as I tried to steady the slippery onion on the end of my knife. 'How have you got to this age without knowing how to dice an onion?'

I shrugged. 'Nineteen years somehow passed me by, onion-wise.' (I am pretending to be nineteen and no one questions that either.) I watched what she was doing, then cut it in half and sliced it in what I immediately saw was a far more sensible manner. I wished then, and I wish now, that the poor couple who adopted me had taught me this stuff. He used to make a Sunday roast from time to time. She would cook constantly, peeling vegetables, making her worthy soups, concocting bland dinners with lentils and ethically sourced meat, baking biscuits that didn't have enough sugar in them. She never taught me a thing.

I try not to think about my Hinchcliffe-Carr heritage. I don't see the TV news or newspapers here. I am starting to learn to speak and write Portuguese: the first full day I was here I got a couple of nine-year-olds to start me off when they were finishing their pictures after the lesson. They found it hilarious that I was so bad.

I focus totally on the children. Any child in the favela can come to classes here as long as they are registered, and there are lots of them. They come into the schoolroom from four years old until eleven, but it doesn't stop there: we go out into secondary schools to teach English, and several times a week we run adult classes in different places around the town. I haven't taught an adult class yet and I'm a bit scared by the idea of it.

I am not starry-eyed about life here, no matter how different it is from the way I pictured a 'shanty town'. I know that these children and their families are up against all kinds of things that I cannot imagine. I know there is a drugs problem. I know there are gangs and guns. I know there isn't enough money. I know this because Ben and Maria talk about it; and from the things they say I know that it's complicated. I haven't seen any of it myself because I stay firmly where I am.

I also know, when I let myself think about it, that if my birth parents hadn't been caught when they were, then my life would have been hell. I would never have been Ella Black: I would have been someone else; and they probably wouldn't have looked after me and I would have died like one of the neglected children you see in online news stories. They might have thrown me into the canal too.

I was saved by the people I attacked, and I find myself wanting to save other children from the troubles their circumstances bring them. I want every child to have the same opportunities to get somewhere in life, no matter where they're born, because otherwise it isn't fair.

I am starting to see how monstrously unjust the world actually is.

As I settle in I start to understand a little more about Rocinha. It is not actually a favela, but a 'favela neighbourhood'; a city in its own right, originally settled by people who came from the north of Brazil in search of work. It used to be run by drug-dealing gangs, but according to Ben and Maria that was actually less scary than it sounds as long as you weren't involved. Some years ago the police came in and 'pacified' the place, which meant they got rid of the gangs and imposed law. People seem to be more ambivalent about this than you might expect.

I still know nothing really. I'll probably never even scratch the surface. It's a hill with a huge number of people living on it, and it is energetic and desperate and brilliant and alive. Rocinha is now my home, and I am going to stay here for as long as I can.

I would probably stay forever if they let me.

I might not be able to leave Brazil actually, since I haven't got a passport and I am probably on some database for attacking that man. Soon my entry permit will run out, I suppose, and I'll be an illegal immigrant.

'Some of us are going out tonight,' Jasmine says to me at the end of the first class of the day. It was an art class and the children are still milling around. 'Nothing massive. We're just going to a bar up the hill for a couple of beers. Do you fancy it?'

I love Jasmine, but I don't even think before saying: 'No, thanks. Hang on a second,' I add to the little girl I'm drawing. 'Stay still. That's right.'

'Oh, that's a shame, Jo,' Jasmine says. 'It would be really nice if you came.'

I have to try hard to remember all my lies: I am Jo, I have been in Venezuela, I broke up with a boyfriend. I stay away from social situations because I'm sure I'll say the wrong thing. I also stay away because I have no money whatsoever. I used the last of the cash I had to buy toothpaste and soap and things like that. At least I don't need shampoo these days.

Jasmine is genuinely lovely though, and I wish I could be a proper friend to her. She reminds me of Lily because she is so kind to me. Without even knowing it she has done me immeasurable good. If she hadn't invited me in when I first turned up I don't know where I would be.

'I'm finishing this tonight,' I say, nodding at the pile of sketches I've been doing of the children. I don't care that everyone thinks I'm weird or that most of the volunteers are nervous around me, probably because of my shaved head. I just want to stay in, out of sight.

I finish my portrait. It's a sketch of a girl called Gabriella. I shade in her plaits and hand her the sheet of paper. She gasps and checks that she's actually allowed to keep it, then says, 'Thank you, thank you, Teacher Jo,' and rolls it up like a scroll to take home.

That evening all the volunteers apart from me go out drinking. I stay behind and clean the kitchen. I may be weird, but this makes me happy.

13

16 days

I wake up smiling because I know it's my birthday. Today I am eighteen, and that is a secret from everyone here. I will celebrate in secret, in my head. I always loved my birthday at home, and today I will love it here in Rio. I would hate it if anybody knew.

Bella sings *Happy birthday to us* in my head and I like that. I hum along, hoping that it won't wake Jasmine. I'm glad I know that this really *is* my birthday. Eighteen years ago I was born, no matter how fucked up it all was. I burst into the world, and I'm still here.

I have been at the school for ten days, and today is the day on which Amanda Hinchcliffe can look me up on the Adoption Contact Register. She will find me there if she does: I applied to add my details a million years ago, when the mother in my head was a wayward teen with a strict family who was going to be a big sister to me.

It feels like a million years ago, and I feel like a different person. It was actually two weeks. Time has gone very strange.

She will look for me now, but the contact details I left with the register were an email address that I will never check and a phone that I stamped on and shoved into a bin.

I am eighteen. I lie in bed and stare at the ceiling. This is me being an adult. It doesn't feel momentous. I had planned a little celebration for today at a pub in Kent to mark the fact that I am officially old enough to drink. There was going to be me and Lily and Jack, and probably a few of the others if they could be bothered to turn up.

In fact my best birthday present turns out to be the arrival of the tiny child who unwittingly turned my life round when I was at my very lowest.

'Ana!' I say when I see her in the doorway. She laughs at the sight of me and runs into my arms. She giggles as I twirl her around.

'Teacher Paula,' she says carefully, beaming at me.

'Oh. Here I'm "Teacher Jo",' I say in a quiet voice. 'Teacher Jo.'

'Teacher Jo.'

'That's right.'

'Teacher Jo-Paula.'

'If you like.'

Ana sits at the front of the class and gazes at me as we sing the songs and point to colours. I smile at her the whole time. If I could change the world for one person it would be her.

Later Jasmine hands me a brown envelope with the word *JO* written on the front. 'I found it on the doorstep,' she says. 'Looks like it's for you.'

There is something small inside: when I open it I find two bracelets with pink flowers on them. They are clearly meant for children.

'That's nice,' I say. I haven't mentioned my birthday to anyone at all. I put the bracelets on my wrist. It must be one of the children, giving me a present in exchange for my portraits or something. The timing must be coincidental.

It must be.

'Someone likes you,' Jasmine says. 'That's because you're so lovely with the kids. Bet it's from one of the little ones.'

I check the envelope, but there's nothing else in there.

'Yes,' I say. 'I guess.'

It must be that. It must be a child giving me a sweet little present. It cannot be anything else. It can't be a birthday present because no one knows it's my birthday. No one knows where I am.

Someone left food on the beach for 'Jo', and now someone has left a birthday present on the doorstep, also for 'Jo'. But when I got the food I wasn't called Jo, and now I am, and so it's a completely different thing.

It is.

It

is.

14

15 days

When I am eighteen years and one day old something bad happens. I am wearing the bracelets, hoping that one of the children will notice and tell me who gave them to me. I am feeling so strange about it that I don't feel like myself. It is horrible. I haven't felt this strange for a long time.

It happens in the first class after lunch. An eleven-year-old called Bruno is cheeky, to make his friends laugh, and it pushes me right over the edge. Not very long ago I did the same thing myself to get Lily out of trouble: somehow I told Mrs Browning that her hair looked nice. But I didn't do it to make anyone laugh. No one ever laughed at my jokes. I did it to get myself into trouble, and Lily out of it.

No one gets to act like that in my class, for any reason.

I am attempting to do some singing, and I know I sound ridiculous blasting out 'Humpty Dumpty', and I also know they're too old for such a babyish song, but this is Heidi's lesson plan, not mine, and I don't appreciate Bruno's giggles behind his hands, his whispers, his stirring up of revolution.

'What is this song?' he asks, pretending to be polite.

'It's about Humpty Dumpty,' I say. 'I know it's a bit silly. But anyway, let's try it again. *All the King's horses . . .*'

'But who is the Humpty Dumpty?' he asks.

'He's an egg.'

There is a moment's silence.

'An egg,' echoes Bruno. 'A fucking egg?' They all burst out laughing. *Fucking* is one English word everyone knows. Bruno has the audience in the palm of his hand and they are laughing at me.

I cannot let that happen.

'Don't use that word, Bruno. It's very rude.' I sound so fucking lame, when I am actually very fucking angry.

Bruno turns to his classmates and does something with his face that makes them roar with laughter. I am Mrs Browning. I try to breathe deeply, but I can't let it go.

'Bruno,' I say. 'That's *enough*.'

'But I didn't do anything,' he says, in Portuguese.

'You know what you did,' I answer, also in Portuguese. I switch to English because my Portuguese isn't up to a lengthy conversation yet. 'You swore at a teacher, for one thing. If you don't want to take part in the class and talk politely, then you can leave.'

He stares at me, as insolent as Bella. I stare back. He reminds me of myself in the grip of my demon and I don't like it. Neither of us looks away. I know he wasn't really swearing at me. But still. My head is starting to ring. I push her away frantically. I thought she was better now. I thought we were on the same side. I mutter the words that sometimes banish her.

270

'No *doubt the universe is unfolding as it should*,' I say jaggedly under my breath, and I don't know if the children can hear me or not, and I don't care. '*The universe the universe the universe.*' Everything swamps me and I want to do something bad because it's all too much. I was a child in a classroom and I was rude to a teacher, and that same day I was taken away by the Blacks in a panic, and then everything I thought I knew crumbled into dust and I can't bear it.

Bella wants to mess this up. She can see that we've salvaged a life here, and she wants to blow it up because that's what happens.

IT WON'T LAST, she whispers.

It will.

IT WON'T. THEY'LL FIND OUT THAT YOU LIED ON THE FORMS. THEY'LL THROW YOU OUT ANYWAY.

No doubt the universe is unfolding as it should.

I thought she was on my side, but now she's not. I have to be the best person I possibly can because I want to stay here. It's my home. I can't be taken over and do something crazy. This mustn't happen.

My vision goes blotchy. Everything disappears around the edges, and I can only see Bruno. I need to attack him. I want to scare him. I mustn't.

LET ME AT HIM.

No.

HE'S BEING RUDE.

No.

HE CAN'T DO THAT. HE NEEDS A LESSON.

He's a little boy. He's fine.

I'M GOING TO TELL HIM.

'You need to leave,' I hiss it in English and then in Portuguese. I have to make this boy go away before I attack him. If I hurt a child everything will be over. I will be homeless, jobless, hopeless, and it will be what I deserve. I am sweating, struggling with Bella, with myself. I point to the door.

'Go on, Bruno. Come back when you can behave and talk nicely. Go home. Go right now.' I can barely get the words out.

I watch him hesitating. He has to leave. My hands are twitching, desperate to grab him. I want to push him up against the wall and yell into his face. I want to pinch his skin. I want to hurt him.

I have to get him away.

Strive to be happy.

The rest of the class sits shocked and silent. Bruno, thank God, gets up and walks out of the room, his shoulders drooping, clearly about to cry, and Heidi, the other teacher, looks surprised but doesn't intervene.

The universe the universe the universe. I have not needed those words for a long time.

I sit down and let Heidi run the rest of the class.

Go away, I say to Bella. I think my lips are moving but it's OK.

CAN'T.

272

Please. Be nice. Help me. You were helping me.

YOU KNOW IT'S ONLY A MATTER OF TIME.

That's why we're taking it one day at a time.

YOU'LL BE FOUND OUT. YOU'LL STILL HAVE NOTHING. YOU MIGHT AS WELL GO OUT WITH A BANG.

No, I tell her. *No no no.*

My head clears slowly, and my ears go quiet, and I swallow back the tears and anger at myself and try to take deep breaths.

She's right. I will be found out any day now. I'll still have nothing. That is all true. She is right.

I go into the loo and wipe my eyes and wash my face. I want to be better than this. I lost control because I saw my bad self in that boy, but it was me projecting, and not Bruno. Bella was trying to sabotage everything, and she is a part of me, and I can't let it happen.

Later in the afternoon I find Bruno's registration forms and ask around until I reach his house. He is sitting on the doorstep drawing a picture. I stand in front of him in the tight alley, and when he sees me he looks away again.

'Sorry, Teacher Jo,' he mutters. He looks back at the door of his house, clearly worried that I'm about to tell whoever is in there that he said 'fuck'.

I sit next to him. He bristles.

'No,' I say. '*I'm* sorry. I am truly sorry. I was mean to you. I was feeling stressed.'

He doesn't understand *stressed*, and I don't know how to say it in Portuguese, so I take his pencil and draw a little picture of myself with claws and fangs and a monstrous expression. I draw Bruno cowering. I draw myself back to normal with a speech bubble saying *Sorry*.

Bruno smiles. I give him a little hug.

'Sorry for fucking swearing,' he says, chancing his luck, and I laugh and he does too.

'You really mustn't say that,' I tell him, and he nods and says sorry properly.

When I get back, two new volunteers are climbing off the backs of motorbike taxis. I am instantly scared (they might know about the violent runaway teenager with the purple hair) but it turns out they are from the States and have come straight from the airport. They're wearing little dresses and high-heeled shoes. Both have beautiful long hair. They stand in the alley.

'Hi,' I say. I watch as the blonde one's nose wrinkles at my shaved head.

'Hi.' She sounds uncertain.

'I'm Jo,' I say. 'You've just arrived? Are you coming to work here?'

'Hi, Jo,' says the other one, who is mixed race with bouncing curls. 'I'm Sasha. This is Amy. Um. Yeah, we've just arrived?'

'Cool. Er, welcome.'

'That motorbike taxi,' Sasha says. 'Amy's still a little freaked.'

'I mean, what the hell?' says Amy.

'It's OK,' I say. 'Honestly it is. Come on in. Do you want a coffee or something?'

'Could we get a glass of water?'

'Sure.'

Maria turns round as we come into the classroom. 'Hi, ladies,' she says. 'Oh – you've met Jo. Thanks, Jo. You're Amy and Sasha? I'll show you to your room.'

I hand each of them a glass of water and watch them carrying their cases up the stairs. Maria winks at me as she goes past, and for the first time since I got here I really, truly feel that I belong.

15

6 days

It's a Monday morning when the phone rings, and I have
been living here for twenty days. The phone is a huge
wireless thing that looks like an antique mobile. It's kept
on its charger all the time, and whoever is closest answers
when it rings. We are supposed to speak in Portuguese but
most of the volunteers can't do that, and so if I'm anywhere
nearby I grab it. It turns out that in eighteen days you can
pick up some rudimentary conversational Portuguese if
you work hard at it.

A class of five-year-olds are coming in for an English
lesson, which means we will be reading a picture book and
looking at the illustrations and talking about the words.
The book classes are my favourites after art: today we are
reading a book about a boy from Cornwall who is captured
by pirates and sold into slavery. I love that book, and the
kids love to act it out after I've read it.

The children run in, jumping around, chattering loudly,
asking about pirates.

Maria, who happens to be here today, claps her hands.
'Stop!' she shouts. 'Everyone out. Walk, don't run.' She

says it again in Portuguese, and the children leave the room and file in more sensibly.

The phone rings. Since Maria is getting everyone to sit in their places and stop being silly, I answer and take the handset into the back room.

'*Alô?*' I say as I walk.

'Oh, hi,' says a man's voice.

My legs give way and I sit on the floor.

My breath isn't coming any more. I gasp for air.

I

say

nothing.

'Hi?' he says again. '*Português? Español?* Do you speak English?'

I try to breathe. I cannot just hang up. Seconds tick by.

I think of the way Jasmine talks.

'Yes, I speak English,' I say in my best, ridiculous approximation of an Irish accent.

'Great. I'm looking for a friend of mine. Just wondering if she might be working with you . . .'

'Mm?'

'Her name's Ella,' he says. 'Ella Black. You might have seen her in the press? She's missing. She has been known to call herself Chrissy. It's a long shot, but have you by any chance had anyone who could be her working for you? I could email through a photo, because she's probably using another name. Last time I saw her she had purple hair. I just want to know that she's safe, and I need her to know that she isn't in any trouble and she doesn't have to hide.'

I don't know what to say.

'There's no one like that here,' I say, in Jasmine's voice, when the silence has stretched out too long.

'If you see her, tell her we miss her and we love her,' he says, 'and she has nothing to worry about when it comes to what she did.'

I hang up even though he is still talking. I lie down and curl up into a ball. My body heaves and shakes. I love him. I love Christian with all my heart. He is looking for me. He found me. He said he loves me.

I love him.

He found me.

I hung up the phone.

I have no number for him.

I can hear Maria starting the lesson.

I

am

heartbroken

all

over

again.

I pull myself together, of course, because I have to. I join in the lesson and, as I ignore my red eyes and puffy face, everyone else does too. I get through the day, sit and chat with the other volunteers during my down time, and go out in the evening to teach the adult class at the municipal hall down the hill.

He said, 'Tell her we miss her and we love her.'

He said he loves me.

I hung up the phone.

I enjoy going down the hill now. As I walk I pass a group of children playing, and they all stop and say, 'Hello, Teacher Jo!' I smile and wave back. A dad I recognize because he regularly drops his four children off for classes shouts: 'I speak English!' from across the street, and I give him a thumbs up. I feel at home. I actually feel like a tiny part of the community. There's nowhere else I want to live.

The sun is low in the sky: it has been a baking-hot day, and the evening sunlight is glorious on my face. As I walk down the hill I catch a glimpse of the sea.

It shimmers in the sunlight. It sparkles. It's beautiful. In the twenty days I've been at the English school I have never been back to the beach, even though everyone else goes whenever they can. I don't want to go there. I haven't been anywhere; I have kept within the smallest possible radius of my new home. No part of me wants to go back to Copacabana, or to go dancing on the streets of Lapa, though that evening will, I am quite sure, remain forever the best night of my life.

I am torn apart with regret. I would give anything to be able to go back and not panic and not hang up the phone. I love Christian, and he looked for me until he found me, and I will always know that, even if *he* doesn't. He said I wasn't in trouble. That must mean I didn't hurt the man too badly. I haven't killed anyone, and it's only as I articulate that thought that I realize how worried I was that I might have accidentally severed an artery or given him an infected cut that spread. That I, too, could have been a killer. The relief that brings me is intense. I feel that the sun has come out inside me. If I'm not in trouble with the police I could get a passport. I could contact the Blacks. I hardly dare imagine the possibilities.

I hope Christian thinks the phone was answered by an odd Irish girl. I hope he's all right.

He told me about Vittoria, and I ran away in the night.

It was terrible behaviour. I want to call him back and say how sorry I am.

I could have told him I was all right. I could have begged him not to tell anyone that I'm here, even if the police were asking. I could have told him that I found out the truth about myself and had to get away, and I wouldn't have had to tell him what that truth actually was. I didn't do that, and now I never will.

When I get to little Ana's café I call in to shout hello to her parents, both of whom come out to kiss me on the cheek, and then I carry on going. I have to put Christian out of my mind. Instead I try to think about what I'm going to cover in this English lesson. We will talk about travelling, about booking tickets, catching buses, all that, in English. This is only the second time I've taught the adult class and I'm nervous. We teach them by walking into the classroom and refusing to speak Portuguese for the entire hour. The classes are free and open to anyone who wants to come along: people often look exhausted and stressed, and I know they are fighting their battles. I am starting to understand that nobody's life is straightforward. I am far from being the only one with demons.

I remember my adoptive mother going out to Italian and Spanish evening classes, anxiously making sure that Dad and I would be all right during her short absence, leaving us with lentil bakes and bowls of fruit, with homework to do or instructions to relax. This class, the one I teach, is the opposite of hers. She went because going to an evening class and learning a language was the kind of thing you did to stop yourself going insane if you'd given up your career (and I don't even know what her career would have been) so you could have a family. When we did actually go to Spain she uttered a few phrases self-consciously, in a terrible accent, and then reverted to English. I smile at the memory. Dad and I cheered her on, encouraging her to overcome her nerves and order for us in Spanish. She was so pleased with herself when she did it. I miss her. She tried so hard, struggled with losing eight babies, adopted me in dramatic circumstances, and then decided not to tell me. I am flooded with empathy for Fiona Black. She did everything she could for me, and I'm here and she doesn't even know I'm alive.

I am eaten up from the inside by the fact that I tried to hurt her, that she will know that for the rest of her life, that it is the last image she has of me.

If Christian is right and I'm not in trouble, I could contact them. I do love them. It's easier to keep the wall up, to feel Bella's fury at them for lying to me, than it is to remember that, no matter what, she is the only mum I have ever known. And she lied to me for good reasons, even if they were misguided.

By the time I arrive at the hall, I am ready to teach the best class ever. These classes are for people who work hard every moment of every day and still push themselves. If you can speak English you can work in tourism. That's why they are here, and that is why I am teaching them to say: 'Would you like a car to the airport?' and 'Shall I book you a tour to Christ the Redeemer?' I'm amazed by the dedication of the adult learners, who range in age from younger than me to older than God.

When I get back to the school, exhausted and ready for bed, I see the volunteers clustered around someone.

'Look,' says somebody. 'Here she is!' They part, and I do not believe what I am seeing, so I blink and try looking again.

'Hi there, Jo,' says Christian.

My heart stops.

He looks the same.

He is Christian.

He is here.

My Christian.

I love him.

I walk up to him and stare into his eyes. He stares back. Everyone else melts away. I say sorry with my eyes. He tells me it's all OK, with his.

'Christian,' I say.

He smiles a very sad smile. 'Would you come for a drink?' he says.

The girls (and the two boys: there are fewer boys here than there used to be in my ballet class) are smiling and looking interested. Everyone is waiting for me to say yes. They are all intrigued. As soon as we go they will start talking about us.

He'd better not have said the words 'Ella Black'. He had better not have said that. I am not ready for any of these people to know anything about my old life.

'Yes,' I say, and I turn and walk straight back out, hoping that he will follow.

'How did you do it?' I say when we are at the end of the alley, on the big road. I am trying to be angry that he tracked me down, but I am delirious with delight. My skin is tingling all over. My muscles are tense. My heart is pounding extra fast. All I want to do is look at Christian. I never thought I would see him again.

Bella is happy to see him too. She is agitated, excited. I feel her stirring inside me.

He looks at me too. 'Sorry, Ella,' he says. 'But really. Hey. What the hell? And where the hell is your hair?'

Christian is angry with me. I am busily trying to be cross with him, but he's the one who's shocked by my behaviour and, from his expression, my appearance, and he is right to be. He liked the girl with the soft body and the purple hair. Now I'm spiky and bald. He liked Ella and now I'm Jo.

'Sorry,' I say. I take his hand. He holds it tightly. 'I'm sorry. I really . . .'

I don't seem to be able to say any more than that.

'Well. I'll answer your question first, if you like. I did this – I found you here – by trying everything I could think of to work out where you might be. We'd talked about the favela. You'd talked about teaching English. When you weren't there on the island I was devastated. Genuinely. And phenomenally worried.'

We are walking up the hill together. I'll take him to a bar I've seen up there.

'Sorry.' It doesn't really feel like enough.

'Look, Ella. I'll just come out and say this – don't be mad. Don't run away. I know who your birth parents are. The bike-shop guy said he'd lent you his laptop, so I borrowed it to have a look, and there it all was in the history. You smashed the screen, by the way. I had to hook it up to my phone to read anything. I gave him money to sort it.'

I cannot say a word. I am hot and shaky.

'It must have been horrible. Finding that out. I can see why you felt the need to bolt. I wish you'd felt that you could tell me though.'

'Sorry.' That seems to be the only thing I can say.

'I went back to the mainland and told your parents everything. I had to. They were devastated in all sorts of ways. They were looking for you, and I'd found and lost you. I tried to leave them to it because I knew it was up to you what you did and when you came·back, but you had to know that you weren't in trouble with the police.' He looks me in the eye.

I don't quite dare believe it. 'Are you sure?'

'I promise. The guy was mad and he did call the police, but they have bigger things than that to deal with. And he wasn't hurt. It was a scratch, it bled a bit, but he was OK. He didn't have to go to hospital or anything. Your parents paid him some compensation and explained a bit about the situation, and he agreed to drop it. So you had to know that.'

I haven't realized until this moment that I've been living on edge for every second of every day. I've always known that I hurt someone and that I could go to prison for it. I lean back and feel weightless with relief. Christian is in front of me, saying the man is all right. I believe him.

'I've been making calls every day. I called about sixteen places I thought you might have gone, and on number seventeen I found a strange semi-Irish girl. Was that meant to be Irish?' Christian puts on a terrible accent. *'There's no one like that here,'* he says. 'And there you were. My Ella.'

'Your Ella.'

'Or my Jo.'

'Did you ask for Ella at the school? Just now?'

'No. Not when you'd made it so clear that you were hiding. I just said I was looking for my friend, and then I saw your photo on the wall, and even without the hair I knew it was you right away. It was your eyes. I said that was you, and they were all, like, *Oh, Jo!* They love you there, but they're a bit scared of you.'

'They should be. I come from bad people.'

Christian shakes his head. 'You are the strongest, bravest, most brilliant person I've ever met, Ella. You are yourself. Nothing anyone else has done reflects on you. You are breathtaking. Maddening too.'

It's nearly dark, and the lights are on all over the favela. The thick cables overhead are working.

'I . . . Look. I can't imagine what it feels like to grow up thinking you know where you come from, and then to discover that you don't, and then, after all that, to find out that your parents are in jail for terrible crimes. I really can't imagine that. I'm so sorry. And I'm beyond happy that you're safe. You really are very strong, Ella. Your parents – would you still call them that? – Fiona and Graham. They are beside themselves. They're destroyed. They're still here at the moment. They tried to suggest that your running away was my fault, but they stopped when they realized how much I knew.'

'They said it was your fault?'

'They were really, really angry that I'd taken you out in secret, and then far more so that I'd been to visit you on Paquetá. I slipped your note under their door that night, but when I went back and you were gone I had to tell them. They thought I'd given you ideas. They said you would never have run off like that before. They made it very clear that I was responsible. Then you called them from a German phone and your mum was sure you were coming back. That was you, wasn't it?'

I take some deep breaths.

I wait for the onslaught.

Bella?

WHAT?

Aren't you angry?

OF COURSE.

But?

BUT WE'RE IN A BAR WITH CHRISTIAN. FIONA BLACK HAS ALREADY SUFFERED.

I smile. She's right. I am angry that my parents blamed Christian, but I don't want to storm around and lash out. Bella tried to hurt Fiona Black with a broken bottle. I can't be angry with them any more. I've done everything I possibly can to hurt them already. They thought they were giving a lovely baby a home; they thought they'd raised a nice girl who had friends and a boyfriend, and who was doing well at school. Now they have a bald daughter who lives in the slums and doesn't speak to them. I can't really imagine how it could actually have worked out any worse for them.

I walk a little way up the hill, just because I have to move. I take some deep breaths. I go back to Christian and take his hand.

'Come on,' I say. 'Yes, it was me with the German phone. Let's get a beer. I haven't had a proper drink since we went to Lapa.'

He looks quite nervous. 'What's it actually like?' he says. 'Living here?'

'It's good.'

'Not scary?'

'Not any more. No.'

'They don't blame me now, you know,' he says quickly. 'As soon as I told them I knew about the adoption, and then about the birth parents, they just crumpled. No one else in their life knows that, it seems, apart from their lawyer. They were devastated that you'd found out. They just want to know you're alive, Ella.'

'Are they at the same hotel?'

'Yes. In the same room, in case you come back. You could call them there. You wouldn't even have to speak. Um. I wrote the number down just in case you wanted to.'

We sit inside a little bar down a side street. It's lit by a dim wall light. Several other people are drinking beer in there. I recognize a teenage boy who drops his younger brother, Gabriel, off at classes sometimes, and give him a wave. There are flies buzzing around in the doorway.

'I meant it . . .' I say. Half an hour ago I thought I'd lost Christian. Now I have him and I need to say it all to his face because I might never see him again and this is important. 'In my note, when I said I love you . . . I *do* love you. I loved you the first time I saw you, and then I loved you more and more. That day on the island. The two of us. It was the most wonderful thing. The best day.'

He looks at me sideways and smiles. 'Wasn't it?'

'Really.'

'We're heading back to the States tomorrow, Felix and Susanna and me. I couldn't go without seeing you. I just couldn't. I had to find you, and so I did.' Christian hesitates. 'Ella – look. You'll probably say no but I have to ask. You could come with me. Back to Miami.'

I look into his eyes. 'I haven't got a passport. It was stolen from my bag. That was . . . Well, I'll tell you about that another time.'

He looks at me. 'Please do. When you feel ready to be Ella again. Tell me. I'll come back for you. If you like.' He is stroking the palm of my hand with his thumb.

I am staring at him. This is the most enormous thing, and my heart fills up and everything goes soft and fuzzy and I will never forget it as long as I live. Christian wants me to come to Florida.

He will come back for me.

He

will

come

back

for

me.

'Yes,' I say. 'Yes. I will.'

'Do you have an email address?'

'No. Not one I look at. I often answer the phone at the school, or you can turn up.' I imagine logging into my gmail account. It would be full of things I don't want to see. I look into his eyes. 'I'll set up a new email. It will be just for you.'

'Here. Here's mine. Please write to me. Text me. Call me. Send a letter with a carrier pigeon. Anything you like. Please keep in touch, Ella-favela. You fabulous girl.'

He hands a scrap of paper to me. It has the hotel's number on it as well as his details, and I take it and have another sip of my beer.

'I will. My fabulous boy.'

'I need to give you one more thing.' He pushes an envelope across the table to me. 'It's not much. I wish I could give you all the money you need. But it's just something to keep you going. I know those places don't pay much in the way of salaries.'

I stare at it. I have no money, but I have food and the things I need.

'I can't take your money,' I say. I have got here by myself. I've done all this on my own, and I have food and a home. I can't be rescued now by a handsome prince.

I haven't paid my fees though.

'Don't be ridiculous,' he says. 'You can call it a loan if you like. When you can, send me some money back. Or bring it to me. If it'll make you take it now. I wish I could give you more. This isn't life-changing money. It's just a little bit of cash. That's all.'

I'll give it to Ben. I take it and smile my biggest smile at him, hoping he can see my soul sparkling through my eyes. Christian pays for the beers, and I lead him up the hill, past the chickens, right up to the place where the children play football at the very top. The city is spread out before us, a string of sparkling lights. The moon lights up the ocean. The mountains are dark. The city is at our feet, twinkling, alive.

Christian laughs at the sight of it, and then we turn to each other. He takes hold of me, and I take hold of him, and we kiss each other for a long time.

I want the moment to last forever. I am Jo, in the favela, kissing the boy I love beyond all words, on a moonlit night on top of a Brazilian hill.

16

5 days

I open the envelope much later, lying on my mattress on Jasmine's floor. The light is off and I hold it into the moonlight that's coming in around the edges of the blind.

Christian has given me money. I have enough cash to go out for a drink on Friday for Jasmine's birthday. I can buy her a little present. I can give some cash to Ben and Maria. I'll pay him back one day. I love him.

There's not only money in there though. When I've stared at the money for a while I take the other thing out of the envelope. It's a photograph of the two of us together, and I never knew that such a thing existed because in all the time I've spent with him I was too busy gazing at him to think about taking a selfie. Selfies belong to a different universe. But this is a photograph of me and Christian, in Lapa, dancing in the street. It was the best night of my life, and it was real. In the picture I have long purple hair and I am looking at him and laughing, and he is looking at me and laughing too, and we are so happy. I stare and stare and stare at us both.

He has written on the back of it:

Susanna took this. The best night of my life ♥

Jasmine turns over in her sleep. I put the photograph under my pillow with the money and lie awake, beginning to feel whole again.

I get up early and, while I'm waiting for the kettle to boil, stare at the English school's phone. I can't call from here because they might be able to trace it. I gather up the few coins that were left from my old stash, and I walk fast along the alley and down the hill to where I know there is a payphone. Then I walk right down to the bottom and call from the phone next to Super Sucos instead. If they trace my call to here they still won't find me.

I take a deep breath and, before I can think about it for a moment longer, I dial the number for the Blacks' Copacabana hotel, from the piece of paper Christian wrote it on. My fingers tremble as I do it. I am breathing rapidly but I don't let myself put the phone down. I force myself to keep it against my ear.

When someone answers I talk quickly.

'Could I speak to Mr and Mrs Black, please, in room 1108?' I say it in Portuguese, because that's only polite.

'Sure,' says the man on reception in English, and then another phone is ringing, and then someone picks it up and says, 'Hello?' and it's actually Graham Black, my adoptive father. My dad. His voice isn't urgent. He doesn't expect it to be me; not at all. It's half past six but he doesn't sound as if I woke him up. I wonder what life is like for them now. They stay in their room and wait. They're not surprised by the phone ringing. They don't even expect it to be me.

'Hi, Dad,' I say. 'Sorry. I'm fine. I'm sorry. You should go home. I'll call you there, I promise. I need to get a new passport. I need some stuff for that. Tell Mum I'm sorry and –'

I click the phone down before he can react. I'm trembling all over. I walk quickly back up the hill, not looking back.

The four-year-olds always make me feel good, and today Ana comes straight up to me and clings on to my legs, and I crouch down and pick her up. She is heavy enough to disguise my still-shaking arms.

She giggles and strokes my fuzzy head. 'Hello, Teacher Jo-Paula,' she says.

'Hello, Ana.'

Ana is my little saviour. She will never know what she has done. She has never so much as questioned my name: she calls me Jo-Paula and the other volunteers smile indulgently when she does it. No one has asked why she calls me that. It is the most innocuous thing, and it is a secret that would unravel everything. I've had several names since I was Ella, and Paula was the shortest lived and most transformational of them all.

'You have small hair,' she says now, touching it with the open palm of her hand.

'It's going to grow,' I say, and I stroke her silky bob. Then I put her down and throw myself into singing nursery rhymes with the little children.

I kissed Christian again. He made a mammoth effort to find me; and now I'm going to have to email to thank him for the money. All this makes me smile all through the afternoon.

If I am going to be Jo I'll need to build a life for myself. A real one. Now I know the man is OK and I'm not going to be arrested, everything is different. Until Christian told me that, I felt like you do when you think you're at the bottom of the stairs but actually there's another step to go, and you step off and panic, feeling as if you've just stepped off a cliff. That was how I was, every moment.

Now I'm beginning to feel like the person I always wished I could be: I am different and bigger and living an actual life that I literally went out and got for myself. I am going to grow into Jo. Jo will not be a Black or a Hinchcliffe or a Carr. She won't be Ella and she won't be Bella. I called her Marsh, off the top of my head, when I arrived here. Jo Marsh is who I will remain.

I look across the room at Jasmine. She is gathering up the leftover stickers from the children's activity this morning, and I go to help her. I need to be open with Jasmine; not in the sense of telling her anything, but in the sense of talking to her and laughing with her and not being so guarded any more. It's difficult because I don't want to say anything at all about my old life, but I'll do it.

'Where are you from, Jasmine?' I say. She looks at me and I realize that it came out all wrong. I laugh. 'I don't mean *where are you from?* in a racist kind of way. I mean, you said your parents live in Dublin, but is that where you grew up?'

She grins. 'You should say: *No, but where are you from originally?* with a little tilt of your head. Yeah, I grew up in the West of Ireland. I was born in Hong Kong, and my dad died when I was little. He was Chinese. So when I was still tiny Mum moved back to Ireland and I was unusual, looking like this while being Irish. I never lived above a Chinese takeaway so that was hard for some people to understand – not only that but I'm literally shit at maths and I can't play the piano. Baffling. So. She and my stepdad moved to Dublin a few years ago. It's good there. How about you? Where are you from? *Originally?*'

It's funny: Jasmine is my best friend now, and without her kindness I would never have stepped through the door of this place. I sleep on her bedroom floor every night, yet we've never even had this conversation. I suppose that shows how much I have shied away from talking about anything personal. For nearly three weeks I've done everything I can to avoid the *How about you?*

'London,' I say. It isn't very imaginative but at least it's huge, and a place I know.

'Oh, that must be cool,' she says.

'It's OK,' I reply. 'I mean, I haven't been there for ages but it's home, I guess. In a way. Not like this is home though.'

'Oh, it's the best here, isn't it? I'm just loving it.'

'Me too,' I say, and I mean it. I knew I would love Rio and, even though none of it has been anything like what I imagined, I do. I know there are things out there that I will have to face soon enough, but for now I can strive to be happy, just as it says in the poem.

17

2 days

On Friday Ben turns up just before we're leaving for the club to say happy birthday to Jasmine. Then he turns to me.

'Have you got a moment?' he says quietly, and he leads me into the kitchen.

One of the girls is making coffee but she takes a look at us and leaves. I don't know what he wants. I gave Maria some money but it wasn't much. Now I'm worried that he has discovered that I'm here under a fake identity and he's about to kick me out.

He fixes me with his all-seeing look. I wait for him to tell me how disappointed he is to discover that everything about me was a lie.

'Congratulations, Jo,' he says, instead. 'We've received the money, and you're a fully paid-up member of the team. I can switch things about and find you a bedroom, or you and Jasmine can move into one of the doubles if you like. You two seem to have hit it off.'

'I owe her. But . . . I didn't give you *that* much money . . .?'

'No, and I can give you back the deposit you gave

Maria, because the full amount arrived. I assume you arranged it from home, like you said you would. Our admin staff said they got a call from someone saying they were paying your contribution, and when they had the details they transferred it straight over.'

Christian.

That's the first thing I think. Christian has paid for me to be here.

The Blacks. That is the second thing. If he's told them where I am, they could have done it.

Ben is still talking.

'Are you going out with everyone tonight?'

'Yes.'

'Good. I hope you all have a good time.'

'Thank you. Was it . . . ?' I try to compose my thoughts. 'Was it a man who paid? An American?'

Ben smiles. 'Your friend who came here the other day? He caused quite a stir, I've heard. No. It was a woman actually. Your mum.'

We pile out into the street together, the seven of us who are going to celebrate Jasmine's birthday. I try to compute what has happened. Christian has told the Blacks that I'm here and that I owe the charity some money. They have called to pay it. That's their way of saying that it's all OK. I'm here legitimately now. If they know I'm here they could have come to get me, but they didn't. They have sent me a message and I love them for it.

I walk faster, to catch up with Jasmine. She is the longest-serving volunteer at the English school: everyone but her has arrived since I did, as the previous set of volunteers moved on to be home, or elsewhere, for Christmas. The girls are dressed in little sundresses and tiny cardigans, with swooshy hair and shiny shoes. I have cobbled together the best outfit I could manage, which involves the denim shorts I wear every day, and the halter-neck top I bought in Rio when I was Ella, which I meant to throw away but never did. I have borrowed a silk scarf from Sasha and tied it around my head. Jasmine lent me her make-up, so for the first time in ages I'm wearing eyeliner, mascara and lipstick. It feels odd, painting on a face. I stepped right away from being like everyone else, and now I'm stepping back into it, just for a night. I worry that I look ridiculous with make-up on, but it's the best I can do really. I'm used to feeling like the odd one out on occasions like this, and the good thing is that now I don't care.

'Oh my God, Jo,' says Sasha when she sees me. 'You look amazing. You really do. I mean, you always look amazing, but tonight you are just . . . Wow.'

Amy, who has got over her distaste of the favela thanks to actually living here, nods. 'Yeah. You do look cool.'

'No one's as cool as Jo,' says Jasmine, putting her arm round me.

I look at the ground. I don't know what to say, so I don't say anything at all. I'm glad they're being nice to me, but I really don't mind whether I look nice or not.

The fat woman is sitting at the café opposite our alley, on the main road. She is always around the neighbourhood, sitting and drinking coffee. I like seeing the same people every day. Now that my Portuguese is better I might try to strike up a conversation with her.

When I smile at her she smiles and looks away. I walk down the hill with the others, all of us heading for the bus stop.

The venue turns out to be much grander than I expected and everyone is showing their passports at the door. When I get to the front of the queue the woman looks at me and says, 'ID?'

'We need ID?'

'It's the law in Brazil,' Jasmine says from the till next to me. 'Any club, anything like that, you have to show ID at the bar. I did say everyone should bring passports.'

'Yes. You did.' Jasmine said that and I ignored it for obvious reasons. 'I'm really sorry,' I say to the door woman, 'but I haven't got it. I forgot. Sorry.'

She looks at me through narrowed eyes. 'You can't go in without ID.'

'Oh, please? I'm with them. They've all got it.'

This is like being at home in Kent, talking my way into being served alcohol. It usually worked then, one way or another, and it works now. The woman makes the silence stretch out a long time, then sighs, says she'll let me in this once, and tells me to bring my passport next time. I promise I will. I pay the entrance fee, which takes up a scary chunk of my precious money, and she takes a photo of me. I don't like that, but it seems to be happening to everyone.

Then we are in. This is a proper old-fashioned samba hall that looks as if it has been here for a hundred years. It is glitzy and glamorous, with chandeliers and polished floors and high ceilings. A man in a white tuxedo leads us up a grand staircase and shows us to a table. The downstairs is a dance floor, and we can look down on it over some railings. There is at least one other dance floor in a room nearby.

'Please,' he says, handing us menus. 'Please, choose a drink.'

I look at the glossy menu. This is a different world – a different universe – and for this night only I'm going to enjoy it. I was expecting a venue like Antonio's, where I met my darling Christian and his friends: a busy, informal bar filled with locals. This is a tourist place, and everything about it is shiny and impeccable. This is the kind of place the Blacks would like.

It's not a place most of my Rocinha neighbours would have access to. It's strange to be here. I feel like an imposter, but when I look around the table I see that no one else does.

I thought the others didn't have money, and yet it seems they do. I suppose these are gap-year students from Europe and America, and they've paid thousands of pounds to join the project, so of course they probably have spending money on top of that for treats. Most of them are going travelling later. They are, I realize, in a completely different situation. It will not occur to anyone that I'm any different from them. They consider my funny hair and my lack of wardrobe to be stylistic or ethical choices. I am a part of the school and I am good at art. They have no idea.

I was always so careful about the way I dressed and presented myself. Right up until Tessa cut my hair and Bella got me to dye it purple, I did everything I could to blend in. I hated attention because it was always bad. There is an English girl here, Lauren, who reminds me a tiny bit of Ella Black; though Lauren seems more straightforward. I often see her watching everyone else, making an effort to do things the way they do them, anxious above all to fit in. She sometimes seems awestruck by me: she thinks I'm older than her, when I'm actually younger. When Lauren looks at me I feel as if Ella Black is gazing at Jo, amazed by what she was able to become.

The waiter in his white tuxedo is standing grinning at us, electronic notebook in hand, little pen poised above it. Jasmine, as the birthday girl, orders first and picks a passionfruit caipirinha at a cost of considerably more than I was imagining I would spend on this entire evening. Lauren orders the same. So does Sasha.

It is my turn.

'The same, please,' I say in Portuguese.

By the time he's finished, everyone has ordered a passionfruit caipirinha.

The drinks arrive, and we all toast Jasmine's birthday.

Jasmine is the only person who knows that I slept rough on the doorstep. She took me in and gave me food and a shower and her bed, and I will always love her for that. I hope she has the best birthday ever.

'Thank you, everyone,' she says. 'And thanks to everyone for coming out with me. Four months I've been in Rio, and this is the first time I've done anything like this.'

Jasmine looks happy. She has put her hair up in a bun and tried her hardest to look like a grown-up (and this is her nineteenth birthday so she very much *is* a grown-up), but she seems to me to be someone who will look better when she's older. Her dress suits her: it has a big full skirt that works perfectly with her tiny waist. I had no idea she had anything like that packed away in our bedroom. I know she's spending another month at the project and then moving on to a different project in Ecuador, and I will miss her hugely when she goes.

I realize that I am assuming I will still be at the school in a month, and that takes me back to my project fees being paid, and that makes me giddy.

'Happy birthday, Jasmine,' I say as our glasses clink together. 'You deserve all the happiness in the world.'

'Oh – thank you, Jo! So do you.'

The passionfruit caipirinhas are wonderful. I take a sip and am instantly back in the street in Lapa, dancing with the love of my life. The fruitiness is different and it's more sophisticated, but it's the same drink.

We are not far from Lapa here. Christian is back in Florida now.

Hours later I finish my third cocktail and look for someone to dance with. I don't feel drunk because I've been dancing more than drinking, and the music and the people and the heat and the joy will keep me going forever. The club, which was a stately tourist place when we arrived, has become a nightclub with wild Brazilian dance music and sweaty people on the dance floor. Hundreds and hundreds of people are here. I have been dancing and dancing and dancing, letting everything out without stopping to think. I've lost the others and I don't care.

The people are a mixture of tourists and Brazilians. Some of the local people are spectacular dancers. I stand at the edge of the dance floor, my empty glass in my hand, and watch their legs and feet, their hips, their arms, the poise of their bodies. It makes me forget everything, and the music goes right through me. It's so loud that even if I did want to talk to anyone I wouldn't be able to.

A man comes over and extends his hand, inviting me to dance. He is handsome, black and stylishly dressed. I take his hand.

I remember dancing with Christian somewhere down the road from here, and following other people's feet, and having the best night of my life.

Now I dance carefully with my new partner. I try to mimic the samba moves with my feet, but it doesn't really matter what I do. He dances in front of me, not touching, and he clearly wants nothing from me but a dance. After a while he tries to talk, but I can't hear what he's saying so I tell him that by mime and we just dance. The song changes and we keep dancing. When I am sweaty and exhausted I thank him, and he gives me a little bow, and I wander away.

I step out on to the balcony for some fresh air. From up here I can see that people are queueing right down the street to get into this place. I watch them standing out there in the tropical heat. There are bars all the way down this road and they have tables outside, and there is a pink flowery vine growing up the building opposite. My head is spinning with the music and the dancing, and the sweat is hot along my hairline.

Someone is next to me. It's a woman – an older woman I saw earlier on the dance floor doing some amazing moves – and she says, in Portuguese, that she's hot. I wipe my forehead and I agree. We talk a little bit about nothing in particular. She asks where I am from and I say London. We stand side by side for a while, staring out at the street, at the hundreds of people wanting to come in.

Then the woman has gone and Jasmine is beside me.

'You all right, Jo?' she says.

'I'm having a wonderful night,' I tell her. 'How about you?'

'Yeah,' she says. 'Yeah, it's epic, isn't it? Will we get another drink?'

'Sure.'

We sit down at a table back at the top of the grand staircase with Lauren and Ted (one of the rare boy volunteers), and I seem to have a bottle of beer in my hand. The music is pounding but up here it's quiet enough to talk.

'So you've had a good night?' Lauren asks Jasmine.

'The best,' she says, holding up her glass. 'I've had the best night. I have. The very best.'

'You deserve it,' I say. 'You know, we should find the bus back at some point. They do go all night, don't they? Or do we have to wait around for the first one in the morning? I'm working at ten.'

'You'd be all right to wait it out, if we had to, wouldn't you?' says Jasmine. 'It wouldn't bother you at all.'

'Of course. It'd be fine.'

She starts to speak, then stops. Then she puts her drink down on the table and leans towards me. 'You're such an enigma, Jo,' she says. I can smell the sweet alcohol on her breath. 'I've known you ages, but you've never said anything. Any time I tried to ask you about your life you changed the subject, and because I saw what you were like when you arrived I thought you'd been really ill and I never wanted to push you. You shout out in your sleep sometimes.'

'Do I?'

'It breaks my heart. And then – there's a woman who called the other day looking for someone working here. She didn't say Jo, but I'm thinking it was you she was after. Because you're the only one who's, you know, a bit mysterious.'

I put down my drink.

My mother paid my fees. And a woman was looking for me. I don't want her to turn up. It is mean of me, but I don't want to see the Blacks. Though apparently I'm happy to take their money.

WE CAN HAVE THEIR MONEY WITHOUT SEEING THEM.

That's not fair.

NOTHING IS FAIR.

'Who did she ask for?' I say.

'Ella. Or Chrissy. I think she's called a couple of times but I've only spoken to her that once. The others said.'

'What did you say?'

'I said no. I said there's no one here by the name of Ella or Chrissy.'

I feel sick. Jasmine, my friend, has pulled the rug out from under me. But she didn't give me away, and that's what matters.

'You're amazing,' I say quietly. 'Thank you, Jasmine. It's complicated. Tonight is about you. When we're in our bedroom tomorrow, I'll tell you about myself.'

I don't know what I'm going to tell her: some part of the truth, I suppose. A version. Not all of it. She looks so happy that I feel guilty about being such a bad friend; but I feel nervous too. I try to stand up but my legs are weak and wobbly, and I quickly have to sit down again.

Someone paid my fees. A woman has phoned, looking for me.

306

Ever since Christian found me, I haven't really been hidden. I close my eyes. The drum beat reverberates through my body. Jasmine is saying things but I don't know what they are.

I don't have to hide from the Blacks. I'm eighteen. I can live in Rio and teach English if I like. I am doing fine.

The police wouldn't take me back to my parents like an abducted toddler because I'm old enough to live my own life, so I don't need to hide from them either.

I'm not in trouble with the police. Christian said I'm not.

I didn't hurt the man.

It's not the Blacks or the police I'm hiding from.

It is not them at all.

I turn back to Jasmine. 'What was her voice like?'

She is frowning because she was in the middle of saying something else and I have no idea what it was. For all I know it might have been a description of the woman's voice.

'Oh,' she says. 'Well. She was talking English, and she had an English kind of voice.'

'Was it an English voice like this? *Have you seen a girl called Ella?*' I do my best impression of Fiona Black, with her Radio Four accent. Instantly I regret saying my real name. My real-ish name.

'No. That's what *you* sound like. It was more like this: *Have you seen a girl called Ella?* No. That's not quite right. It was an English accent for sure, but not your one.'

I swallow. I have no idea what my birth mother's voice sounds like, but I do know she is English. I know she is from Birmingham, and Jasmine's attempt at replicating the accent sounded a bit like it might be a Midlands kind of thing. One thing is for sure: if she didn't sound like me, then she wasn't Fiona Black.

And all of a sudden I begin to panic. How could someone who did the things she did and then spent half her life in prison be able to track me down like Christian did?

I cannot imagine it; but that doesn't mean it's not possible. I do know that she wanted to see me. The parents whisked me out here to keep me away from her, and I love them now for the madness of that plan. I have no idea if my disappearance got any coverage in Britain, but if her lawyer was able to write to the Blacks it wouldn't have been difficult for her to find out that I was in Brazil. I told Michelle I was calling from abroad. It wouldn't be hard.

She could be looking for me. The woman who led five innocent people to be tortured and murdered could be ringing the right number and asking for the right person.

Lauren is leaning forward. Lauren, the Ella Black of the favela, has been listening in from Jasmine's other side.

'Oh yes,' she said. 'I meant to say. I spoke to this woman on the phone. She said she was looking for Ella or Chrissy. After you had that gorgeous boy turn up asking for Chrissy but actually meaning you, I thought it might be you, so I asked if she meant Jo.'

I stare. 'When was this?'

Lauren pulls a piece of her hair into her mouth and

chews it. 'A few days ago. Sorry, I meant to say. Anyway she said she probably did mean Jo actually. She was nice.'

'Please tell me that didn't happen.'

'I was trying to be helpful.'

'It wasn't helpful.'

'Sorry. I wasn't to know.'

I am on my feet, filled with Bella. All of me is Bella. For a long time I've been Ella-Bella. But now I hate Lauren. I hate her more than anyone right at this moment. I cannot lose control here in public, but I cannot look at her either.

'You have no idea,' I tell her. 'You have no idea at all what you've done. None. Oh, fucking hell, Lauren.'

I want to say more, but I can't because everything that has kept me strong has funnelled itself into anger, and I am white hot and my ears are ringing and my eyes are going and I have nothing left. I can't do this any more. The monster is going to find me. The monster is part of me. The monster is coming.

I turn and run. I run down the stairs, past the other dance floor, and follow the sign to the exit. I have to pay for my drinks before I can go, and so I hand my piece of card over to a man and give him the money for the cocktails. Then I am out on the street by the queue of people, and I don't know where to go or what to do but I know I can't stay at the English school any longer. I'll need to move before she gets here.

My head is ringing. My vision is going. My mother is coming, and even my demon has no idea what to do.

*

Jasmine grabs me by the arm and pulls me to a table and pushes me down so I'm sitting on a chair. She reaches across and holds me and pats my hair. I know what I am really hiding from now. I should have known I couldn't shut it out. We are out on the pavement, a few metres from the people who are still queueing to get into the samba club.

Jasmine and Lauren have actually heard Amanda Hinchcliffe's voice down the phone. That is impossible. I grew inside her, and she called them and they spoke to her about me.

That

is

contact.

It's direct contact between my birth mother and her lost baby.

I cannot control myself.

I don't think I will ever control myself.

'It's OK, Jo.'

Jasmine followed me and she is looking after me and I can't let her because Bella might hurt her. Her long hair tickles my face as she leans over. I lean away. I have to hurt myself so I won't hurt her.

'It's OK, Jo,' she says again. 'Don't worry. Whatever it is, we'll make it all right. I promise.'

'You can't. I have to go. She's found me.' I can barely speak through my sobs. My plastic chair is wobbling back and forth, one of its legs shorter than the others.

'Who's found you?'

'That woman.'

Jasmine doesn't ask any more. I don't say anything. She hands me a pile of the tiny squares of tissue that they have in dispensers on café tables, and I try to mop myself up a bit, watching the tissue disintegrate into papier-mâché on my fingers.

'Sorry,' I say. 'It's your birthday. You should be in there, having fun.'

She rubs my back. Her hand is reassuring.

'As if I'm going to let you run out into the night in that state. Honestly, Jo. I'm so sorry we upset you, Lauren and me. I didn't mean to, and I know Lauren didn't either.'

'It's not you,' I say. 'It's me.' I stop and laugh at the triteness of the phrase. Nothing is coming out right. 'Oh, Jasmine. I'm so scared. I'm so, so scared.' I take another tissue from her and wipe it carefully along the underneath of my eyes.

'Who is she?'

A waiter is standing beside us. I don't want a drink, but Jasmine asks for two caipirinhas and then he goes. I mop my eyes a bit more and try to take control of myself, but it's difficult because I keep hearing Lauren's clipped voice saying: *I was trying to be helpful.*

I need to get away quickly because she knows where I am. I cannot let her walk in. I cannot I cannot I cannot. I can never see that woman.

Never.

Never.

Never.

Never.

N
e
v
e
r.

The drinks arrive. I don't want any but I take a sip anyway and it tastes like rocket fuel and I know I'm going to be sick. I stand up and look around. It's a hot night and we are outside and there are too many people. I turn and run into the building and look around for the loo, and see a sign pointing up the stairs. There is an empty cubicle, and it smells and the flush isn't working and it's blocked with paper, but I lean over it and am noisily, hugely sick.

My soul, my future, my happiness all pour out of me, down the toilet.

Jasmine's hands rub my back. I didn't know she was following me.

'There you go,' she says. 'It's OK, Jo.'

I cannot speak or look round. I just feel her hands and hear her looking after me. The place stinks even more now, and I want water and I want to be in bed and I want to sleep and to be safe and I don't know what I want.

After a while I stand up. Jasmine squeezes my hand.

'Come on,' she says. 'I'll pay for those drinks, and then we'd better go.'

We walk together down the street, past the queue of people waiting to go dancing in the heady Rio night. It doesn't take long, and then we are in proper Lapa, in the same places I went to with Christian. I am wobbly.

'I need to go away,' I say. 'From here. Right away.'

'Do you? Where to?'

I shrug. 'North, I think. North Brazil.'

'You can come to Ecuador with me if you like.'

I manage a smile. 'Thank you. I'd need to get a new passport. But she'd still find me.'

'Who is she?' Jasmine asks again.

My. Mother. I can't say those words.

'A monster,' I say instead. 'A monster who is coming after me.'

18

12 hours until she dies

I am up early in spite of my hangover. I watch Jasmine sleeping and I envy her calm face and the way she breathes so evenly. She looked after me last night and I owe her a massive explanation. I think I'm going to tell her everything. I creep out of the room to make myself a coffee and plan my escape. Everyone knows I'm Ella now. Amanda Hinchcliffe knows I'm here.

I take a Brazil guidebook and sit on a tiny chair in the classroom, and wait for the painkillers to kick in. I try to shut it all away, but the fact remains: my birth mother, who went to prison for nearly eighteen years, knows where I am. She paid for me to be here and she's been calling for me and I have to go. I need to pack up my few things and leave this place right now.

But she'll follow. If I don't turn and face her she'll follow me. I am hidden here but she found me.

I open the book at random and decide to go to a place called Salvador. It sounds like an interesting city. I will go there and find some work and . . .

I sigh. I can't turn up in a strange Brazilian city with a limited grasp of the language and without a plan. I can't run away forever. Things don't actually work like that. If I'm running away from here, then the place to go is Florida, and love.

So I'll need a passport.

Ben comes into the room and says: 'Morning, Jo! You're up earlier than you should be, surely?'

'Do you know anyone in Salvador?' I say.

'Salvador?' He sits on the table beside me. 'Are you on the move?'

'Not sure. I might be.'

'Just when your mum's paid all that money?' He sees me flinch and shakes his head. 'Sure – I'll see if I can do anything. I don't know anyone up there doing what we do here, but I'll do some research. I'd happily give you a reference. You should think about doing a TEFL qualification, you know.'

'Thank you.'

I won't really go to Salvador, but now Ben might tell anyone who asks that I was thinking about it.

Because it's Saturday, there's just a class of teenagers to teach at ten. And then I'm free and after I've had a proper conversation with Jasmine, that's when I'll leave. Everyone who's not working stays in bed. Lauren teaches with me but we ignore each other as best we can, and the moment the students have left she goes out. Jasmine's not up yet. I will be embarrassed to see her, and I know I have to tell her a version of my full story now.

The school's computer is in the back room. I haven't done this since Paquetá, but I take a deep breath and type the name of my birth mother into the search engine.

Amanda

Hinchcliffe.

I hate those words. I cannot bear writing them, and I hate the words that come up, and I also hate the pictures. However, I need to take a proper look at them. I need to have an idea of what she might look like if she comes here to find me.

I am looking for pictures of her on her release from prison, but however many pages of Google images I scroll through, they are all old ones. In the end I read some articles instead, and discover that she has been 'given a new identity' because public feeling about her crimes is too intense for her to be able to live safely.

There are no photographs of what she looks like now so I have to look at her when she was seventeen. She was younger than I am now when she was arrested, and eighteen when she went to prison. When she was my age she was heavily pregnant. Now that I'm that age I am living under an assumed name in Brazil. That's definitely a thing that criminals do: perhaps we are alike in a way.

That thought is enough to propel me into fury. I am like my mother. Not so long ago I smashed a bird apart with a hammer. I attacked Fiona with a broken bottle. I slashed a man across the face. I stole a tourist's bag from a beach. I slept rough. I lied and lied and lied.

I am not going to be like her.
I am not I am not I am not.
YOU ARE.
I don't want to be.

I stare at the photos. When I did this before I was looking for signs of myself in her face (and they are there, I know it; they are there more than I let myself see before). This time I am looking for signs of anyone I have ever met since I've lived in Brazil, or even before the Blacks whisked me away here.

I stare at the grainy pictures, and it's difficult to tell anything really. She could have made the calls and paid the money from anywhere. If she was here she would have come to find me by now.

I read old articles about her life before she went to prison. She was the eldest of three children, with a younger brother and sister and an abusive father. She met Billy Carr (and I skip over him and everything about him and I always will) when she was fifteen. They did the bad things.

If I let myself think about the things they did I would never think of anything else. If I thought about the fact that I was there – embryonic and innocent, but me, and on their side – then I would never be able to live a life.

'Oh,' says a voice behind me, and it's Jasmine. 'That's that woman, isn't it?'

I turn round and look at her. She doesn't seem scared of me. She doesn't look as if she hates me now, after last night. In fact she puts a hand on my shoulder.

'What's that?' I say. Jasmine has caught me looking at my birth mother. She knows who 'that woman' is. That woman from the news. That woman who did the killing.

'That woman. That's a long time ago – but isn't it the woman from, you know, out there?'

It takes me a while to get there. Jasmine is pointing vaguely towards the outside world, in the direction of the Estrada de Gávea. I turn and look at her, at Jasmine, at my friend. Her face is open and she's smiling a little. She is dressed for the day in a black dress and strappy sandals: she's not wearing her Favela English School T-shirt because she's not working.

I hear the class next door singing the ABC song.

Jasmine pulls up a chair and sits down beside me. 'What are you looking at this for?' she says, and I realize that although her words have stabbed me through the stomach there is nothing that seems different about me yet. 'Oh, God, is she from *prison*?'

'Which woman?' I say, and I hear my voice sounding light and casual, which is odd.

'Oh, you know. She stopped me in the street a few weeks ago and asked where the language school is. She's always around the place. Big woman.'

I stare at Amanda Hinchcliffe's face.

I think of the fat woman.

I stare at her face.

I think of the woman.

I stare.

It doesn't make any sense, but the thing that Jasmine saw instantly is there: they are the same person. She has put on weight, but prisoners probably don't actually spend their time doing press-ups in their cells and striding around a yard. She has the same face now as she had back then, and parts of it are my face and I never noticed it even though Jasmine did.

Mentally I scroll back through the times I've seen that woman. She was there when I was homeless. She was there when I met Ana and came here for the first time. She is always around, sitting in cafés drinking coffee, watching, half smiling. I thought she was local. I was going to strike up a conversation with her.

'Fucking hell,' I say, and Jasmine looks towards the classroom, but they won't have heard me because they're chanting the colours. 'Jasmine. Look. I promised I'd tell you the truth and I will.'

Jasmine is rubbing my shoulder, and just for a second I lean back and let it happen.

I tell Jasmine everything. I actually don't leave out any of it. I tell her that my name is Ella Black, that a month ago I had purple hair, and then I tell her all the things that are harder to say than those ones are. I tell her that I was unhappy at home, that my only friends were Lily and my gay boyfriend, Jack. I tell her a bit about Bella. People start to come in and use the office so we move upstairs to our bedroom, and I talk about the mysterious dash to Rio, and show her the photograph of Christian and me dancing in the street. I tell her that I found out I was adopted, and attacked my mother, and then found out who I was adopted from. I tell her that I slept rough and a man grabbed me by the ankle and I stole a bag from the beach.

I tell her that the monster is my mother.

As I speak I stay calm, because Jasmine is there, listening to every word I say, biting her lip and not shrieking or looking horrified that she's shared a room with me all this time, lending me her things and making me coffee when I most needed it. I know that Bella is in me, but she doesn't need to take me over yet because Jasmine is here. Bella is saving herself for later. I know that.

'So,' says Jasmine, and she is so gorgeously calm about it all that I want to hug her. 'What do you want to do?'

I take some deep breaths.

FIND THE WOMAN.

Later.

WE HAVE TO FIND HER.

I know we do.

OK. LET'S DO IT THEN.

I can't fly into a rage and attack the woman because that would make me as bad as she is. However, I know that nothing I do or say will stop Bella going out there to find her, and I don't want to try, because I am Bella and Bella is me and we are going to find our monster and look her in the eye and we have agreed on that.

'I'm going to go and look for her,' I say.

'I'll come with you.'

*

320

For once she isn't at the café. She isn't at the other café either. We walk down the hill but we don't see her. That woman is the only person who has always been around: she is the first 'local' person I recognized. And now she's not here.

'We'll find her,' says Jasmine. She walks over to the nearest motorbike taxi and starts talking in her basic Portuguese, miming someone larger than herself, asking where she is. The guy shrugs and asks his friend. I sit at a table in Super Sucos, overwhelmed. This happened quickly and I cannot get my head round it; I try to convince myself that this woman might not in fact be Amanda Hinchcliffe. Surely she's not allowed to come out of prison and fly straight to Brazil? I can't begin to make sense of it.

The motorbike-taxi guys are talking about her. They do at least seem to know who Jasmine is looking for. One of the waitresses from Super Sucos gets involved in the discussion. I don't tune in properly. I would only understand half of it. I know enough to realize that Jasmine hasn't told them why we're looking for that woman.

'We need to go up past the welder and turn left,' she says when she comes back to me.

I stand up and we do. We walk up the hill to the welder and turn left and walk for a little bit, and then Jasmine stops and asks an elderly woman who is sitting on her doorstep with a baby on her knee whether she's seen a woman who speaks English and is quite big anywhere around here, and the woman nods and points and explains something too quickly for us to understand, but in the end

I manage to catch it. We do our best to follow her instructions, and when we find ourselves in a tiny alley with a sign in front of us that reads PENSÃO, we look at each other.

'Give it a go?' says Jasmine. 'That means guest house. So we could go in and ask. If you want to.'

I open my mouth to reply, but nothing comes out, so I take a deep breath and nod, and then I force some breath out of my lungs and say: 'I want to.'

Jasmine takes my hand and squeezes it. I squeeze back.

'Thank you,' I whisper.

'She might not be here,' says Jasmine. 'But she might. It's worth a try. I think you have to see her, don't you?'

'Yes.'

My legs tremble as we walk up the path. I can't knock on the door so Jasmine does it, and there's a woman standing there who is not the woman we're looking for. This woman asks if we want a room and Jasmine says yes, and I don't know why she does that but I follow them in. The landlady is talking, showing us stuff. She takes us into a room with two beds in it and points to things, and although she's talking slowly because we're foreign, and although I can understand what she's saying, I don't focus. I slip away, out of the door, and look around.

There is a bathroom. It's small and clean and white. I go through another door and walk into a kitchen, which is empty, with a pot bubbling on the stove. The door next to it is a bedroom, perfectly tidy with the sheets pulled tightly over the bed.

Then I push open the door next to it.

And I stop, and I stare. The ringing in my head is so intense that I can't do anything except stand there. My vision is blotchy around the edges, but I can't have that.

You don't need to do this. You don't need to take control. We can do this together.

WE'LL GO IN?

Yes.

JOINING FORCES?

Yes.

WE'LL SORT THIS OUT.

Together.

The other rooms here were immaculate. This one is quite messy.

That is not the thing.

There are clothes spilling out of a suitcase.

That is not the thing.

There is a glass of water beside the bed, a book of meditations, a bead necklace, a tiny teddy bear.

Those are not the thing.

The walls. The walls are the thing.

The person who lives in this room has covered the walls, which are wallpapered in green and white. She has covered them with pictures.

She has covered the walls with

pictures

of

me.

I stand there, swaying, and stare at the largest photo on the wall opposite me. It's a photograph of me when I was Ella Black. I know when it was taken. I am wearing school uniform, and I am smiling at a camera and holding a little cup.

I won that cup for cross-country, and a girl called Margot, who came second, was furious with me. The photo was on my school's website: I have never had an actual copy of it. Amanda Hinchcliffe has printed my photo from the school website. I am trying to remember whether my name was on it. I think it was: it was from a 'news' section, because my victory in the cross-country was news.

I am trying to remember because this feels important. Did this picture say *Ella Black* underneath it? I cannot be sure. If it said *Ella Black*, she could have googled me and found it, but if it didn't, she could only have found it by knowing my school and what I looked like, and monitoring the website for sightings of me.

This whole room is evidence. The person who lives here is obsessed with me in all my incarnations. Ms Hinchcliffe was so desperate to see me that the Blacks moved across the world to get me away from her. This is Amanda Hinchcliffe's room.

She lives here. She isn't here now, but she lives here. She followed me. She found me when no one else could find me. She has never spoken to me, but she could have done. She could have done anything she wanted to me. Anything at all.

There are pictures of me everywhere. Some are posed (me in a school photo; me smiling into the camera on Copacabana, in the picture I last saw in the newspaper at that other guest house), but more of them are not. I see myself getting out of Fiona Black's car in my school uniform, walking down some pavement with Lily, and hand in hand with Jack, my lovely fake boyfriend.

There I am in Rio, but still Ella, with purple hair. I am sitting sketching on the beach while the Blacks are fuzzy in the background, talking to one another. I am sitting at a bar looking bored, with the two of them on either side of me.

There is no picture here of me joining the zombie parade, or on Paquetá. But there is one photograph of me homeless. I am on the beach that I now know as São Conrado, sleeping. That must have been around the time my money was stolen.

She stole my money. She might have stolen my money.

Then I realize that she gave me those cheese balls. She was my benefactor. She might not have been, but I know she was.

There are a couple of photos of me in my Favela English School T-shirt, and that's all. After that, I suppose, she knew where I was, and then she didn't need to stalk me and take photographs because she could just look at me in real life.

She doesn't get to do this.

She doesn't get to be my mother.

You don't get to do this.

You don't get to be my mother.

I am saying the words under my breath, and then I am in the room, tearing down the pictures, ripping them apart and throwing the pieces all over her stupid bed. I tear every picture of myself off the wall, and I know the woman whose house this is is shouting, and Jasmine is standing there not really knowing what to do and probably talking to me, but I can't stop, and it's the whole of me because Ella is the same as Bella, and I don't try to stop myself because I don't want to. I shake them off when they touch me. Every picture of me has to be off this wall because I don't belong to this woman and she doesn't get to lie in her bed and look at my face and pretend I'm her baby.

In the corner of the room, by the table, is a really bad drawing of a baby. She didn't have a photo of me so she drew me, her lost baby. That makes me pause for a second, and Jasmine grabs my arm and leads me out of the room, and the woman is yelling at me, and Bella wants to go back and carry on smashing things up but she can't because even Bella is feeling too sad.

Someone took those pictures and I never noticed. She had someone on the outside taking my photograph and I never had any idea. No wonder the Blacks had all that security. I wonder whether they saw people taking my photo, whether they suspected this might be happening.

I long for my real parents, the ones who looked after me.

I am lost.

I

am

lost.

Jasmine is talking to the landlady, explaining that I am the girl in the photographs, and the landlady already knew that because there aren't many baldish white girls around the place. She is talking fast and I'm not listening.

The door opens.

She is there.

19

5 hours

I see bits of myself in her face. This is my mother.

'Jo,' she says.

'Ella,' I say.

We stare at each other. I don't know what to do. Bella is coursing around me, raging, and while I'm staring I have an internal argument.

LET'S JUST SMASH HER UP.

We can't.

WE CAN.

We can't.

WHY?

Because then we'd be just like her.

That stops it: even Bella doesn't want to lunge at her now. I don't want to turn it inwards and hurt myself either. Actually I do a bit, but I am not going to because I have to be better than that.

Jasmine takes my hand and squeezes it hard. I let her do that. I am staring into Amanda Hinchcliffe's eyes, and she is smiling at me.

'But you're Jo,' she says, and her voice is soft and different from the way I thought it would be. 'You're my Jolene.'

I cannot say a word. I am not her Jolene.

'My baby,' she says.

I am not her baby. I was though. Once.

I walk out of the door and down the alley and away from her.

Bella knows she can't attack this woman, but as soon as we are out of the door bad things start to happen. It's not like I can't control myself, because I can these days. I've had to incorporate my Bella into my being, just to get through. I've used her strength, I think, for survival. That's why, for the first time in my life, I've felt like a whole person.

But I cannot cope with this. Neither part of me can deal with seeing my birth mother's bedroom. I walk along the alley, away from the guest house, away from that woman, who isn't coming after me, away from my wonderful Jasmine, away from the poor landlady. I don't know where I'm going. I know I can't hurt anyone or I would be like her. I know I can't kill myself because I tried that before and I couldn't do it. I know I can't run away and live off my wits because I did that and it wasn't fun. I don't want to go back to the Blacks. Not now; not like this.

When I get to a bigger road I head uphill. This is where the drug dealers live. I carry on walking to the very top. It's not sunny today. There are clouds in the sky. No one would expect me to be here. I hope they won't look for me here. I can see rainforest on the other hills, and a distant Christ the Redeemer with his back to me.

I sit down at the edge of a stony path and just stare out at Rio. It's wonderful, beautiful, alive. It's everything I imagined it to be and a million things more. I take a sharp stone in my hand and draw shapes in the sand. Drawing calms me down. It always has done. That's why I do it.

I can't go back to my old self. I don't know what to do.

I have looked my birth mother in the eye.

It isn't enough. I have a lot of things I need to know, and I'm never going to get another chance to ask her because after today I cannot see her ever again.

20

1 hour

I thought the fat woman was a local person who watched
the world go by. I thought that one day I would talk to her,
now that I could speak Portuguese. I didn't imagine she
would speak English because she looked like someone who
had been in the favela, drinking coffee, part of the scenery,
for her whole life.

I never thought for a moment that she could possibly be
Amanda Hinchcliffe. To my eye she looks nothing like the
teenager in the newspaper clippings, though Jasmine saw
it. She looks nothing like the mother in my head. She is not
actually gigantically fat, but she looks much older than
thirty-six. Her eyes are sad and her face is jowly. She looks
like a woman who has had a hard life. Not a murderer; not
a released prisoner; not my mum.

We sit opposite each other in Super Sucos. The air is hot
and heavy: there will be a storm later. Jasmine is nearby,
poised. I stare at Amanda Hinchcliffe. She has a mole on
the side of her face with a little hair growing out of it. Her
hair is short and thick. It's not as short as mine. I look at
her nose. I know it's like mine. I check my lines of escape

again. I can leave easily. I can get out of this place, and vanish back into the favela, in no time. I can run faster than she can, particularly uphill.

'Jo,' she says, and her voice breaks. I see myself in her eyes. In the weirdest, most disturbing way, meeting her is like coming home. I know that this is where I grew from an embryo into a foetus, into a baby. I know this is the first person I ever saw. I know it.

I know that this is my curse.

They took me out of her arms and gave me to the Blacks, but this woman is my mother. I don't know what I feel, apart from that certainty. The woman in front of me, the woman I have seen almost every time I ventured out of the school, just sitting at a table or walking slowly up and down the hill, is the woman who conceived me in between murders.

'Did you name me Jolene?' That is the first thing I want to know.

She smiles. She is just staring at my face and smiling. It's horrible.

'Yes,' she says. 'Jolene. I liked to listen to Dolly Parton. I always loved Dolly. You know the song? It was old before you were born. It was old before I was born too. And then you called yourself Jo. That's a sign, my chick.'

'It's not a sign and I am not your chick. You did that, didn't you? You left me food and money on the beach. You wrote *Something to help you Jo* on the bag. That's why I called myself Jo. It's not some mystical sign. I would have picked another name if I'd known.'

She is unbothered by that. I hate her. I hate her but I can't take my eyes off her. This is like a horror film come true. The monster is sitting opposite me and calling me Jolene.

'How did you find me?' That's the other thing I need to know. 'How did you do that? You were here when I was sleeping on the beach. You found me when no one else did.'

'I stopped that man from attacking you,' she says. 'Do you remember?'

I close my eyes. Of course I remember. I nod the tiniest nod. I am not going to thank her. I remember her voice, yelling at him in English. She was watching me all the time. Every single moment.

All the time.

Like a cat with a mouse.

Like a cat with a baby bird.

'How did you find me?'

She sighs and finally looks away. She is evasive.

'Do you remember,' she says, 'when you lost your phone? Then you found it because someone handed it in to the police and they gave it back to you.'

I do remember. It was annoying to lose it, then nice that somebody found it for me. That seems less heart-warming now.

'You got a tracker put on it.'

'My sister. Yes. She took those pictures of you. She got it from your bag. It's easy to install a tracker if you know what you're doing. She has a friend who knows what he's

332

doing. She took your other mother's phone too and did the same, and put it back in her bag and she didn't even notice. We knew they'd take you away from me when I got out. I had to see you, my chickie. I *had* to. You see . . .'

I don't see anything. 'So you knew as soon as I was in Rio.'

'Yes, we did.'

'And you came here.'

'I just needed to see you. I'm not going to be around much longer. You see, I'm ill, and –'

I don't want to hear her stories. I am incandescent with rage. Everything about me is boiling over. I'm entirely on Team Bella. She has broken the law a million times over and I can send her back to prison and I will. I will. The police will be on my side now. The blood is pounding through my body. I am hot all the way through, to the core, and Bella wants to reach across and push her to the ground and smash her with a hammer like I smashed that bird.

But I can't do that because that would make me as bad as she is.

Also I don't have a hammer.

'You got someone to put software on my phone and my mother's phone so you'd always know where I was. If I'd thrown it away in Paquetá you wouldn't have found me here.'

'No, I wouldn't. And that would have been a shame for you, my chickie, because I did help you out as best I could. I gave you that food. I chased off that man. I paid your fee for the English school.'

I want to say it would not have been a shame for me, but actually she's right. It would. That man's hand around my ankle. She sees me hesitating and jumps in. 'Jo,' she says. 'Jo. I've been waiting all your life to talk to you. I'm so sorry, but I have to. I don't know if you'll believe me, but everything I've done has been for you, as best I could. It wasn't much.'

'No, it wasn't.'

'I didn't like the things we did, me and your dad. I mean, at the time it was all I knew. It was strange.' She has a horrible reminiscing expression on her face, and I look away. 'Anyway I couldn't let the baby be born when all that was happening. I was pleased when we were caught, for your sake.'

I hate her. I hate her so much I want to die. I screw up my eyes and will her to stop talking. I look at Jasmine, who asks, with her face, whether I want her to call the police. We have agreed that as soon as I've found out the things I want to know, Jasmine will call them. I shake my head. Not yet.

'You had a good life. I was so proud. My sister. Audrey. She kept an eye on you. She's been here too. It wasn't so hard to find out where you were, not if you know people.'

'She took those photos of me.'

'I wanted to look at your face. My baby girl.' She reaches out to stroke my face. I lean back so she can't.

I am not her baby girl. I am myself, but I don't even know what my name is. I think I need to go back to being Ella Black. I can't be Jo, now that I know it was the name of Amanda Hinchcliffe and William Carr's baby.

'You were doing well.' She looks up. 'You had a bloody amazing life. Excuse my language.'

'I wasn't happy.'

'You were perfect. Jo. My Jo. My Jolene grew up perfect.'

'I did not.'

'You would have had no life. You don't understand.'

I clench my fists. 'I wasn't happy though. I had a kind of . . .' I stop. 'I had weird thoughts. Did you . . . ? When you were doing the bad things, did you feel like you had another self who took you over? Did you have ringing ears?'

She looks blank. 'No, my chick. I was always myself. *I* did those things.'

The relief is so intense that I can barely stay upright. I had no idea that this was what I wanted to ask, but now I see that it was the only thing I really needed to know. Bella is just mine. She's not a genetic inheritance.

She stares. Then she shakes her head and takes a deep breath. 'Let me be in your life,' she says. 'It wasn't my fault, not all of it. I know I can't really be your mum. Let me be a friend. I only want the best for you.'

'No,' I say. 'Just no. I don't care if you say you're dying or whatever. I don't care. No. No. You don't get to do that. No.'

I stand up. I can barely see. I have to get away from her so I walk out of the café. I don't look back, although I want to. Part of me wants to ask a million more questions, even though I know the answers would be awful. This is too much.

I nod to Jasmine and she gets out her phone. I can't wait. I just have to get away from Amanda Hinchcliffe, so I run down the hill.

There is no taxi and I can't get on the bus that's waiting there because she would get on it too, so I decide to keep walking. I walk towards the tunnel so I can flag down a cab as soon as one arrives.

When I look round I see that she is coming after me. Her face is crumpled and she looks so distraught that I want to help, but I know I can't because I know that to make her happy right now I would have to call her 'Mum', and I will never, ever do that. I think of the other women who felt sorry for her, the ones she lured to their deaths, and I keep walking towards the mouth of the tunnel.

'Jo!' she shouts. 'Jo. Just wait a minute.'

I don't. I keep going. I need to get away from her.

'Jo.' She has nearly caught up right at the mouth of the tunnel. Cars come out of it fast, then slow down if they're stopping at Rocinha. They whizz by so quickly that I feel the wind in my fuzzy hair. She grabs my arm, and I try to pull away, but I can't because her grip is very strong. 'Jo. Listen. You don't have to see me. You can do what you like. I just needed to see you, and I promise I'm ill and I won't be around for much longer. Just . . . just know that I love you. I've thought of you every day. I was your age when I went to prison, and I've been there all your life and it's . . . Well, I got out and I came straight to find you. Audrey and I got a different passport each – you don't need to know. Just know that I would do anything for you. I'd die for you, Jolene. If you need anything, tell me. I'll get it for you. I'll get you whatever you want. I need to give you eighteen years' worth of birthday and Christmas presents.'

'You don't. Please don't.'

'I want to. You're a better girl than I ever was. Just – live your life. Live it and do things and be happy. Don't put your trust in a man. Look forward, not back. My Jo. You can do anything.'

I cannot stand the greetings-card sentiments. I know she is trying to say things that are important to her, but I can't listen. I have nowhere to go, and so I run into the tunnel. There is actually a little pavement in here, and I follow it alongside the road, hoping that she won't follow. I'll run through and out the other side, and then I'll find a cab.

I need to stop running away. I'll stop running just as soon as I've run away from the murdering monster that is my birth mother. Jasmine will have called the police by now and they will arrest her.

I am not looking back. The traffic fumes are making me choke. The car headlights dazzle me. The sound of all the engines is amplified and it fills my ears so if she was running up behind me shouting I wouldn't be able to hear her.

I don't know for sure that she's there until she grabs my arm.

'Jo,' she says. 'I'm sorry. I'm sorry for being me. Just let me hug you. Just one hug.'

She attempts to grab me with both arms. She pulls me towards her. I try to escape. This is mad: we are in a tunnel that is clearly forbidden to pedestrians. I see a police car coming the other way, slow down opposite us and then speed up. It's going to do a U-turn and come to rescue me. Another siren sounds from the other direction. I am finally ready for the police.

I pull away. She tries to grab me again. I step backwards, wanting more than anything else in the world to get away from her.

It happens fast. There is the long note of a car horn. The screeching of brakes. Her grip on my arm pulling me back, shoving me into the wall of the tunnel so I hit my head. A thump and a thud and an echoing crash of cars driving into each other.

Then there is just me, and I am standing with my back to the tunnel wall, and she is lying in the road, and most of the cars are swerving to avoid the pile-up and just carrying on in the other lane.

Then the siren is deafeningly loud, and then there are police.

I sit down and try to breathe.

She did say she would die for me.

One Year Later

Dear Fiona and Graham,

Thank you so much for your email. I was really happy to get it this morning and incredibly pleased to hear from you both sounding kind of upbeat. I'm glad Humphrey is OK. Give him a big kiss from me and tell him that, no matter what he might think, I actually haven't forgotten him. And the same goes for you two. Thank you for the photo of the three of you. I'll print it out when I can.

Life here is good. Who would have thought I'd still be living in Rio? I bet you regret bringing me here.

I know we've been in touch more and more lately and now I want to say a few things, because I've been thinking about them a lot. You can stop reading now if you want. It might be easier for you. If you want to come back and read it another time then do that.

I try not to think about the past and my origins and all of that because honestly if I start thinking about it then I never stop and I get sucked into all sorts of destructive stuff. But I'd like to get this down, and then maybe we can never talk about it again.

You did an amazing thing nineteen years ago. You adopted a baby from the middle of something unspeakable, and you gave me a home and all the love in the world. You did everything you could possibly have done for me. You gave me a home and healthy food and a family and an education. You protected me: you protected me like mad because you knew the dangers that had surrounded me. You knew what I'd been part of, before I was born. If it wasn't for you – well, I wouldn't have been born into that world because I would have been adopted by someone else, but you did a lot for me and those other people might not have been so nice.

So – thank you for that. Sincerely, and with all of myself. I mean it.

I wish you'd told me though. The other people might have told me. That will always be the thing, and I will never quite get past it. You knew the day would come when I'd find out and you must have known that the longer you left it the worse it would be. An adult needs a birth certificate from time to time. I bet you kind of pushed the issue aside through my childhood thinking 'it'll be OK' and 'we'll tell her later'. But it was always going to happen, and, truly, the longer you left it the worse it was going to be, and then it was bad, wasn't it? You took me to Rio, and my birth mother tracked me there because her sister had stolen my phone, and then it all blew up and here I still am.

I know it was difficult, when I saw you before you went home. Fiona, I realize that the way this happened has been devastating. I wish I could be your real daughter. I wish I could have said it was all OK, that we could go home and I'd finish my A levels and we'd go back to normal but with no secrets this time. I do wish that. I hate to think of you at home, at a loose end, just waiting for me the way you used to do when I was at school.

But . . . although things can't be the same, maybe they can be different. It'll be New Year soon, and this could be a year when we see each other. You know I'm studying online (I am doing a much better picture of Rio for my A level than the one I did for GCSE, that's for sure). I'll work out where to apply to university soon. I do appreciate your offers of financial help. I'll pay you back, I promise. I don't even know which country to study in, let alone anything else. But I'll probably stay in Brazil if I can: Christian is living here too, now. We're getting a flat together in Rocinha. It's the place where I feel I belong.

And finally – this is the difficult bit.

You hid a huge thing from me, and I hid one from you too. I did everything I could to fit into the world you'd made for me. I've been seeing an English-speaking counsellor out here, a friend of Maria's, and talking it through with her has made me understand a bit more. So you know I studied hard and I had my friend Lily and my boyfriend Jack (he was never my boyfriend btw) and I did well at school and I was never wild and never difficult? Well, I kind of separated myself out a bit – because remember that I did actually know I was adopted, because you used to tell me when I was small, but I shut it out and refused to hear it and you stopped telling me?

And what I think happened is that I made myself so resolutely 'good' so that you'd keep me, but then my 'bad' side had nowhere to go. So I separated it out from myself, and kind of fenced it off, and gave it a name. I called it Bella. I know to most people that means 'beautiful' but to me it means 'Bad Ella'. Bella would overwhelm me sometimes. I would shut myself away and give in to her. A couple of times she tried to make me hurt myself, but I could never actually do it: I lashed out instead. I killed creatures that Humphrey brought in. I broke things. I smashed things to pieces with a hammer. I destroyed my stuff.

It was getting worse. I wanted to lash out and I was so scared that I was actually going to hurt someone else, that people would see the real me and everyone would hate me. It would happen at school and I would fight myself to control it and I know I would have failed, in the end.

And then it happened. I lashed out at you, Fiona, and then I hurt the man in the café. I will feel terrible about that for the rest of my life. The fact that you forgave me at once without question is a testament to the people you are. It really is. For what it's worth, I am so so sorry.

Then when I was alone in Rio I used Bella's strength to get me through. She and I worked together. It's not always straightforward, but finding out the truth about myself has helped me pull the two sides of myself together. I feel like myself, now. I've never felt that before.

So – I do think of you in Kent, and I do miss you, and I would like to see you. I'm not ready to come back, but could we meet next year, maybe?

Lots of love,
Ella xx

Nineteen Years Earlier

Fiona was trying to concentrate. She realized she had drawn a weird, rambling picture without meaning to: she was just sitting, waiting, and her doodle had taken on a life of its own. It had covered a whole sheet of paper. It was lines and flowers and then trees and birds and cats and waves and beaches. She was drawing everything that wasn't a baby thing. It was a strange sprawling mess that covered the paper she was supposed to keep by the phone so she could make notes if the call ever came.

Everything was riding on this. She felt certain it was their last chance. She was thirty-five and that wasn't old. Everyone said that. *You're still young*, they said, as if eight miscarriages counted for nothing. She had given up on that now. It wouldn't work. Her body didn't work. She was not going to have her own baby. That was beyond any doubt.

There was a dark voice inside her that told her it was all her fault, that wanted to make her go out and do terrible things to make everyone see how messed up she was. She ignored that voice as best she could, but it had been difficult over the years. Sometimes she had to shut herself away and let it all out.

But that had finished now. She was going to give a home to a baby that needed one. Or a child; everyone knew that you hardly ever got a baby. She and Graham had been through so much together, and she was constantly crippled by the thought that he could leave her and have a family with someone else, with someone whose body did work properly; someone who did not have secret horrible thoughts. But he hadn't done that, and he said he never would and she knew he was telling the truth. They were solid. That was one thing Fiona didn't worry about.

Today, though, there had been talk of a baby. That was why she was sitting by the phone. That was why she was drawing and staring and waiting. That was why she had cleaned the house from top to bottom and done everything else she could think of until she had run out of jobs. That was why she was just gazing at the phone, waiting for something that might never happen.

If they got this child she would look after him or her forever. She would feed them healthy food and make sure they had everything they needed. They would send their child to a good school and make sure they were always warm, never hungry, always safe. She would do everything for this baby. He or she would always be happy and nothing bad would ever happen.

The phone rang.

Acknowledgements

Thank you so much to Ruth Knowles for being the most amazing editor. All the teams at PRH, in editorial, foreign rights, publicity, production, design: I am incredibly lucky to have you all on my side and am in awe of everything you do.

Enormous thanks to Steph Thwaites at Curtis Brown for the constant support and brilliance.

Thanks to Colin Ramsay and Conor Foley for different types of technical help.

Thank you to Kat Pieper and everyone at Project Favela in Rocinha for welcoming us in and letting us spend time in your classes, then answering lots of questions. The Favela English School of this novel is entirely fictional but visiting you helped me ground it, in some ways, in reality.

At home, Craig Green makes it possible for me to get these books written, with constant support, love and coffee.